His Brother's Wife

"When are you going to take me riding again, Peter?" Margaret asked boldly.

"Are you sure you want to, Margaret?"

She smiled and almost in a whisper, she asked, "Don't you, Peter?"

Her face flushed pink. Neither spoke. Then Peter moved towards her. Her fragrance, the softness of her gown, the shining hair made him ache to hold her. Suddenly her arms went around his neck and he clasped her close to his chest.

"Margaret, Margaret," he murmured into her hair.

She clung tightly to him and he could feel the warmth of her body next to his. Then he found her mouth, and her body trembled.

"Oh, my love, my love," she murmured.

We will send you a free catalog on request. Any titles not in your local book store can be purchased by mail. Send the price of the book plus 50¢ shipping charge to Belmont Tower Books, Two Park Avenue, New York, New York 10016.

Titles currently in print are available in quantity for industrial and sales promotion use at reduced rates. Address inquiries to our Promotion Department.

HAWKES NEST

Jean Hayward

BELMONT TOWER BOOKS ● NEW YORK CITY

A BELMONT TOWER BOOK

Published by

Tower Publications, Inc.
Two Park Avenue
New York, NY 10016

Copyright ©1979 by Jean Hayward

Prologue

Peter Hawke stood on the solid, darkly stained deck at the stern of the *Bristol Cloud* staring at the black and heaving sea. A wide and frothy wake followed as the ship sailed through the dark night. There were few stars and only a sliver of moon. Wind and spray needled his face with cold. He pulled his grey cloak closer about his shoulders and continued to watch, fascinated by the rhythm and power of the ocean. Peter was astonished at the enormity of the Atlantic. Nothing but endless water which sometimes was grey, sometimes deep blue, always fathomless black at night. There were times when the sea appeared smooth and calm as a lake. More often it moved with deep rhythmic swells, causing the ship to roll heavily. All that Peter had read and heard had not prepared him for the vastness, the seemingly endless body of water, a feeling of being separated from any form of civilization beyond the *Bristol Cloud*. He felt tense as his eyes searched the darkness. The huge sails above him appeared as monstrous birds with wings outspread, hovering over the ship.

"Bit brisk tonight, Sir."

The ship's First Mate spoke to Peter, suddenly appearing next to him on the deck.

"Yes, rather."

"You fixin' to stay in Boston, Sir?"

"New York, perhaps. I'm not certain," Peter replied.

Usually a gregarious person, ready to engage in conversation at the first instance, tonight Peter did not feel like making an explanation of his plans.

"Boston's a right proper place, Sir. A right proper place."

Peter did not have the vaguest idea what the man meant, nor was he particularly interested in a meaningless conversation, so he made no response.

The two men stood motionless for a few more minutes, each listening to the sound of the wind in the sails above them and the steady swishing of the sea as the ship broke through the water. Then Peter turned to speak to the ship's officer.

"I believe I'll go to my cabin. It's getting quite chilly. If you will excuse me," he said, bluntly putting an end to the possibility of any further talk.

"Yes, Sir. Good night, Sir."

Peter found his way below to his cabin, no small task in the darkness of the ship. Sleeping was difficult, as it had been since the first night out of Bristol. The roll and pitch of the ship was a disturbing sensation, although he had not been ill as were many of the others on board. He now was two weeks out of Bristol, two weeks away from England, and a lifetime away from Margaret. Her pale and stricken face still was vivid in his mind; her eyes, dark and pleading, as they had been the day he told her and William he was leaving for America on Lowell Howard's *Bristol Cloud*.

Peter's heart quickened even now as he remembered Margaret coming to him in his room. How he loved her! Only time and great distance would ease the pain of wanting her. If, indeed, anything ever would. Could he be making a mistake leaving England, going thousands of miles to a land where he would be a stranger? Admittedly dreaming for years of doing that very thing, now

6

that he was on his way doubts kept creeping into his mind.

His life at Hawkes Nest had been so comfortable, so settled and orderly. At least it had been until Margaret came. He guessed now that he really had no choice but to leave his home.

Peter did not want William ever to know or suspect anything between himself and Margaret, but to stay in the same house with them would have been impossible, if not disastrous. He knew he would miss his brother and Hawkes Nest more than he cared to speculate. As for Margaret, his whole body ached at the thought of her. Peter closed his eyes, trying to force sleep, but her face was always there. He thought he could smell the lavender she always wore and he imagined he could hear the rustle of her silk gown.

Sitting up in bed, Peter reached for the bottle of brandy he had in his travelling bag. Perhaps a swallow or two would help him get to sleep. He cursed loudly as the ship rolled hard and he spilled some of the liquid on the bedclothes. Nothing like a soused blanket, he thought, muttering to himself. The brandy didn't help much, except to warm his insides. He still was wide awake. His long legs felt cramped in the narrow bed. He tried thinking about the other passengers on board. There was a family from Bristol named Craven. A man, his wife and three small children. There were two young Irishmen who kept to themselves, and there was a middle-aged spinster who was going to her brother in Boston, no doubt with the hope of finding a mate in a new land. Completing the passenger list, besides Peter Hawke, were two Englishmen, both of whom were planning to settle in New York. Their families were to come later.

Tossing about in the hard and uncomfortable bed, now smelling of brandy, Peter wished the voyage didn't take so long. It seemed interminable. Boston still was almost three weeks away. He sighed heavily and closed his eyes, willing himself to sleep, for sleep was all that could separate him from the events of the past months which had brought him to this ship rolling and surging across the Atlantic.

Part One

● 1 ●

It was late February. Mist lay like a fine grey veil over
the countryside, blurring the horizon. The valley seemed
almost to be receding in the fading light of day. Only the
occasional tinkle of a cowbell broke the stillness as the
animals made their way to the barns. Day was ending in
Woodbridge and soon the lamps and candles would
light the windows of the village houses which clustered
together as if they had a common wall. Wisps of smoke
drifted from the chimney pots and melted into the dull
light of the sky. The little village of Woodbridge was
nestled in a narrow valley some thirty miles northeast of
the busy seaport of Bristol. The cemetery behind the
stone church bore moss-covered headstones dated 1710,
1715, so it was known to have been there for more than
one hundred years. No particular interest ever had been
shown as to its beginning. Woodbridge was quite simply
a small English village.

After weeks of rain the narrow and curving road was
flowing with mud which spattered to the soft grass
growing thickly along the edges whenever a carriage or
cart or horse and rider passed by. People in Woodbridge
grumbled that never had they known such a winter. The
sky seemed permanently set in a palette of greys, pale
and smoky to near black. Branches on the trees hung
limply, their leaves slick and shiny. The air was still and
quiet. A narrow stream running just east of the village

was swollen from the constant rains and had spilled over into some of the gardens behind the houses. Woodbridge shops and craft houses hovered close to the winding road which the coaches used on their way to and from Bristol. The British road system was being improved so rapidly that coaching routes were spreading from one part of England to another. Now every village, no matter how small, offered an inn for travellers. These, in turn, became gathering places for the villagers themselves. In Woodbridge it was The Bell.

The village also had Hawkes Nest. The largest house in Woodbridge, it sat well back from the road on a slight knoll. From this perch one could look over the rooftops, past the church and across the valley to the river which flowed slowly on its way to Bristol and the open sea. The house had been there almost as long as Woodbridge itself. Three generations of Hawkes had called it home. Built of a soft, honey-colored stone, half-timbered, with a deeply thatched roof, dark with age, the house had latticed windows, tall and narrow. The facade was broken in the center by a wide and heavy oak door. Chimney pots straddled the tops of two large brick chimneys which were partially covered with creeper and lichen. A cobbled stone path leading from the road had a patchwork of flowers and wild grasses on either side. Surrounding the house was a thick hedge of dark yew.

There was a large sitting room with dark panelled walls and a deep black fireplace. A wide, diamond-mullioned window looked out through the trees to the road below. Next to this room was a small parlor which **Mary Hawke kept closed except for visitors.**

"The walls and furniture will be all but ruined by dust and soot if we don't keep the parlor door closed," she had insisted, with some regularity.

The kitchen was large and comfortable with a long

rectangular table where the family had its meals. There were two china cabinets on one wall filled with the flowered china Mary Hawke cherished.

There was an upper story which had four bedrooms of modest size, although each had nooks and deeply recessed windows which gave the appearance of more space. Heavy dark beams of chestnut crossed the ceilings.

A large square wing had been added to the kitchen. This was used as a workroom and study by Henry Hawke. Here he kept the books and tools and materials he used as a wagon and coach maker as his father had been before him. The room smelled of leather and tanning acid and varnish and paint.

Coach and carriage making had become a profitable business in England. Most of the carriages throughout Europe were English, partly because the craftsmen did such fine leather and skin work and also because the French no longer were making carriages.

Black was the most popular color for a carriage, followed by grey and then brown. Often there were red, blue or green stripes used for decoration. Public coaches were much heavier and not as elaborate or as finely finished as private vehicles.

Henry Hawke's father built coaches for the Post Office which did not own the vehicles but hired them from the builders for so much a mile. After his father's death, Henry continued the work and the reputation of the family grew and the business prospered.

Wheels of Hawke coaches seemed to last much longer than those of other coach builders, which helped to enhance Henry's reputation throughout England. He used the best woods he could find, tracked down the strongest harness and finished his work with a fine hand.

Robust and strong, Henry Hawke was an impressive

man who was proud of his imposing stature and proud of his work. He apprenticed his two sons at an early age as wheelwrights and then to make wagons and carts of all description. In the farm country where the Hawke family had lived for three generations, this continued to be a lucrative business.

William and Peter grew strong and sinewy and soon took the same pride in their work as their father had done all his life. However, Peter often talked of moving on to some unknown place, to some unknown opportunity. Henry Hawke was aware of his son's restlessness and seeming dissatisfaction with wagon and coachmaking. The work offered little stimulation to Peter's desire for a new world to conquer.

This day Henry Hawke's two sons returned from their father's funeral, driving the family carriage up the road to Hawkes Nest. As they reached the house, Peter indicated he would tend to the horses and William stepped down and walked up the stone path to the wide oaken door. He stood quite motionless, momentarily, then opened it and went inside. The house was quiet except for the steady, measured ticking of the clock in the hall. There was an almost eerie stillness. William entered the kitchen to find that the fire had been out for hours and the room seemed damp and cold. Moving towards the coal bin, he put some black chunks in the stove. A fire and some hot tea would help to ward off the chill in the room. He lighted one of the lamps on the long dining table.

Peter came in, letting the door fall shut behind him. Neither of them spoke. William sat down in the rocker which had been his mother's. It seemed too small for him and he realized that he had not sat in it since he was a boy. Peter moved towards the high-backed chair his father kept in the kitchen since the boys' mother died. Before her death it had been in Henry and Mary Hawke's bedroom.

The two brothers were silent, each with his own thoughts. They had been a close family, the boys working with their father as he taught them his trade. Henry Hawke had been a rather stern man, but never was unkind or cruel, and seldom had they questioned his word. His wife, Mary, was a gentle and virtuous woman. The boys' sister, Henrietta, married six years now, lived on the outskirts of the village.

Like the Hawkes, most of the people in Woodbridge were second and third generation, so one's background and family statistics were common knowledge. Since only a few of the adult population of the village could read and write, information was passed by word of mouth, one to another. The children were learning some reading and arithmetic at the Church school.

The Hawkes were more fortunate than most of the families in Woodbridge. All of them had had some schooling. This was most noticeable in their speech and gentle manners.

Woodbridge was inhabited mostly by craftsmen. Farmers lived in the outlying areas of the village, the surrounding country being all farmland and forest. On Fridays most of the farmfolk came to the market-place in Woodbridge to trade and to purchase. Henry Hawke and his two boys nearly always spent Fridays at the square. Henry and his wife secretly hoped the boys might find wives at these village gatherings, but beyond one or two romantic escapades neither William nor Peter seemed particularly interested in any one person. Their father often reminded them that they were now in their twenties and ought to be thinking about having families of their own. Certainly there were any number of young women in the village who would have welcomed their attention.

Since Mrs. Hawke's death the boys' sister, now Mrs. James Stokes, came once a week to do laundering and cleaning for her father and brothers, as well as other necessary chores. Lately her visits were coming farther apart. Expecting her third child, she had been feeling rather poorly. The last day she had come she told her brothers they must think about hiring a housekeeper, someone to do their laundry and prepare meals. Someone to come every day to keep the house in order. William had agreed and said he would see to it. Now he stood up and poured the hot water into the teapot.

"Is there anything to eat with the tea?" asked Peter.

William put some bread and butter and a small piece of plain cake on the table and the two ate together, alone in the house for the first time.

They bore little resemblance to one another. William had his father's great height, well over six feet, and his massive chest and shoulders. Hair and mustache were thick and a ruddy brown in color. His lips were thin, but finely drawn above a strong chin and sharp jaw. He had very dark brown eyes under heavy brows.

Peter was considered the more handsome of the two. He had his mother's finely chiseled features and bright blue eyes. Also over six feet in height, he seemed smaller than William due to his more slender build and long slim legs and arms. His hair was thick and straight and dark blonde in color. He had a full and well-shaped mustache and his eyebrows were not as heavy as William's. Peter's mouth was slightly curved, even sensuous.

The clock on the kitchen wall struck four and William raised his head to look at it. This particular clock probably was the family's favorite. Made of rosewood with a charming, hand-painted face, it had a lovely soft bell which rang the hours.

"Peter—"

Just as he spoke, the oak door opened and their sister walked into the house, followed by her husband James, and their two small children, Patience and Andrew.

16

William quickly offered his chair to his sister.

"This house is cold as a tomb!" Henrietta gasped and put her black-gloved hand over her mouth, realizing too late that her remark, to say the least, was inappropriate.

A faint smile crossed William's face.

"Would you like some tea?" he asked.

Henrietta shook her head and seated herself in the rocking chair. Her pregnancy was obvious now and she moved awkwardly. As William looked at her he saw that she was becoming more and more the image of their mother. Her blonde hair and blue eyes, and her ready smile, make it impossible not to recognize her as Mary Hawke's daughter.

"We are on our way home and only just stopped by to tell you that we have found someone to come and care for the house," said Henrietta. "We stopped to speak with Reverend Thomas," she continued, "and we asked him if he knew of anyone who could help you. He suggested Ellen Davis."

"Ellen Davis?" William could not identify her in his mind.

"She's been a hired girl at the Crowley farm for three or four years now. Reverend Thomas says Mr. Crowley's selling the place and moving to Liverpool to be with his daughter, and Miss Davis has nowhere to go."

Henrietta scarcely stopped for breath.

"Well, I've arranged for her to come and see you tomorrow morning at nine o'clock. You'd best work out some arrangement with her, William. Reverend Thomas says there's a small cottage right on the edge of the road, not far from the church, and he says she probably can let that. It's empty right now."

"All right, Henrietta. I'll take care of it."

William sounded a little impatient.

James turned towards his wife.

"We had better be on our way, Henrietta, to get home before dark."

He had been standing next to her chair, silent and stoic, his hat in his hand. James Stokes was a rather nondescript man, short and muscular, with a solemn, somewhat brooding face. He had a very heavy mustache and a small beard. His eyes were a watery blue and deepset. Now the children were beside him, tugging at his coat.

"The road is full of mudholes and they make handling the wagon more troublesome than usual. I really think we must go, Henrietta."

His voice was quiet but firm.

Henrietta nodded her head, shooed the children ahead of her, and they were all gone as quickly as they had arrived. As the door closed behind them, Peter exclaimed, "You'd think we were bloody babes!"

"She's only trying to be of help." William remarked. "And you must agree that we can't manage here without some assistance." he added quickly.

"No, I suppose not," Peter admitted.

William poured the remainder of the tea into their two cups and leaned back in the rocker, resting his head against the top of the chair, his legs stretched out in front of him.

"Well, Peter, I suppose we should make some plans about father's business. He has left equal shares to us and Henrietta. Hawkes Nest comes to me, as the eldest, of course, and he no doubt figured we would continue the work here. I realize you have little interest or enthusiasm for the trade. I think father was aware of that too, but I certainly could use your help for the next year or two at least. We will have to send letters advising that we plan to continue father's work here, and we shall have to finish the orders he left."

He looked squarely at Peter as he spoke, searching his

face, wondering what his answer would be. William knew that Peter often was restless and had talked of leaving Woodbridge at one time and another. Many days he had left the house, his work unfinished, and been gone for hours walking the nearby hills or riding across the valley. His father eyed him curiously when he returned, but Peter always continued his job and finished the particular item on which he had been working.

Peter now leaned forward and put his empty cup on the table. Raising his eyes, he looked directly at William.

"Of course I'll stay on a while." Then he smiled. "Who knows, I might yet like it."

Peter's remark seemed to end the conversation as he got to his feet.

"I think I'll go for a walk. I shan't be long."

He made no mention of William joining him. Walking into the hallway, he took his coat and hat from one of the hooks on the wall, and went out the door. It now was quite dark. The rain had stopped. Lamps shining through the windows of the village houses made the narrow road barely visible. He thrust his hands into the pockets of his coat and started along the muddy road. Most of the people behind the windows he passed had been to his father's funeral this afternoon and he knew he could stop at any one of the houses and be welcomed. However, he chose to walk on alone.

The three Hawke children never had known any other house than the one in which he now lived. And Woodbridge had been the only place he had known, aside from two trips to Bristol with his father.

Ah, Bristol! Peter found the activity of the town fascinating. Carriages coming and going on all the streets. Wagons and carts of every description. The people wearing clothes such as he had never seen. Handsome and colorful. The ladies like bright birds in velvet and wool cloaks with matching, high-crowned bonnets trimmed with feathers and ribbons, and men wearing soft grey or brown wool coats over long, slim, closely fitted trousers. And such beautiful houses. Tall and shuttered with polished fittings on the doors, and some had many chimneys. Not so welcoming as Hawkes Nest, he thought, but much more grand.

Peter wondered who might live in those beautiful houses. Probably shipping merchants, men who owned trading companies, or perhaps the owners of ship-building firms. Certainly most of the wealth in Bristol was connected in some way with the ever-growing trade with the New World.

The harbor was the best of all. A forest of tall-masted ships in a maze of rigging and sail. Ships waiting to be loaded or unloaded, as the case might be. Ships going to America, to the West Indies, to Australia. Peter had listened to the shouts of the men on the decks as they directed the cargo-carriers below them, and his eyes widened at the myriad of sights and sounds. What had excited him most was the anchor being raised on one of the ships, lines slackened or tightened, and the ship moving out, slowly, away from the dock, everyone shouting at once. Such an adventure, going to sea! Peter had been sixteen at the time.

He thought about that now as he walked slowly down the road away from his home. He was free to go if he chose. William would not prevent it, much as he might want him to stay. The boys had been taught to be independent and responsible for themselves, to make their own decisions. Peter stopped suddenly as he had arrived at the church. In the darkness he barely could see the bell tower. He thought about his father, buried in the churchyard this day. Peter had loved his parents. Now they were side by side behind the church. He remembered well the happy days all of them had shared.

The birthdays with special things to eat. The festivities at Christmas, lasting for days, with parties and singing and special services at the church. His mother had cut branches from the trees surrounding the house and placed them over the doorways. She had sprigs of holly in bowls and cups on the long dining table where they gathered for meals. There were anise biscuits and wonderfully fragrant spice cake they had only at holiday time with raspberry shrub. The house had been full of people sharing with them, and candles shone in all the windows.

Everyone in Woodbridge had looked forward to the Christmas season, partly because of the gay festivities at Hawkes Nest. Since Mary Hawke's death there had not been the parties and gaiety associated with the family and the house itself.

Peter sighed deeply and thrust his hands further into the pockets of his coat. He knew he would not leave. At least not just yet. His desire for freedom and adventure was great, as was his loyalty to his family, each one constantly pulling against the other in his mind. He turned and started walking briskly back towards the house. Perhaps in a few years. . .

● 2 ●

Ellen Davis looked out the window of her bedroom, resting her arms on the sill. The wet grass in the meadow sparkled in the sunlight and the flowers by the fence hung their heads, heavy with last night's rain. Mr. Crowley's dairy cows were moving about in the thick grass, the earthy wet smell filling the air with the freshness of the countryside. There was a crispness in the morning light and a hint of spring. Perhaps the dismal winter with its grey skies and misty days finally was over.

This was the day Ellen was to go to Hawkes Nest to see about a position. She really didn't know much about the family. The Hawkes bought eggs and milk regularly from Mr. Crowley, and she knew that Mr. Hawke was a widower. Ellen also knew there were two sons and a daughter, but she never had seen them. Always so busy on the farm, she scarcely had time for socializing.

Round and sturdy, with strong arms from lifting milk containers and working the churn, Ellen's cheeks shone with a healthy glow and her blonde hair usually was curled damply about her face and neck. She had a generous, well-shaped mouth, slightly curved at the corners, and her eyes were a soft brown, sometimes turning to green in the sunlight. When Ellen looked at herself in the mirror, she knew she was not beautiful, but she hoped someone might say she was pretty.

Ellen was left an orphan when her parents died within two months of each other. She had a legacy of a few hundred pounds, a tidy sum to be sure, which she felt she must not touch in the event she should not marry. This thought occurred to her quite frequently since she now was twenty-one and there had been no young man enter her life and little possibility one would so long as she remained in virtual isolation on Mr. Crowley's farm.

Adam Crowley had been a long-time friend of her father's and she had come to work for him soon after her parents died. The Crowley farm was nearly fifty miles from her own village of Wexford, but with no family she felt fortunate to have someone to turn to for help. And how lonely she had been! Her father and Mr. Crowley had been friends since they were boys and when Adam Crowley learned that Ellen Davis was left an orphan he immediatley made arrangements for her to come to his farm. In exchange for her room and board she was to help with the chores and be of assistance to his wife.

Ellen was so relieved to have someone look after her that she became a most willing and efficient servant. She was very lonely and missed her home the first year or two. Then she settled into the routine of the farm and began to feel more secure.

Now Adam Crowley's wife was dead and his children had moved to the cities, having no interest in dairy farming. He decided to sell the farm and go to Liverpool to be with his eldest daughter. Ellen's legacy would have paid for the place, but she was uncertain about being able to keep it profitable, even with two hired hands. Dairy farming was one of the most rewarding occupations for women in England in terms of financial return, as well as one of the most arduous. After much thought, Ellen decided she did not want to part with her money, that she would rather find work in the village.

The clock struck seven and Ellen turned quickly from the window. Her appointment with William Hawke was for nine o'clock and she still must dress and allow enough time to walk to Hawkes Nest. Perhaps she could ask David, one of Mr. Crowley's hired hands who worked about the farm, to take her to the village in the wagon. On second thought, she decided he had far too much to do and Mr. Crowley might not like him to leave even for a short while. Besides, the sun was shining and the walk would do her good.

Ellen took great pains with dressing for the appointment. Her brown wool dress with its narrow lace ruffle at the neck was most becoming to her rosy cheeks and blonde hair. Anyway, it was her only nice dress. Over it she wore a brown wool cloak with black braid trimming, a gift from Mrs. Crowley one Christmas. Ellen knew it had belonged to one of Mrs. Crowley's daughters, but she was grateful nonetheless.

Ellen looked in the mirror as she tied the ribbons of her black bonnet under her chin. She wished she had a better one, she thought to herself, noticing the frayed edges of the ribbons. But perhaps Mr. Hawke would take no mind of it, in any event. She studied her reflection carefully and pushed back some shining tendrils of hair which had managed to escape from the bonnet. Picking up her one pair of gloves from the bureau drawer, she walked out of the room towards the kitchen.

David entered the kitchen almost at the same instant and set a large basket of eggs on the long table in the center of the room. He glanced at Ellen and his grey eyes fastened on her, an expression of surprise on his face. Never had he seen Ellen looking so fine. Usually her round figure was covered by a large apron, while she worked the churn or was busy with the cooking, her hair concealed by a ruffled cap.

"Where would you be goin'?" he asked, inquisitively.

"This is the day I go to Hawkes Nest to see about a position. You know, David, I told you I wouldn't be staying on. With Mr. Crowley leaving, and the new people probably not needing me, well, I just can't stay on." she explained.

"Would you like me to take you in the wagon?" David inquired.

"Oh no, it's such a fine day. I think I'll enjoy the walk."

"Well, the road's a fright with the mud," he stated, flatly.

"I'll walk on the grass along the edge if it's too muddy."

Ellen's voice was cheerful and eager. "I'll be fine," she added.

David watched her as she went out the kitchen door and along the path leading to the road to Woodbridge. He remembered well the day Ellen had come to the farm. Barely seventeen, she seemed thoroughly frightened in her new surroundings, so shy and quiet that at first he was not sure the girl could speak. Gradually Ellen began to accept the sympathy and understanding the Crowleys were so eager to give. She still did not talk much, David thought. At least not to him. He was easily old enough to be her father, but he always felt he would have enjoyed her companionship. Still, Ellen kept mostly to her room when she wasn't busy about the house. Obviously, she was not aware of his loneliness.

David had been with Mr. Crowley almost thirty years, ever since he became lame after an accident on the farm.

He long ago had discarded the idea of having a place of his own and had become somewhat of a recluse, always disappearing from view whenever anyone came to the farm. He never went into the village unless on some errand for Mr. Crowley.

Ellen continued down the road to Woodbridge, the morning sun warming her cheeks. Hawkes Nest had been described at some length by Reverend Thomas, although Ellen had seen the house two or three times. Not so large and imposing as the manor houses near Wexford, nonetheless she thought it was the most beautiful place she ever had seen. Ellen had passed Hawkes Nest on her infrequent appearances in the village. Walking up the stone path to that very door, her heart was pounding. Never had she applied for a position before. Raising the brass knocker on the door, she tapped it twice. She looked down and smoothed the skirt of her coat, and waited. No one came. Ellen tapped the door again. Surely this was the right day, the right time. Could she have made a mistake, she thought, with some apprehension. Suddenly footsteps sounded and the door was opened. A very tall young man with bright blue eyes stood looking down at her.

"Mr. Hawke?"

"Yes, I'm Peter Hawke."

"My name is Ellen Davis. I've come to see Mr. William Hawke about a position." Ellen's voice was soft and a little shaky. She hoped she did not betray her nervousness.

The young man seemed to be staring at her. Then he smiled.

"Yes, of course. Please come in and sit down. I'll fetch him."

Ellen stepped through the doorway into the entry hall of the house. It smelled of candle wax. The woodwork was dark and highly polished. Hats and coats were hanging from brass hooks on one wall and there was a large clock on the opposite side.

Peter quickly disappeared. He was a most attractive man, Ellen thought, as she sat down on the small settee just inside the door. Indeed he was! She folded her hands in her lap and waited. Glancing about she noticed several closed doors. There must be more than one parlor. Leaning forward slightly, she could see into a large room with a deep black fireplace and shining panelled walls. There were large chairs and a round table near the windows. Ellen wondered if the rest of the house was as handsome.

William Hawke appeared in the hall and Ellen jumped to her feet as if she had been pulled up by a string. Her stomach felt quivery and she clasped her hands together nervously.

"Miss Davis?" he inquired.

She nodded, aware of the fact that he was a very large man. He directed her into the room she had noticed just before he entered the hall, and motioning her to a chair near the windows he sat down opposite her. Ellen observed that he was wearing some kind of heavy apron so she guessed he had been working somewhere in the house.

"You have come well recommended by Reverend Thomas," William began. "We require general cleaning, laundry, and meals. This house has nine rooms. We rather like a large breakfast, a fair mid-day meal, a proper tea and a light supper," he continued. "Do you think you can manage all that?"

"Oh yes, Sir. I've been doing all of those things at Mr. Crowley's. It will be no trouble, Sir," Ellen was quick to respond.

William took notice of her clear, rosy skin and fine blonde hair. Her clothes were neat and clean. She appeared capable. He mentioned the compensation, to

27

which Ellen quickly agreed.

"You speak as if you've had some schooling, Miss Davis," said William, matter-of-factly.

"Yes, Sir, a little. I fancy reading, Sir," she replied.

"How soon may we expect you?"

"Well, Sir, I have a few things to move from Mr. Crowley's. Reverend Thomas has been kind enough to arrange for the cottage near the church where I can stay. I could start Thursday morning. Would that be agreeable, Sir?" Ellen asked in reply.

"Of course. We shall expect you at seven then."

As an afterthought William asked if she needed help with her moving.

"Oh no, Sir. I haven't much."

"Very well, then. I'll return to my work. Thank you for being so prompt, Miss Davis."

William stood up and the interview was over. He led her to the door.

"Thank you, Sir," she said as she started down the path.

"We shall expect you on Thursday morning then."

"Yes, Sir. Thursday at seven. And thank you again, Sir."

Ellen waved her hand shyly.

William watched her until she disappeared among the trees which partly hid Hawkes Nest from the road. He thought she had a sweet face and a pleasant voice. That was a definite asset in a woman, he had decided.

Ellen walked down the road on the grassy edge. She felt strangely exhilarated. How easy it had been to apply for a position! Why had she been so nervous, so wary? She knew she was going to enjoy taking care of so fine a house. And Mr. Hawke seemed like a very kind gentleman. Tall and important looking he was. Not so handsome as the blue-eyed one, but he seemed right pleasant.

Ellen was eager to get started with her new tasks. Now she would be able to go to church regularly, make some new friends, become a part of the village. She walked briskly as if anxious for the day to be over and be on with the next. There were a few threatening clouds in the sky, but she was certain she would be back at the Crowly farm before there was more rain. The air was fresh and cool to her face. She bent down to pick a wildflower growing beside the road and now was twirling it between her fingers. The sound of turning wheels interrupted her thoughts and Ellen stepped to the far side of the road so as not to be spattered with dirty water. The wagon slowed to a stop beside her. Seated up top was Peter Hawke.

"I'm going right past Mr. Crowley's and I'd be pleased to let you off there," he said, looking down at her, his hands resting easily on the reins.

"Oh, thank you, Sir." she replied.

Peter reached for her hand and helped her to the seat beside him. Ellen suddenly was at a loss for words. She could think of nothing at all to say. Thank goodness they had only a short distance to go. He surely would think her stupid.

"We're very pleased that you will be coming to the house, Miss Davis," Peter began, after a few moments of silence.

"Thank you, Sir. It's a fine house and I'm happy to be of service," Ellen replied in a barely audible voice.

She clasped her hands together in her lap. Now there was only the sound of the wagon's wheels and the rhythmic gait of the horses as they continued on down the road. When they at last reached the Crowley farm, Ellen started to move from the seat and Peter spoke quickly.

"One moment. I'll help you down."

He came around to the other side of the wagon and reached for her arm.

"Now that I'm here I may as well take back some eggs," he said, tethering the horses to the fencepost.

"Oh, yes, Sir. Mr. Crowley can help you with that."

Ellen was so unused to being around young men that she wanted desperately to escape to her room.

"Thank you for bringing me home, Mr. Hawke," she added.

"You're quite welcome." Peter replied and headed towards the barn to find Adam Crowley.

Ellen hurried to the house, untying her bonnet as she went. When she reached her bedroom she looked out the window and saw Mr. Crowley and Peter talking and gesturing to one another. Then they began walking towards the house. Ellen was trembling. She unbuttoned her coat and got out of her brown dress. What on earth was the matter with her? As she fastened an apron about her waist, she caught sight of herself in the mirror. Her cheeks were flushed and her hair was curled damply around her forehead. Her hands felt cold, but her face was moist with perspiration. Ellen suddenly was embarrassed. She reached for the hairbrush and smoothed her hair, then looked out the window again. The wagon was gone. Straightening her skirt, Ellen started for the kitchen to prepare the evening meal. It would be the last one she would cook at Crowley farm. Tomorrow she would move to the cottage and on Thursday she would be starting a new life.

• 3 •

The tiny stone cottage into which Ellen Davis moved her few belongings had only two rooms. A kitchen-sitting room and a small bedroom. It appeared that no one had lived there for some time as the little house smelled mouldy and damp from having been closed up without heat or air. Cobwebs nestled in the corners of the windows in delicate, fanciful designs. A pale print covered the settee in the small sitting room. There was a rocking chair and a round table by the window. Ellen assumed the table must be for one's meals since there seemed to be no other. There was a tiny fire grate in the wall. The floor was bare and the curtains at the two windows were thin and worn and smelled of dust.

Ellen sighed heavily and looked about the room. The kitchen seemed adequate, but she certainly would have to do something to make the place less dismal. Fresh curtains and some kind of floor covering would help considerably. The brass tea kettle which belonged to her mother would brighten the kitchen, and the oil lamp she had in her bedroom at Mr. Crowley's could sit on the round table by the window. Mr. Crowley had given the lamp to her when she left.

The bedroom furniture was meager also, but the bed was comfortable and one could be thankful for that at least. No matter. In a few weeks she could make the little house more cheerful.

Reverend Thomas had explained to Ellen that the owner of the cottage had gone to Bristol and decided to stay in that city. However, he would not sell the house, but only let it.

Ellen's first morning at Hawkes Nest was spent cleaning the supper dishes which had been left the night before, and preparing breakfast for William and Peter Hawke. She had awakened with the first light of day and hurried with her dressing so she would not be late. The brothers greeted Ellen as they appeared in the kitchen, but ignored her from that time on. They were so busy talking about all of the letters they must write to their father's customers, and how that must be done within the next few weeks, and of the necessary arrangements they must make. They pushed their chairs back from the table when they had finished with breakfast, and were still conversing as they left the room.

Ellen was a little disappointed to have become a fixture quite so rapidly, but then she shrugged her shoulders as she realized that there was a vast difference in being a hired girl for a man who was a friend of her father's, and being a housekeeper for two men to whom she was a stranger. She hardly could expect to be taken into any conversation as she had with Mr. Crowley.

After adjusting the strings of her apron and fastening them more tightly about her waist, Ellen picked up the empty teacups from the table and put them in a pan of water to wash. She began singing softly as she washed Mary Hawke's flowered china.

The muffled voices of William and Peter drifted out from the workroom occasionally and then there was silence. Ellen could hear only the ticking of the clock on the kitchen wall. Such a pretty one it was, with its hand-painted face and softly ringing bell.

Finished with the dishes, she looked about the room.

The floor could stand a good scrubbing and the curtains needed washing. Pulling the curtain aside to look out the window she could see it was again a bright, sunny day, making it hard to stay inside after the long, gloomy winter. Maybe she could pick some flowers first for the dining table before she started her chores, and perhaps she would be allowed to take some home to brighten her own room. Going about her tasks Ellen stopped often to admire the beautiful objects in the house. She sighed, wondering if she ever would have so fine a home.

Peter Hawke's voice roused her from her thoughts by saying that he and his brother would not be taking tea today, but would like an early supper instead. There he was standing not five feet from her as she stood looking into the parlor from the hallway. She had opened the closed doors to see what was behind them. Embarrassed and flustered, Ellen quickly closed the doors.

"Of course, Sir. I'll have it ready at five. I'm sorry, Sir, I only looked in to see if—"

"It's quite all right." he interrupted. "You'll be doing that room in time anyway," he added as he walked away.

Ellen's face was flushed and she felt that same strange feeling she had had in the carriage the day he had driven her back to Mr. Crowley's. William Hawke didn't make her feel so flustered and foolish. He was easy to talk to and seemed so gentle and kind. Of course Peter Hawke had not been anything but kind and gentle, too. She must stop this nonsense, she thought, shaking her head.

As soon as Ellen had prepared the evening supper she put on her hat and coat and hurried away, forgetting to ask about the flowers. The soft cool air felt good on her warm cheeks. As she walked towards her little cottage the varied smells of cooking wafted from the houses in the village and she was eager to get home for her own supper.

When Ellen reached the cottage she was surprised to feel fatigued. The work had not been all that hard the first day. Certainly not as strenuous as at Mr. Crowley's, she thought to herself.

After hanging her coat and hat on the hook in the bedroom she decided to sit down in the rocking chair for a few minutes before she started to prepare her supper. She rocked slowly back and forth, occasionally brushing a wisp of hair from her face. In spite of being tired, she thought, I feel happy.

"I'm going to like it there," she whispered to herself.

Henrietta Stokes came to the house the very next day to meet Ellen and to satisfy herself, so Ellen believed, that Hawkes Nest would have proper care. Mrs. Stokes seemed unduly concerned about Mary Hawke's china and offered considerable advice as to its care.

"You know this china is of the finest quality and not one piece has been cracked or broken," Henrietta remarked as she held a dainty cup in her hand.
"If you put only one piece at a time in the wash water, I'm sure nothing will happen to it," she suggested.

After noticing Mrs. Stokes' obvious condition, Ellen thought it would be far better if she kept to her bed instead of fussing about her mother's china.

Already the word had spread through Woodbridge that the Hawkes had hired a housekeeper, and a young one at that. The usual gossip and sly remarks were made, fortunately not within Ellen's hearing. Some raucous fellows at The Bell were wagering over their tankards of ale as to whether it would be William or Peter who would bed her down first.

"The Hawke brothers'll be fightin' and scrappin' over than 'un, I'll betcha. Those peaches look mighty full an' ripe an' I'll wager she could put up quite a hassle," said Adam Barton, wiping his mouth on his sleeve.

Laughter rang through the room, but neither the

Hawke brothers nor Ellen were aware that they were the object of such great merriment.

The next few weeks passed rapidly. Ellen was learning that much needed to be done at Hawkes Nest. Besides the laundry and cleaning and cooking, there was brass to polish and many windows to wash. Aside from her work she found she was waiting anxiously each day to see Peter. He always had a bright smile and a cheery "Good morning." Just looking at him made her feel happy. When he smiled his eyes twinkled and she found that charming.

Ellen had decided that no doubt Peter always would have the best of life because he seemed to expect it. When he walked his step was springy and graceful, belying the strength in his body. When he laughed it was with great vigor and enjoyment. He would slap his hand against his leg and roar with delight at a humorous remark or joke.

"Do you really think it's all that funny, Peter?" William would ask, smiling at his brother with amusement.

Now Ellen folded Peter's cothes with extra care when she laid them away. Of course she gave William Hawke's clothing the same attention, but not with the warm feeling which came over her whenever she touched anything belonging to Peter.

When one considered the usual lot of domestic servants in England, Ellen was most fortunate to be employed by considerate and thoughtful masters. Her wages were paid weekly, her Sundays were her own and she was treated kindly. Indeed she was most fortunate.

Ellen had spent considerable time in the village shops selecting some plain thin fabric for window curtains, a few pieces of earthenware and some cooking utensils. There still was no floor covering at the cottage, but with summer coming she decided she could manage until the winter months. Having never before lived completely alone, Ellen found that she rather enjoyed the independence. She admitted to herself that at times she longed for someone to talk to in the evenings, but always there were her books to fill that void. The books numbered only four and she had read and re-read them so much that she had almost memorized the pages. Nonetheless, reading was a joy to Ellen.

She had great imagination and sometimes her thoughts bordered on fantasy. Oh, to be a great lady in a manor house with dozens of rooms and many servants, with balls and parties to go to, and handsome young men eager for her hand. When Ellen became quite carried away, she always managed to smile at her own illusions and face the true reality of her life. Coming from a family of quite modest and ordinary background, even though her father had managed to save something for her legacy, she realized that her dreams were far beyond possibility. In fact, they were as unlikely as some of the stories in her books.

Today Ellen had baked bread, the tantalizing fragrance permeating the entire house, and William and Peter had eaten ravenously. Watching them at the table she was pleased with her efforts. Walking home to her cottage later she wished with every step that she really could be the mistress of Hawkes Nest. What a happiness that would be!

After having some bread and tea for her supper, Ellen sat down in her rocking chair. Feeling drowsy, she leaned back, listening to the sounds of the village. Footsteps on the street, children's voices at play, somewhere a barking dog, and the sound of a wagon's heavy wheels behind the clip-clop, clip-clop of a horse. All the sounds of living, she thought. Different from the Crowley farm. There it had been mostly animal sounds. The cows and the chickens, the goat and the pigs. Raucous and shrill sounds. She liked it much better here in Woodbridge.

Ellen leaned forward in her chair, startled by a knocking at the door. It now was very dark so she must have dozed off. Who could be coming to her house? She quickly lighted the lamp and looked through the thin curtains at the window, but she could see nothing in the darkness. The knock sounded again.

"Who is it?" she called.

"Peter Hawke, Miss Davis."

Ellen caught her breath and opened the door. The oil lamp on the table cast a soft glow over her face. She felt the color rush to her cheeks as she saw Peter standing on the step, tall and startlingly handsome, a grey cape buttoned close about his shoulders.

"I'm sorry to both you at this hour," he began.

"Oh, it's no bother at all, Sir," Ellen was quick to respond. "Won't you come in?"

Peter stepped into the cottage and glanced about the tiny room. Then he smiled directly at Ellen, his eyes bright in the lamplight.

"William and I will be leaving early tomorrow morning. He has decided to go to Bristol with me after all and we wanted to tell you that you will not be needed at the house for a few days. I shall be away at least a week. William probably will be back by Sunday."

"It's very kind of you to come and tell me, Sir," said Ellen. "I'll have everything in order when you return."

"Is there anything we can get for you in Bristol?" Peter asked.

"Oh, my, I wouldn't know, Sir. I've never been to a large city like that," Ellen laughed in reply.

"Very well then. We shall see you in a few days."

As Peter moved towards the door his eyes held Ellen's for a few brief seconds. He seemed about to speak further, then he was gone out into the blackness.

Ellen's heart was pounding in her breast as she slowly closed the door. The sensation she felt was bewildering. Could she be falling in love? Is this what it was like? A feeling of happiness and sadness all at the same time? The tightness of her throat? The tingling feeling which seemed to run all over her body?

Ellen opened the door again and looked out into the dark night. She realized she had been so surprised at her own reaction that she had not even heard Peter's footsteps as he walked away from the cottage. It was almost as if he had not been there at all, as if she had been dreaming. Could she just have imagined he was there? But no, she remembered clearly his saying "Is there anything we can get for you in Bristol?"

● 4 ●

The two brothers boarded the coach to Bristol where Peter planned to continue on to Salisbury and William would return to Woodbridge after one or two days' business. They found the seaport more congested than ever with people and wheeled conveyances of every description. There was an air of excitement, however, at the sight of the ships crowded into the harbor.

England's mercantile fleet now was the greatest in the world. Docks were being built in every port town of any size, and lighthouses were established to aid in safer voyages. The demand from America for goods was astonishing. Ships' holds were filled with fine cotton and woolen fabrics, English cutlery, hardware, books, twine, spices and seeds for planting. The new country was expanding with unprecedented speed. She needed iron and steel and a thousand different kinds of manufactured goods. The ports of England and Europe were eagerly responding to those needs. Fortunes were being made by the shipowners and tradesmen.

It took almost forty days for the voyage from England to America, a little less for the return trip. The three-masters crowding the harbor were known as packets, so-called because they carried mail and packages. These ships surging across the Atlantic were also known for their bad food and stagnant water. Their crews often were a mixture of ruffians from the waterfronts of Liverpool and New York, and inexperienced young boys looking for adventure. The robbing of passengers or the knifing of a ship's officer was not an uncommon practice.

Still, the sight of the ships being loaded or unloaded seemed ever fascinating to the crowds of people milling about the docks watching the activity. Occasionally one would hear the harrowing tale of being chased by scavengers on the run to the West Indies, or of a howling gale that was the near finish of the ship itself.

While William was engaged in a business discussion, Peter had walked to the dock area and was sitting on an empty keg watching a ship about to set sail for Boston.

The last of the cargo had been taken aboard and the first mate was barking orders to the crew. Suddenly a large black carriage came riding so fast by Peter that he jumped to his feet and stepped backwards to avoid being hit. The thought occurred to him that so impressive a carriage with its beautifully matched pair of greys surely must belong to someone of considerable importance.

His curiosity forced him to move closer to where the carriage had lurched to a stop in front of the Boston-bound ship. A rather short and rotund man bolted out of the door and hurried to the side of the three-master. He was wearing a flowing black cape and a tall dark grey hat. Peter could not guess his age from where he was standing, but assumed by his movements and bearing that he would be in his late years. He was carrying a rather large box and apparently was most anxious to have it sail with the ship. However, he was having difficulty making himself heard by anyone on the deck high above him.

Then Peter's attention was again drawn to the carriage as another person stepped down from the open door. It was a young girl. She appeared very small and fragile to Peter in her long blue velvet cape, especially in the midst of the crates and barrels where she stood. She spoke to the older man, urging him not to step too close to the edge of the dock. Peter thought she called him "Father."

He watched her closely as she approached the man with the box. He could just glimpse her very dark hair **curling from under the edge of her high-crowned blue** velvet bonnet. As Peter was about to offer his assistance, one of the crew took the box and it was safely aboard.

The girl turned to go back to the carriage and as she did so she glanced squarely at Peter. She seemed rather **surprised that anyone had been watching her.**

Peter was startled by her beauty. Her eyes were very dark, framed with thick, sooty lashes, under smooth well-shaped brows. Her skin was the palest ivory and her lips were full and rose-pink beneath a small, upturned nose. Peter could only guess at the figure under the voluminous velvet cape, but her hands and feet were small and delicate in appearance.

In an instant she was inside the darkness of the carriage with the elderly man following her. They were quickly gone. Peter's eyes followed the carriage as it rounded the corner and disappeared. He heard a hoarse-voiced laugh behind him and turned to face an old man puffing on a long pipe.

"They jolly well *better* take the package," he muttered. "He owns the damn ship!"

Peter was about to ask him who the shipowner was, but the old man shuffled off, shaking his head, and Peter decided that it was very unlikely he ever again would see the girl or her father so there was no need for further inquiry. He turned and started back up the street to meet William.

Later that evening when they were having an ale at the

Rose and Crown Inn, Peter remarked suddenly to William that this afternoon he had seen the most beautiful girl he ever had set eyes on.

"Where?" asked William.

"Down by the docks. I went there while you were at Eldredge's. She got out of a carriage, a most handsome one at that, and I still can hardly believe I really saw her," Peter explained.

William laughed. "Maybe you really didn't."

"Oh, but I did. Her father's a shipowner, I was told. At least I assume he was her father. She was really beautiful, William."

"Why didn't you find out more about her?"

"Well, I'll most likely never see her again. I decided there was little point in asking. Now I wish I had."

"Well, cheer up, brother," said William. "Maybe you'll find her in Salisbury."

William set his empty tankard on the table and got to his feet.

"Right now I'm off to bed," he continued.

Stretching his long arms above his head, he started for the stairs. Peter decided to follow him. He didn't feel like having another ale anyway.

Unable to get to sleep right away, Peter lay on his back, his hands beneath his head, watching the shadows on the ceiling. The sight of the girl in the blue velvet cape still was vivid in his mind. He wondered who she was and where she lived. What might her name be? Why hadn't he asked the old man who they were? Peter was annoyed with himself for having let such an opportunity escape him.

Then a faint smile crossed his lips. He couldn't imagine where or how soon, but he knew he would see the girl again. He suddenly felt very sure he would see her. Peter wondered if she would remember him at all or any part of the incident on the dock. She had glanced at him only a matter of seconds. He would just have to wait and see.

Peter's journey to Salisbury was uneventful. The ride in the coach was rough and tiresome and he was thankful for a stop at the inn where he could change to a fresh shirt and enjoy a glass of ale. He visited two places of business whose proprietors were most solicitous regarding his father, and Peter assumed they were sincere in their sympathy.

He found it increasingly difficult to keep his mind from wandering back to the docks at Bristol and to the girl in the blue cape. However, he accepted the fact that seeing her there a second time was only the remotest possibility and he ought to turn his eyes elsewhere. To the round and buxom chambermaid, for instance, who brought him clean towels and a ewer of water. He smiled to himself as that thought occurred to him. She looked quite ripe for a toss in the quilts.

On the way back to Woodbridge the coach stopped briefly in Bristol, but hardly long enough to walk to the docks. Besides, it was most unlikely the big black carriage would be there. So Peter reconciled himself to returning to Woodbridge and settling down to some long and tedious work. At least he had some good news to pass on to William. Mr. Thomas Pevesey had ordered a new carriage.

● 5 ●

While William and Peter were away on their business trip, Ellen Davis went to services at the small stone church. It was her first visit since coming into Woodbridge. Reverend Thomas greeted her warmly and inquired about her new surroundings. Ellen was grateful that he did not mention that she had been so long in coming to church. She had waited until she had a new bonnet to wear with her brown coat.

Several of the older members of the congregation introduced themselves. Other stared at her dumbly. The young people, particularly the young ladies, eyed her with suspicion and curiosity. She supposed this was not unusual since she hardly was known in the village.

As Ellen walked back towards her cottage she was aware of footsteps behind her. She ignored them and continued on her way. She listened again. The steps were still coming. She slowed her walk, hoping whoever it was would pass her by. Then she stopped suddenly and turned around. No one was in sight. Whoever it was had simply disappeared.

Ellen couldn't see anyone except some people still standing on the steps of the church. How strange. Could it have been the echo of her own steps? She continued walking down the road and heard no sound behind her. Perhaps no one had been there at all. Yet she was so certain she had heard footsteps following her. Whoever it was may have gone into one of the houses along the road and that could explain why she never saw ayone when she turned around. Maybe someone had intended speaking to her and then had not.

Ellen reached her cottage and went inside. After preparing her mid-day meal, she decided to make some spice biscuits to take to Hawkes Nest. William Hawke just might be returning to Woodbridge from Bristol before dark and she could surprise him with something nice to eat with his tea. She sometimes wondered why William and Peter had not yet married. They both were unusually attractive and seemed to be well-liked by most everyone. Ellen had seen three or four pretty young ladies at the church this morning, all looking demure and feminine in their lace-trimmed bonnets. In fact, she felt plain and uninteresting next to them. Their pale and fragile looks made her even more conscious of her healthy and rosy appearance. Young ladies of the time strived to appear delicate and helpless, and as a matter of social pride were expected to do as little domestic work as possible. The "Sheltered Lady" ideal was spreading to the smallest town. Even some farmers' wives were considered "too fine to work." Delicacy was a much sought after virtue. Since Ellen was employed as a housekeeper, she would not be thought of in the same terms as the other young ladies in Woodbridge, even though many of them came from farm families. She realized her social standing would be very limited. No matter. Ellen already knew what her life was going to be, and she knew her place.

Wrapping a clean cloth around the spice biscuits, Ellen started out on the short walk to Hawkes Nest. As she passed the row of houses in the village, she thought she again heard steps behind her. She turned around quickly this time and saw a young girl, about ten or twelve, standing a few feet behind her.

"Good afternoon," said Ellen.

"Good afternoon," was the reply.

"Did you want to speak to me?" Ellen inquired.

The child stared at her, not answering right away. She was not a pretty little girl. Her hair was limp and a muddy brown, obviously in need of washing. Her eyes were small and rather beady. However, Ellen noticed that her clothing was clean and her face and hands looked well scrubbed. Then the child asked her if she was the lady at Hawkes Nest.

"Yes, I do work there. I'm on my way to the house now," Ellen explained.

The child's face brightened noticeably.

"I'd so like to see inside that house. Could I go with you?" she asked.

Ellen hesitated as she looked carefully at the little girl.

"Are you the one who followed me from church this morning?" she asked.

The girl dropped her eyes and her face flushed with color.

"I heard Reverend Thomas say something to you about the house. That's all," she replied softly.

"Who are you?" asked Ellen.

"I'm Molly Barton. I live right there in that house. My father helps Mr. Arthur. He's the blacksmith," she explained.

Ellen searched the child's face again. Then she smiled.

"All right, Molly Barton, come along then. But you must not touch anything."

The little girl's eyes widened and her mouth dropped into a broad smile. The two of them went on down the road, the child kicking a pebble now and then with her shoe. Ellen smiled down at Molly Barton and realized that she had just made her first new friend in Woodbridge.

• 6 •

After an unusually long and cold winter, spring seemed late in coming. Now the flowering fruit trees in the surrounding orchards were blossoming profusely, the spent flowers drifting down in the gentle breeze, creating a snowy carpet beneath the branches. Rose-bushes were a mass of bud and bloom, the full-blown flowers filling the soft spring air with a heady perfume. Sweet William and tall phlox crowded against each other in the tiny gardens behind the village houses.

The yellow climbing rose by the big oak door at Hawkes Nest gave Ellen the greatest pleasure each morning as she came up the walk to start her round of duties. She stopped to admire the flowers and to smell their fragrance. Her life was falling into a routine now and she felt as if she had been in Woodbridge much longer than a few months. She went to the church regularly, but had not yet attended any of the social functions, though she had been asked. She visited with the people in the shops and they seemed friendly towards her.

Ellen had convinced herself that she was secretly in love with Peter Hawke. Of course Peter had not the remotest idea what was going on in Ellen's mind. He saw her usually only twice, maybe three times a day, and there was practically no conversation in any event. She kept the house in immaculate order and she was a fine cook. There seemed no reason to discuss her duties at all. William had commented on more than one occasion that Ellen was wasting her talents on them. She really should marry one of the fine lads in the village.

Ellen had smiled, but said nothing. She didn't tell them that she had been escorted home from church twice by Ben Hammond and that he had invited her for tea at The Bell. She found him rather dull, however, and admitted to herself that they must appear strange together. He was short and slightly built with very slender hands and feet. His boots seemed almost feminine, they were so narrow. Still, he was someone to talk to and she realized that she was noticed when she was with him. Also, she did enjoy their teas at the inn.

So the weeks went by and Ellen was quite content with her life in Woodbridge. She saw Peter every day and she was becoming more and more necessary to Hawkes Nest. Both William and Peter mentioned that the house had never looked better since their mother died and they really never could manage without Ellen.

William seemed to be away on a business trip every few weeks. At these times Ellen noticed that Peter was very restless and spent a good part of his time riding across the valley. Often he would not return until just before dark when she was about to leave for her cottage. His supper was ready, for which he always thanked her, but there was rarely more than polite conversation.

Now William was taking the coach to Bristol again. He had received a letter from a Mr. Lowell Howard inquiring about an order for a two-wheeled cab or chaise. He had asked that William come to Bristol on Thursday to discuss the matter. When William mentioned Bristol, Peter inquired if he would like him to go along.

"Well, Peter, I'd really appreciate it if you would finish the harness for Mr. Pevesey. I'd like you to take it to Salisbury in a week," William replied.

Peter nodded his head. It really didn't matter anyway and certainly there was no need for both of them to go to Bristol. William seemed to be more skillful with the specifications and financial arrangements with their customers, a part of the business which Peter did not care about.

This particular day was warm and sunny and Peter found himself more and more often looking out the windows of the workroom at the beauty of the countryside. The sun was sparkling on the river in the distance and the green of the trees and grass seemed a softer color than he had remembered. It was during one of these lapses that Ellen suddenly appeared at the door of the room, something she rarely did when they were working.

"It's so beautiful outdoors, Sir, I thought you might like to have your noon meal in the garden," she suggested.

"That's a most pleasant idea—if you will join me," he replied, putting his tools down and stretching his long arms above his head.

Ellen was startled and felt her heart leap.

"If you wish, Sir," she said, softly.

Peter carried a small table and then two chairs from the kitchen to the garden at the side of the house. Bees were buzzing about the rose bushes, and now and then a butterfly fluttered its wings gracefully as it meandered lazily from bush to bush. The air was still and the sky a cloudless brilliant blue.

Ellen had taken special care with luncheon this day. Roast chicken with baby carrots from the garden, and small boiled potatoes with fresh butter. There were scones with strawberry preserves and a large pot of tea.

"Ellen, this is truly delicious. How did you learn to cook so well?" asked Peter as he finished the last of the scones.

"My mother taught me to cook when I was very young. She never was very well and I had to learn most everything when I was quite small," Ellen explained.

"I'm surprised Mr. Crowley didn't take you with him to Liverpool. On the other hand, I'm very glad he didn't."

"Well, Sir, he is with his daughter and there was never any thought that I might go up there."

"One of these days you will meet the right fellow and we'll lose you too," Peter remarked. "I've seen you with Mr. Hammond on more than one occasion," he added.

Ellen's cheeks flushed pink.

"He's just a friend, Sir."

Peter leaned back in the chair, his arms folded across his chest. His shirt sleeves were rolled up to his elbows and now the sun glinted on the reddish blonde hair on his forearms.

"Do you like it here, Ellen? I mean in Woodbridge."

"Oh yes, Sir. I wouldn't care to leave at all. Would you?" Ellen asked, breathlessly.

Peter looked up at the blue sky. He appeared lost in thought and it seemed a long time before he answered. Ellen studied his face, waiting.

"There are times, Ellen, when I should like very much to go to America. I sometimes feel that I don't want to spend the rest of my life at the same trade. I want to do something different. Of course I've had no training in anything else, but there's so much that's new in America I'm sure I could find something for which I'm fitted. If it were not for William, I'd go now."

Ellen felt her body go slack against the back of the chair as he spoke. The thought of Peter going so far away and perhaps never coming back made her feel suddenly weak.

"Of course if he should marry, I wouldn't hesitate,"

Peter continued, "but neither of us has found a wife."

He laughed then, his big marvelous laugh.

"I guess we both are looking for something that doesn't exist, really. If we were smart we'd marry a fine cook like you. Father always said we'd wait too long and end up with the short end of the stick!"

Ellen could think of nothing to reply so she got to her feet and began gathering up the lunch things. Peter stood up too.

"Here, let me help you with that."

He never had offered assistance before, but then this was the first time they had shared a meal together. Ellen was very conscious of Peter's tall muscular body next to her as they stood by the small table stacking the empty dishes. As she turned and started towards the kitchen door she caught Peter's eyes watching her. She returned his gaze, not moving.

"Your hair is beautiful in the sunlight, Ellen. Looks like molten gold."

"Does it, Sir? My, I'd be rich if it were, now, wouldn't I?" she laughed.

Their eyes held each other for a moment more. Then he turned back to the table to pick up his own pile of dishes and Ellen went on into the house. When they had returned everything to the kitchen Peter remarked that it had been most pleasant and when William returned they should do the same thing again. He went back to his work and he suddenly wondered what William might be doing this day in Bristol.

• 7 •

William Hawke walked along Worcester Lane in Bristol
looking for Lowell Howard's residence. The street was
fairly wide with rows of fine houses on either side.
William supposed that tea merchants and woolen manu-
facturers or shipowners probably lived behind the finely
detailed doors of those houses.

Lowell Howard's home was named "Seagull's Point"
and William saw the name over the door of a large white
house on the corner, a thick boxwood hedge outlining
the entire property. He raised the shining brass knocker
on the door and tapped it twice. Then again, and the
door opened. A young girl stood facing him. He barely
could see her because of the small amount of light in the
hallway, but he guessed she was about seventeen.

"Yes, Sir?"

"I have an appointment with Mr. Howard. My name
is William Hawke."

"Oh yes, Sir. He's expecting you. Come this way,
please."

William followed the girl along the dimly lighted
corridor. She opened a door and directed him to enter.

"Father, this is Mr. Hawke."

Lowell Howard stood up and stretched out his hand
in greeting. William took a long stride towards him and
shook his hand. Mr. Howard was a small rotund man
and his coat and trousers were straining to cover his
large stomach and very ample legs. His hair was almost

white and was thinning on the top of his head. He had a pleasant smile and William judged him to be a man of good humor.

After motioning his guest to a chair beside the fire burning in the small grate, Mr. Howard turned to the girl who still was standing by the door.

"Margaret, would you be kind enough to ask Mary to bring us some tea?" Then he turned to William. "Perhaps you would prefer sherry."

"Tea is fine. Thank you," William replied.

"Some of both, Margaret."

"Of course, Father," said the girl and she quickly disappeared.

With a sweeping glance about the room, William concluded that Lowell Howard obviously was a man of considerable means. The carpet was thick and richly patterned. Draperies at the windows were a heavy brocade. A finely carved desk stood against one wall and on its top were some beautiful leather-bound volumes and a crystal paperweight. The room was comfortable and very masculine. The smell of tobacco was prevalent.

After a brief reference to the spring weather, Mr. Howard began an explanation to William as to why he had requested him to come to Bristol.

"When I learned that you planned to continue on with your father's business, I decided you were the man to call upon. My daughter will be having her eighteenth birthday in a few months and I should like to give her a really fine vehicle. I was thinking of a two-wheeled cab, nothing so large that she can't learn to handle it herself. Can you do something for me?"

"Certainly," William replied. "I'd be most pleased. Have you decided what fabric and wood you would like?"

Before Mr. Howard could respond, the girl

reappeared with the tea tray. William quickly got to his feet, took the tray from her hands and set it on the small table next to the fire. Only then did he really look at her. He scarcely had taken notice of her when she led him from the hall to the sitting room, but now William was astonished that he could have missed seeing at once how beautiful she was. Standing in front of her with the tray, he realized she was very small, not quite reaching his shoulder. Her large round eyes were a very dark brown with heavy lashes, and her hair seemed to form a halo of dark tendrils about her pale face. Her lips were full and gently curved and just faintly pink.

"Mr. Hawke, this is my daughter, Margaret."

She curtsied slightly as William acknowledged the introduction. As she bent down he could see the small rounded breasts pushing against the smooth bodice of her dress.

"Mary was busy upstairs, Father, so I brought the tray myself," she said as she smoothed her skirt. "Would you like anything else?"

"No, dear. Thank you. This will be fine."

Mr. Howard did not invite Margaret to share the tea with them, to William's disappointment, and as she walked out of the room he watched her small body sway from side to side as she moved. She seemed so fragile and so feminine. He could not recall ever having seen anyone quite like her.

Lowell Howard continued to discuss the plans for the carriage while they sipped the hot tea and ate ginger cake, and William assured him that he would be able to do whatever he wished. William would return to Bristol within a week to choose the finest wood, leather and brass fittings, and they could make the financial arrangements at that time.

As their conversation waned, Mr. Howard stood up and indicated the meeting was over. William hoped

Margaret would return to the room or perhaps see him to the door, but she did not. As he went down the steps and turned into the street, he caught a glimpse of her peering from behind the curtains at what must have been the parlor window. He smiled to himself and continued walking down the street.

The wheels of the coach rattled along the road with a monotonous rhythm as they carried William back to Woodbridge and he found that he could not get Margaret out of his mind. She seemed so gentle, so lovely. There surely was no one like her in Woodbridge. Perhaps on his next visit to Bristol he could arrange to see her again for a proper visit.

When William returned to Hawkes Nest he learned that Henrietta had died giving birth to her third child, a stillborn son. James Stokes, deeply grieved, did not want to see or talk to anyone. Finally, Reverend Thomas persuaded him to see his wife's brothers. William and Peter tried to be understanding and sympathetic, but their efforts were less than successful because of their own feeling of loss.

Henrietta's two young children, Patience and Andrew, appeared bewildered and frightened. Peter put his arms about the two tiny bodies and hugged them close to his chest, wordlessly trying to comfort them.

The day of the funeral was cloudy and grey. As Ellen Davis stood in the crowded churchyard she remembered that Henry Hawke had been buried there only a few months ago. Now his daughter was placed beside him and his wife. Such a sad year for his sons.

Later that afternoon Ellen carried the tea tray into the sitting room at Hawkes Nest where William and Peter were talking in low tones. William thanked her and as she started out of the room he asked her to remain and sit down for a few moments.

"Ellen, you could be of considerable help to Mr.

Stokes the next few days," he began. "He has decided to take the children to his mother in Worcester until he can make arrangements about the house and his business. Right now he feels he would like to leave Woodbridge," William explained. "He may change his mind, of course, but Worcester is his home and his mother could be of help with the children. If you could go to his house and bundle up the children's things and whatever else he needs for the journey, we would be most grateful," he continued.

"Of course, Sir. I'll do whatever I can," Ellen remarked. "The poor little ones. How sad for them," she added.

"You needn't be concerned about us here, Ellen," said William. "We can manage for a few days without you.'

"I can drive you out to the house tomorrow, if you like," Peter volunteered.

"Very well, Sir."

By the end of the week James Stokes and his two children were on the coach to Worcester. He vowed he would keep in touch with Henrietta's brothers, but since his business was saddle and harness making he could set up most anywhere, and William and Peter doubted he would ever be back in Woodbridge. While they never had shared a close relationship with their brother-in-law, they knew they would miss seeing the children.

After only four days at home, William was again setting out for Bristol, for two reasons. He had told Lowell Howard he would return within a week, and he had promised James Stokes he would consult a solicitor about handling Henrietta's share of her father's will. So he expected to be gone for several days.

Peter was becoming used to William's frequent absences and had settled down to his work with unexpected concentration and interest. He made no further comment about leaving Woodbridge. Ellen secretly hoped that while William was away she and Peter could share another picnic in the garden, but the June days had turned cool and misty.

Peter worked a full day, then spent the early evening with friends in the village. Sometimes when Ellen returned to the house in the morning she would find his supper untouched. He had not talked with her again other than a polite "Good morning" or "Good evening." She supposed she had no right to expect more. There really was no need for discussion other than that related to one's duties. So Ellen went on with her work, experiencing happiness in seeing Peter each day and dreaming her own fantasy that she was mistress of Hawkes Nest.

Molly Barton had been coming to Ellen's cottage more and more often. The two of them would sit on the step when the weather was fine, and talk or just watch the twilight pass into the night. When it was rainy or cool they sat by the tiny fire grate and Ellen read one of her books aloud. Molly seemed to enjoy the reading most of all.

One evening the child's parents stopped by the cottage. This was the first time Ellen had seen them.

"We're Molly's folks, Miss Davis," said Amy Barton.

She was a tall, thin woman with dark hair and pale grey eyes.

"Molly, git home an' help yer mother with the supper."

Adam Barton spoke gruffly, taking no notice of Ellen. He was stocky and muscular, as one would expect a blacksmith to be, Ellen thought later.

"Molly seems to enjoy being with you, Miss Davis," said Amy Barton. "Talks about you all the time, but if she gets too bothersome you just shoo her out."

"I enjoy her company, Mrs. Barton. We like to read together. She's really no bother at all," Ellen remarked.

Also, Ellen thought to herself, the child kept her from being lonely. The people in the village seemed friendly enough, but everyone seemed so busy there was little time for visiting.

Ben Hammond continued to walk home with Ellen after church. They still would have their teas at The Bell on Sundays and sometimes on the fairest days he would suggest they walk down by the stream and pick the watercress which grew so abundantly there.

Peter would be at the church too on Sunday mornings, but since he sat in the family pew at the front and she usually was near the rear of the sanctuary, they rarely spoke to one another. At the close of the service he always was caught up in a crowd of people offering him invitations to Sunday dinner or to tea later in the day. The young ladies waited from Sunday to Sunday, each hoping he would walk home with one of them or accept a family invitation. Since Sunday was Ellen's day off from Hawkes Nest, she never knew how many of those invitations Peter accepted. How she envied the fluttering, sighing and giggling that went on from the young girls as they and their parents clustered around Peter, and William too when he was there, on the steps of the church each Sunday.

Ellen watched Peter smiling and nodding his head, being gracious and charming to them all, and she felt miserable and unattractive as she walked away, Ben Hammond by her side. She told herself that somehow, some way, she would have to rid herself of her strong feelings for Peter. Nothing whatever could come of their relationship. She was a servant in his house and there never would be anything more between them than polite conversation and casual interest.

When she was feeling particularly unhappy she

thought that perhaps the best thing to do would be to marry Ben Hammond. He had asked her, to her complete surprise, after only a few months' acquaintance. So far Ellen had resisted his advances. Even now, walking beside him, she persuaded herself that she really was needed at the Hawke household and that regardless of the consequences she would stay.

8

William had invited Lowell Howard and his daughter, Margaret, for tea at the Imperial Hotel in Bristol and now was in the grand salon awaiting their arrival. As he saw them coming through the door, he quickly got to his feet and went to meet them, his hand outstretched toward Mr. Howard. Bowing slightly to Margaret, William again was taken by surprise at her unusual beauty. Her dark eyes seemed even more luminous and the deep red of her velvet bonnet and cape made her lips appear a softer pink than he had remembered. Her hands were encased in a small brown fur muff which matched the collar on her cape.

Leading his guests to a table by a window, William indicated to a waiter that they were ready to be served. He had talked with Mr. Howard the day before concerning the details of the carriage, so this was to be purely a social afternoon.

Since Lowell Howard had not volunteered any information as to the nature of his business, William politely had not infringed on that privacy. They discussed England's politics, trade with America, the fine spring weather, as well as the social season in Bristol, which William knew little about.

"My club is having a cotillion on Saturday, a week. Perhaps you might like to join us, Mr. Hawke?" suggested Mr. Howard.

William glanced quickly at Margaret.

"We should be most happy to have you as our guest," she said, her voice soft and low-pitched.

"I am highly honored," William acknowledged.

Just at that moment he wondered how his father knew that Mary Adelaide Evans was the one he should take for a wife. Since young women were brought up in a most delicate, secluded manner, it often was difficult to know much about them. They were taught music and embroidery and the social graces to help them be attractive to men. Yet so many marriages were arranged and the young girls were kept so closely chaperoned, one did not truly know one's wife or husband until after marriage.

William was aware that Margaret was watching him closely as he conversed with her father. What might she think of him? Indeed he hoped he was making a favorable impression.

The tea hour was over all too soon as Mr. Howard reached for his hat and gloves on the chair next to him.

"I'm afraid we shall have to take our leave, Mr. Hawke. We are expecting guests for the evening and we shall have to be home in time to change," said Lowell Howard, getting to his feet.

"This has been a most pleasant interlude," he continued.

"My pleasure, Mr. Howard, Miss Howard," William remarked, bowing again to Margaret.

"Saturday, a week, then?" Lowell Howard said, matter-of-factly. "At the Gloucester Club on Windham Road at eight o'clock."

"I shall be delighted and again I thank you for the pleasure of your company this afternoon," said William, his eyes meeting Margaret's.

He walked with them to their carriage, conscious of Margaret's tiny figure beside him. He wanted to touch her, but knew he could not. As they drove away,

William's spirits rose to such a state he felt like shouting after them. Saturday, a week. At the moment that seemed like an endless length of time. Thinking of the Cotillion, William knew he must see a tailor for the proper clothes at once. He turned and walked briskly down the street. He could not remember when he last felt so light-headed and gay.

"Well, what do you think of him?" asked Lowell Howard of his daughter as they settled back in their carriage for the drive from the Imperial Hotel.

"He's very nice, Father. A gentleman," Margaret replied.

"He's certainly taken with you, my dear. He could hardly keep his eyes off you all afternoon," continued Mr. Howard, chuckling.

"Oh, Father, really," Margaret said, pretending indignation.

She had felt the attraction also. William Hawke was considerably older than the young fellows with whom she danced at various parties, and seemed so masculine, but she quickly decided that probably was due to his maturity. Margaret still could recall the firmness of his jaw and the strength so evident in his large frame. And she thought his thick ruddy hair and mustache most attractive. Certainly everyone at the Cotillion would take notice when she walked in with so impressive an escort.

"He has a good business and I think he has a very sound mind."

Her father broke into her thoughts with his continuing conversation.

"You could make a very sensible marriage there," he added.

"Father!" Margaret was shocked. They had only just met the man, three times at most. "Besides, he may already have a wife."

"He doesn't, my dear, believe me, he doesn't."

Reaching Seagull's Point, they hurried inside to freshen up before their guests arrived. Margaret dawdled with her dressing. She really was in no hurry to break the spell of the afternoon. William Hawke had indeed kept his eyes on her throughout their time at the hotel. She was used to admiring glances from men, and even from some women, but this man was different. She felt strangely drawn to him and already was thinking about the Cotillion and wondering what that evening might bring.

When Margaret was five years old, her mother had died as a result of a miscarriage. Since then, Margaret had been raised by the family housekeepr, Mary Rhodes. Lowell Howard adored his wife and never again did he find anyone he wished to marry. There had been a number of spinsters and widows who had considered him a most eligible husband, but he had managed to avoid any entanglement. Now that he was past fifty years of age, he was anxious that Margaret marry and have someone to take care of her. His business had been very lucrative and she would have a substantial inheritance. Therefore, he was most concerned about her marriage to someone of integrity and responsibility. At this time in England a wife's property became the property of her husband upon their marriage.

Lowell Howard had a small shipping company, two packets which plied the Atlantic from Bristol to Boston and back again. Perhaps William Hawke might be just the man he had been hoping for to take over that business and enlarge the company. Many offers of other ships had been made, particularly on the run to New York. Mr. Howard wondered if the man knew anything at all about trading. He'd make it a point to find out on his next visit.

William had written Peter that he would be staying on in Bristol for another week. He did not mention the Cotillion, only that he had more business to attend to and needed additional time.

The days dragged on interminably for William. He slept late at the inn, had a leisurely breakfast and then walked to the tailor's to see if his new clothes were about finished. He was informed that he could expect them ready on Friday and not before. Receiving the distinct impression that he was becoming a nuisance, William vowed he would not return to the shop until Friday.

He had not seen Margaret since their tea at the Imperial Hotel. Because it had not been suggested that he visit Seagull's Point prior to the Cotillion, William felt he must not impose upon them. Finally, Saturday arrived. William dressed with special care and when he glanced in the mirror at himself he decided the new clothes had been a good investment. He hoped Margaret would think so too.

Arriving at the Gloucester Club at ten minutes before eight, William elected to wait on the long veranda for Mr. Howard and Margaret. The place was swarming with young men dressed in tightly fitting trousers and beautifully made coats like his own, and young ladies in billowing dresses of every hue. Such a clatter of noise.

Carriages were lined up one behind the other, waiting to unload their passengers at the steps. William could hear the music already playing inside the building. His heart quickened with excitement and anticipation. Then he saw Mr. Howard alighting from his carriage. And Margaret. William went forward to meet them.

"Ah, Mr. Hawke, how noble you look," said Lowell Howard, tipping his hat in approval and smiling broadly.

William's eyes turned to Margaret as she started up

the steps. He scarcely could believe her beauty. Her hair was drawn back in a mass of thick, glossy curls and fastened with silk flowers. Her dress was heavy white silk, the full skirt festooned with pink rosebuds and tiny leaves of pale green satin. The neckline of the dress was wide and deep, showing the soft curve of her throat and the firm roundness of her young breasts. Resting lightly on her shoulders was a blue velvet cape.

Much later when William returned to the inn and lay on his bed, he knew he very likely would not sleep any the remainder of the night. He felt sure he was in love with Margaret Howard. Never had he been so exhilarated by a woman. The thought of making love to Margaret was intoxicating to him. William knew he wanted her for his wife.

Lowell Howard had invited him to come after church services and share their mid-day meal.

"I'd be delighted, but I shall have to be on my way by three o'clock. I've been away from Woodbridge almost two weeks now and I have much to do there."

William sat up in bed and looked out the window. Daylight was filtering into the darkness of night, giving the sky a transparent look. He must come to a decision today about Margaret. He would speak to her father.

At the dining table at Seagull's Point, William glanced at Margaret as often as he could and still pay attention to her father's conversation. She smiled at him and her eyes were soft and glowing. William felt she was attracted to him also.

Margaret was remembering last night. She had enjoyed every minute at the Cotillion, watching the other young ladies eyeing her with the tall distinguished looking gentleman they had not seen before. She knew they must make a handsome pair. When asked about him, Margaret would only say that he was a friend of her father's. Having all eyes on her whenever she was dancing with William Hawke was exciting and she wanted to make the most of the evening. They all would soon know who he was anyway. Now her thoughts were interrupted by her father's voice.

"Please excuse us, Margaret. I wish to speak with Mr. Hawke in the library."

William was startled. What could Lowell Howard have to say to him in private? Now would he have the opportunity to ask for Margaret's hand? Or had her father already guessed and was planning to discourage him? William excused himself from Margaret and followed her father out of the room to the library, where they had first been introduced.

Mr. Howard motioned William to a chair and then began fussing with his pipe, puffing hard to get it lighted.

"William," he began, "May I call you that?"

"Of course, Sir."

"You seem to have a good head on your shoulders and I want to make you a proposition. You'll have plenty of time to think it over as I'm in no hurry at the moment."

William's curiosity was mounting.

"I've been offered the sale of two more fine packets with the thought of expanding my business into New York and opening an office there, but I need help, someone to take charge. I just don't have all that energy any more. I thought perhaps you might be interested enough to think about it. There could be a partnership eventually."

William was astonished. He hardly knew what to respond. He knew nothing whatever about the shipping business and here this man was offering him the opportunity for wealth and prestige and a possible partnership!

"I don't know quite how to answer that, Mr. Howard," he said, finally. "I certainly can't pretend to know anything about shipping and I do have a responsibility to keep our family business intact. I would have to discuss it with my brother. We have a way of life at Hawkes Nest, that's our home, of which I'm very fond, something I would not find easy to give up. I've always been happy with what I'm doing. Actually, my brother might be more suited to your purposes than I."

"Well, of course I've not met your brother," Lowell Howard responded. "In any event, think about it. We still have plenty of time," he continued.

William watched the old man as he enjoyed his pipe and he decided to speak up right then about Margaret.

"Sir, I have a proposition too, and one that can't wait. I want to marry your daughter and I'm asking you for her hand."

William was surprised that his voice sounded so thin. His heart was pounding and he waited nervously as the silence lengthened.

"William," began Mr. Howard, "I'm delighted."

He set his pipe down on the table next to his chair.

"You seem to be a man of integrity and honesty," he continued, "and I'm delighted."

Both men got to their feet simultaneously and clasped hands.

"Of course you must speak to Margaret," said her father. "I'll send her in."

Mr. Howard walked towards the library door and went out into the corridor. William was standing by the fire, looking down into the softly burning coals when he heard the rustle of Margaret's silk shirt. He turned to face her.

"Did you wish to speak with me?" Her voice was soft. "Father said—"

"Margaret, I think you know what I want to say,"

William interrupted as he walked over to her and took her hands in his. He looked down at her upturned face and did not speak for a few seconds. Her lips were parted and they appeared incredibly soft and smooth.

"I think you already know that I love you and I want you for my wife," he continued.

His brown eyes under the heavy brows seemed almost black.

Margaret smiled up at him, then moved so close to his body that her breasts just brushed against his coat.

"Yes, William, I do know and I will marry you.'

Her voice was hardly more than a whisper. She dropped her eyes and the long lashes were a fringe upon her cheeks. Then she looked up at him again as he put his arms about her and drew her tiny figure close to his own and kissed her. A tingling sensation coursed through his entire body, so much so that he did not want to let her go. Margaret's lips responded to his, but soon she drew back, breathless.

"My goodness!" she exclaimed.

"Forgive me," William said, smiling down at her. "But I've wanted to kiss you for days."

They stood looking at each other for a matter of seconds.

"How soon?" William asked, anxiously.

"I shall have to discuss the plans with father," she replied, "but it shan't be long. A month, perhaps?"

"No longer I hope. Now I must start back to Wood-bridge. Will you write me immediately when you know your plans? The date?" asked William.

"Of course, dear."

The words of endearment sounded strange to him. He never had been in love like this before. His feelings for Margaret were almost overwhelming to him. Now she reached up and put her arms about his neck and her lips were close to his again.

"Kiss me again," she whispered.

He pressed his mouth hard against her own and felt her tremble against him. Then he quickly let her go.

"I must leave, Margaret, or I shall miss the coach to Woodbridge. Let me bid goodbye to your father."

They walked out into the hallway and found Mr. Howard to tell him their news. He was visibly pleased for his daughter. Margaret promised she would write William within the week and tell him the date for the wedding as well as all the arrangements.

When Peter received William's letter saying he would not be back at Hawkes Nest for another week, his curiosity was aroused. Why had William not told him more about the additional business matters which were detaining him? It must be especially important that he had to stay and could not handle the matter by post. All things pointed to a substantial new order.

Peter had finished the work for Mr. Pevesey in Salisbury and was ready for delivery. However, he wasn't particularly looking forward to another long coach trip. On this Sunday afternoon he had been with Reverend Thomas and his family. They had invited him to come after church, and it had been a pleasant interlude. The Reverend's daughter, Frances, was a rather comely lass, Peter thought afterwards, although she scarcely had said two words the whole of the afternoon.

Now Peter was awaiting William's return and was in the workroom going over their accounts. He put his pen down suddenly and looked up from his work. For some unexplainable reason he found he was thinking about the girl in the blue velvet cape, the beautiful girl he had seen in Bristol. Strange. She had not come to Peter's mind since he returned from Salisbury.

His thoughts were interrupted by the sound of the light summer rain brushing softly against the window.

William would be arriving soon. It was almost dark and the lamps should be lighted and a fire started in the kitchen stove. Undoubtedly there would be much to talk about.

The coach ride home to Woodbridge that Sunday afternoon seemed endless. William wished he were still in the library at Seagull's Point, holding Margaret in his arms. The coming weeks were going to seem more like months. He decided he would not mention his approaching marriage until Margaret wrote to give him the actual date when the ceremony would take place. William had thought no more about the shipping business and the offer Lowell Howard had made. It was as if the subject never had been mentioned.

William's mind was on Margaret and Hawkes Nest. They would make his father's room their own since it was the largest of the bedrooms. Peter would remain where he was and William's room would just be a spare room until they had a family. The other bedroom in the house was not being used except for storage.

He wished his father and mother and Henrietta were alive to share in his excitement. They would have loved Margaret too. To think he actually would bring home so **beautiful a bride would have pleased them all. They** would have been especially surprised that it would be William before Peter. All the time the boys were growing up, Peter seemed to be the one fate smiled upon. He was extraordinarily handsome with an unusual charm which set him apart from everyone else in Woodbridge. William's shyness had kept him in the background.

Looking out the coach window, he could see Woodbridge in the distance and he moved restlessly in the seat. Darkness was about to overcome the paleness of twilight and a very soft rain, hardly more than a drizzle, was marking the window.

The coach lumbered to a stop and William quickly stepped down from the open door. He reached for his luggage and hurried off towards Hawkes Nest. He could see the lamplight in the windows and felt a warm glow as he approached the house. Dark smoke was curling from the chimneys. William wondered at that moment if Margaret would love it here as he did.

"What kept you so long in Bristol?" Peter had asked as they sat down to tea in the kitchen.

"Well, a number of things. I had to see a solicitor about Henrietta's share of father's will, as James had asked, you remember, and I had several meetings with Lowell Howard about the cab he has ordered. And if all goes well, I'm going to have a real surprise for you in a week or two," explained William.

"Now what the devil does that mean?" asked Peter.

"Well, if I told you it wouldn't be a surprise, now would it?"

William's eyes were sparkling with merriment. Peter's face took on a puzzled expression. William never had been one for teasing.

"Games? That isn't like you, brother," Peter remarked and since William offered nothing further by way of explanation, the matter was dropped.

The next few days William waited anxiously for the post, knowing young women about to be married seemed to have endless details to work out before anything definite could be settled.

The weather had turned warm at last. Summer seemed almost as permanent as winter had been. The air was soft and drowsy. William found concentration difficult. Peter thought his brother's behaviour somewhat unusual. At any rate, Peter was leaving on Thursday for his trip to Salisbury and expected to be gone a week again.

● 9 ●

Ellen was startled out of a sound sleep by a fierce pounding on her door and a voice crying her name, over and over. She quickly pulled a wrapper about her heavy cotton nightdress and hurried to the door. The shrill voice still was calling her name. Opening the door she saw the terrified face of Molly Barton.

"Come help me, Miss Davis! Come help me! He's beating my mother."

Ellen most certainly did not want to become involved in a family quarrel, but the child obviously was so frightened that she was hysterical. Her little face looked grotesque with fear. She pulled on Ellen's arm and kept crying for her to come.

Ellen wondered if anyone else was about on the street. The night still was very dark and she assumed it must be well past midnight. Ellen hurried along, Molly urging her to go faster, until they reached the Barton cottage. The door was ajar and Ellen could hear awful sounds coming from within.

Molly pushed the door open wide. As they entered the candle-lighted room, Ellen could barely see Mrs. Barton cowering in the corner, her husband swinging at her with his heavy belt. The woman screamed as he hit her again and blood spurted from her cheek. The two little boys in the bed on one side of the small room were crying loudly.

Ellen ran towards Adam Barton and grasped hold of the arm holding the belt. He seemed so startled that anyone was there that he dropped his arm limply and looked at Ellen. She could smell his foul breath as he leaned towards her. Obviously he was very drunk.

"Wot call you got to come meddlin!?" he growled at Ellen.

Molly had gone to her mother to help her to her feet. The woman was both relieved and embarrassed to have Ellen in her home at such a time.

"That brat, that brat—" Adam was pointing at Molly.

"She come to get ya', didn't she? A bastard, a dirty little bastard, that's wot she is."

His big head seemed to be retreating into his thick bull neck and heavy shoulders.

Mrs. Barton's face was a white mask. The blood from her cut cheek was running down to her chin and there were spots on her dress.

"I took 'em in, I did, when they had nothin'. Nothin', ya hear me?" Adam continued his yelling.

He raised his arm again and Ellen thought he was about to strike her. She quickly put her hands up before her face. She hardly knew what to do. Molly was clinging to her mother, her face hidden in the skirt of the woman's dress. Now Ellen knew that Adam Barton was not Molly's father. Very cautiously she took hold of the belt in Adam's hand and drew it away from him. He was weaving about the room and then found his way to the bedroom, went in and slammed the door behind him.

The little boys stopped crying immediately and stared at Ellen with big round eyes. She went over and tucked them down in the bed, patting each one on the head. Then she turned to Molly and her mother.

"Mrs. Barton, you better get some water on that cut and clean it off," she suggested.

Amy Barton could not speak. She was profoundly ashamed to have Ellen a witness to her husband as a drunken brute, but there was no explanation she could make. It was as if she had been struck dumb. She sat down in a chair at the table, shaking her head back and forth, her hands clasped tightly together.

Ellen walked over to Amy and laid her hand on the woman's shoulder.

"Mrs. Barton, please don't worry. Not a word will be said by me about this night. I'll go home now and you try to get some sleep."

As Ellen put her hand on the doorlatch to leave, she felt Molly tug at her skirt.

"Miss Davis, can I still come and read with you?" she asked, her eyes pleading.

"Well of course, Molly. Of course you can."

When Ellen slipped back between the covers of her own bed, she wondered who Molly's father might have been, how it all could have happened. Very likely she never would know.

● 10 ●

Margaret was sitting at a small mahoghany desk in her bedroom writing a letter to William. She had decided on a small wedding at home with only some close friends of her father and a few of her own young acquaintances. She indicated to William that he could invite whomever he wished from Woodbridge. The date was set for July 8th, three weeks hence, because it would take that much time for her wedding dress to be completed.

"My dear," she wrote, "I am eager to see Hawkes Nest, of which you seem so fond, as I never have been to Woodbridge. But if you love it, I'm sure I shall too. Please respond as soon as you find it convenient so I shall know if my plans are satisfactory to you." She signed her name "With profound affection."

William received the letter on Friday, the day after Peter had left for Salisbury. Now he would have to hold his good news for at least a week. He wanted his brother to know before he told anyone else. William could imagine the surprised look on Peter's face when he told him he actually would be bringing a bride to Hawkes Nest.

He took the letter to his room, lay down on the bed and read it again. He could visualize Margaret beside him and knew the next few weeks of waiting for her to be his wife would seem interminably long. His body tingled at the thought of taking her into his arms and kissing her soft mouth again.

At breakfast the next morning William told Ellen he wanted her to start cleaning his father's room thoroughly.

"Please wash the curtain, Ellen, and take the rug and beat the dust out. Also, will you remove the bedding and put it into one of the other rooms? I'm getting all new linen for father's room."

"Perhaps you could do that for me at Mr. Hammond's," he added. "I'm sure you would know better than I what to buy."

"Of course, if you like."

Ellen was curious when he did not explain this sudden surge of activity regarding a room that hadn't been used for over four months and could hardly have got very dirty in that length of time. She had cleaned and dusted that same bedroom once a week and always kept the door closed to keep out the dust and coal soot from downstairs. However, she did not ask any questions. William must have good reasons for his request. Someone must be coming for a visit, she surmised.

Ellen missed seeing Peter's bright smile every day and his cheery "Good morning." The house always seemed so quiet when he was away. Usually he was boisterous and of good humor when he was about. One always was aware of his presence.

"Would you believe I could get this dirty pounding nails?" he would say, laughing as he came through the kitchen to wash up for meals.

Ellen had been seeing a great deal more of Ben Hammond than she really cared to. He seemed always to be nearby to escort her home from church, to carry her parcels from the village, or to stroll by when she happened to be sitting on her front stoop, sometimes reading to Molly Barton. Ellen wondered how he could spend so much time away from his tailor and textile shop. Since he had the only shop of its kind in Woodbridge, he had a reasonably lucrative business. She could do worse than to marry him. Still, he no doubt would expect her to leave Hawkes Nest and she most definitely did not want to do that. Ellen felt about that lovely old house now as if it were her own. She found joy in each thing she did to add to or preserve its beauty. Her real home always would be there, she thought idly, and she hoped she never would have to leave it.

Molly Barton had not mentioned the night Ellen came to her house to rescue her mother from Adam Barton's belt, nor had Ellen, although she wondered if his beatings had occurred before and if he ever had laid his belt on Molly.

Ellen realized that women had very little recourse against a cruel husband. Should Mrs. Barton leave her home, there was little or no assurance that there would be any support or help of any kind from Adam. Ellen was suddenly grateful that she was not facing any such burden.

Ben Hammond had secured a copy of Jane Austen's "Pride and Prejudice," a book which was enjoying enormous popularity, and he had given it to Ellen. She now sat in the rocking chair deeply engrossed in that book. Ellen had hesitated taking it as a gift from Mr. Hammond because she did not want to feel beholden to him in any way. However, she was so eager to get into the pages of the story that she had been unable to refuse. She knew that eventually she would have to invite him in for tea. Perhaps Molly and Mrs. Barton could be asked too.

After her intrusion in the early hours at his cottage, Ellen had never spoken to or acknowledged Adam Barton again. She thought him a drunken, bad-mannered brute in any event. She often wondered what had befallen Amy Barton that she would marry such a man. Ellen saw Amy as a gentle and kind woman and hardly in her husband's lowly class. Still, she remembered Adam Barton shouting to her that night that they had nothing when he took Amy and Molly into his house. No doubt they had been destitute and any help would have been welcomed.

Ellen had been reading so long that her eyes were tired from the dim light of the lamp on the table beside her. She put the book down, after marking her place with a small piece of cloth, and went to the cottage door. She opened it and stood out on the stoop. The long twilight was almost gone, lasting late into the evening as it did in the summer months. The air was still warm and soft.

Just now appearing in the fast-fading light of the sky was the evening star. It sparkled and shimmered as it held its solitary brilliance until darkness would allow other stars to share its space. Ellen suddenly wondered where Peter might be and if he could be enjoying the same lovely sight as she.

Sometimes her heart ached from her own longing and frustration when she thought of **Peter's handsome face, and her loneliness became** almost unbearable. Ellen missed him dreadfully whenever he was away. Perhaps tomorrow his tall, graceful figure would come through the door at

Hawkes Nest and he would smile "Good morning." Or perhaps the day after.

Ellen was reluctant to close the door on the ending day, but if she did not the flying insects would be flocking inside her cottage towards the lamplight. So she went in and closed the door, her thoughts still lingering on Peter's whereabouts.

● 11 ●

"You're getting married!" Peter's voice was loud and incredulous. "I must say that is a fair piece of news. Who is she?" he asked.

"You remember Lowell Howard who wrote and asked about a carriage. Well, she's his daughter. Her name is Margaret and she is beautiful. Really beautiful, Peter," William explained.

"Well, I'm very happy for you, William. When is the wedding to be?"

"July 8th. In Bristol," William replied.

"In Bristol? Is that where she lives?" Peter asked, his voice quieter now.

"Yes, Mr. Howard has a small shipping company. By the way he wants a partner. You might be interested in that some day."

Peter hardly had heard what William said. My God, it couldn't be, could it? Could it possibly be the girl in the blue cape who was to be William's bride? The girl he had seen on the dock at Bristol? William clearly had forgotten that Peter ever mentioned the incident. Of course it had been discussed in the tavern and seemed only idle conversation at the time. He could not expect William to remember such a small encounter, particularly when it had not happened to him in the first place.

"I hope you will go to Bristol with me for the

wedding," said William, putting his hand on his brother's shoulder.

"This certainly has happened fast, William. I'm a bit taken aback. How have you kept this secret for so long?" Peter asked.

"No secret, really. And it hasn't been long at all. I've only known her a few weeks, but wait till you see her. Then you'll know," William replied.

"Will you be taking a wedding tour?" Peter asked.

"Only a few days in Bath," replied William. "It's so lovely here now that I want Margaret to see Hawkes Nest in full bloom. You'll like her, Peter. I know you will. Now I've got to find Ellen and tell her. I want her to make some changes in father's room."

Margaret had written again, saying that she would like to bring her own mahogany desk and of course her dowry chest, so certain things would have to be moved out of Henry Hawke's bedroom to make room for a bride's whimsies.

As Peter reached his own room he busied himself unpacking his travelling case, still almost disbelieving of William's news. He had felt all along that he would again see the girl in the blue cape, but never this way. Of course he still could not be certain it was the same girl, but the coincidence of Bristol and her father being a shipowner was too strong to be ignored. However, Bristol was full of people involved in trade and shipping. It could be someone totally different. Questions and suppositions were whirling about in Peter's mind. He suddenly stopped what he was doing and sat down hard on the blanket chest at the foot of his bed. What he thought was really going to make no difference. William was bringing home a bride and there was nothing to be done about it, whoever she might turn out to be.

"Oh, I'm so happy for you, Sir." Ellen's face was beaming at William's news. "Will she be coming soon?" she asked.

William explained that he would be bringing Margaret to Hawkes Nest in about a month. Of course Ellen was to continue on just as she was.

"She's very young, Ellen, and she's had no experience in managing a household. We shall need you more than ever, I've no doubt."

So Hawkes Nest was going to have a mistress again. It had been many years since Mary Hawke's death and everyone in Woodbridge had missed the gay hospitality the house had when she was there.

The news of William's coming marriage would bring both surprise and disappointment to some of the villagers. Young ladies who had been hoping he someday would choose a wife among them would be bitter indeed. And some of the menfolk who had assumed that he would remain single would no doubt express surprise over a glass of ale at The Bell. At any rate, the news spread quickly through Woodbridge once William had told Reverend Thomas of his plans. Friends came by to offer their congratulations. William was elated and his usual steady and quiet composure was caught up in the excitement.

Peter was quite amazed at the change in his brother. Obviously this was a kind of love and devotion Peter had not yet experienced. The two of them decided to open a bottle of wine that evening before supper. William even offered a glass to Ellen.

"Oh no, Sir, thank you, but I don't take to spirits. I might get squiffy."

The two men laughed at her remark and poured themselves another glass.

Ellen enjoyed seeing their obvious happiness and pleasure together. Peter's eyes had taken on a sparkle as well as William's. She decided it must be the wine.

Secretly, Ellen was thankful it was William who was getting married and not Peter. She would find it quite impossible to work in the same house with a bride of Peter's. She bid them good evening after serving their supper and wishing William every happiness.

Walking through the tall dark trees to the road, Ellen wondered what the new Mrs. Hawke would be like. She hoped very much that the lady would like her and life at Hawkes Nest could go on just as before.

Ellen had no way of knowing that Peter was sharing her thoughts and wondering what lay ahead for all of them now that someone new was entering their lives.

Margaret Howard lay in the richly carved poster bed in her room at Seagull's Point listening to the sounds out in the street. The windows were open to the soft summer air and she could hear the day starting. Carriages and wagon wheels, horses' hoofs, loud voices, laughter, shattering profanity, the squeal of a dog who got in someone's way. She wondered if she would be happy living in the countryside.

Bristol was an exciting place with all that was going on and the city was growing at a furious pace. Margaret was not at all sure she could find enough to do in Woodbridge. What would the people be like? Where could she wear all of her pretty clothes?

Her closest friend, Hetty Langley, had made her believe she might be going to a completely different world where there were no parties, no dances, no social graces, nothing but farms and animals and hard work!

"But, Hetty, William Hawke is not a farmer. He's a wagonmaker," Margaret had protested.

"All the same, why doesn't he have his business in the city if he's not a farmer?"

"Because he loves where he lives. Besides, Bristol isn't all that far away. We shall have to come and visit father on occasion."

Hetty wasn't convinced that Margaret's marriage to William Hawke was at all prudent. Margaret secretly believed that Hetty was only jealous. After all, Hetty was a year older than Margaret and still had no steady caller. As a matter of fact, Margaret was the first one among her close friends to be planning a wedding.

The noise in the street was now such a clamor that she decided she might as well get up and dress and go down to breakfast. The final fitting on her wedding dress was to be today and her father had agreed to go with her.

Looking in the mirror as she brushed her long dark curls, Margaret studied her reflection carefully and concluded that William Hawke was indeed a fortunate man. She could not deny the beauty of her dark eyes and creamy fairness of her skin nor the fullness of her mouth and the soft shadow between her breasts. As she continued to brush her hair Margaret wondered what it was going to be like being married. No one had told her anything about what to expect or what was expected of her. Beyond a kiss or two, she knew nothing whatever about marriage or having children or being a wife. When William had kissed her in the library she had enjoyed it and had kissed him back.

"I don't see how you can get any sleep at all in the same bed with a man," Hetty had remarked. "I hear it's just plain awful!" Her tone was both emphatic and sympathetic.

Margaret had smiled and patted Hetty's hand.

"I can't think it's all that bad, Hetty."

Still, Margaret was curious. She supposed she could go to Mary, their housekeeper, and ask her a few questions. At that thought she remembered that Mary was a maiden lady so she dismissed the idea. Now she tied a ribbon through her hair and went downstairs to have breakfast with her father.

"Margaret, have you decided which pieces of furniture you wish to take with you to Woodbridge?" asked Mr. Howard.

"Oh yes, Father, just my desk and my dowry chest. If I find that I want something else from my room after I arrive at Hawkes Nest, perhaps I could have it later?"

This last was a question and her father indicated that would be perfectly agreeable to him. He always had been most generous with Margaret. She was so much like her mother had been that it gave him great pleasure to indulge her. As a result, Margaret had more beautiful silk and satin and wool dresses than most of the young women in Bristol. Often she was surprised with a new bonnet or a small fur tippet with a matching muff. Since he had no one else on whom to spend his money, Lowell Howard delighted in giving to his beautiful daughter.

Now that she was putting a wedding trousseau together, the shopping was almost a daily ritual. Margaret insisted that he come with her, not only to pay for her purchases, but to bring all the packages home in the carriage so they could be opened and looked at a second time. He seemed to take almost as much pleasure as she in the frilly silks and lace-trimmed garments. As he watched her holding each lovely piece for him to admire, he thought she looked incredibly young, still like a little girl. He hoped with all his heart that she would be happy.

"Margaret, you really want to marry William Hawke, don't you?" asked her father, soberly.

"Well, of course I do, Father. Besides, it's so exciting getting married. All the girls are so envious."

Lowell Howard shook his head from side to side, smiling. The joys and innocence of youth!

Peter decided he would, after all, go to Bristol with William for the wedding. His brother seemed most anxious for him to come and Peter did not want to disappoint him. Besides, he really could not give a valid reason for remaining in Woodbridge on that particular day.

So the two of them boarded the Bristol coach on the morning of July 7th. They would spend the night at the inn as the wedding was to be the next morning in eleven o'clock. William planned to take his bride to Bath for three days and then they would return to Hawkes Nest. He had gone over every detail of the bedroom with Ellen so things would be in order when he and Margaret returned. There were new curtains at the windows, all new blankets and linen for the bed, and he had purchased a delicately flowered ewer and bowl for the washstand.

"I expect we shall be back on the 12th, Ellen, and would you please put some flowers in the room on that day?"

"Of course, Sir. It will be a pleasure," Ellen had responded.

She had run her hands over the soft blankets and the smooth linen when she made the bed. The pillows were very large and she guessed they were filled with down. She admired the dainty ewer and bowl and decided then she must find something for a wedding gift. Whatever could she give them? As Ellen looked about the room she could see that William had thought of most everything. Well, perhaps something would come to mind later.

Peter had very mixed emotions as he started with William to go to Seagull's Point for the wedding. He wondered what his reaction would be if, in fact, William's bride turned out to be the girl in the blue cape. After all, he really knew nothing about her. He remembered that she was exquisite to look at and that was all he really knew.

Peter went up the walkway on Worcester Road with William and turned with him towards the boxwood enclosed house named Seagull's Point. Then suddenly the door was opened and the two of them were ushered inside. Peter's heart was beating wildly. He didn't know what to expect. Immediately he was being introduced to Mr. Howard. He couldn't be sure it was the same man he had seen on the dock. Without the flowing cape and the tall dark hat he just didn't know.

They went into a large and elaborately furnished parlor. There were perhaps a dozen people in the room. Then he and William were introduced all around. Peter took note of three young ladies, one named Hetty Langley, who eyed him curiously. And then he saw William's face brighten and he turned to see a young girl enter the room. Margaret Howard. The girl on the dock. Peter's heart leaped and he felt suddenly as if all his blood had drained out of him. He wondered if his reaction was noticeable. It was indeed the same girl. She was even more beautiful than he had remembered. In her white silk and lace dress she was breathtaking. William took her hands in his and then led her over to where Peter was standing.

"Margaret, this is my brother, Peter."

She curtsied slightly and expressed pleasure at meeting one of William's family. She showed no recognition of ever having seen Peter before. It was just as well, he thought. Later, Peter could not remember what had happened next. He only knew that William and Margaret were married and the room was buzzing with excited voices. And suddenly Lowell Howard put his hand on Peter's arm and spoke to him.

"William tells me you might be interested in the shipping business."

"Well, Sir, I think I could be. Right now I know nothing whatever about trading or ships."

"It's really not difficult, but it takes a strong hand, Mr. Hawke. You have to deal with all manner of men. However, there's a good profit to be made if you are interested."

"I'll think about it, Mr. Howard."

Peter spoke without any particular enthusiasm. He actually wanted to break off the conversation. He could not concentrate or concern himself at this moment. He was wondering if he and William and Margaret would be able to live together at Hawkes Nest. Peter walked back towards them. At that instant he wanted most of all to return to Woodbridge.

As he approached his brother, Peter noticed the broad smile on William's face. Then his brother's eyes grew brighter as he saw Peter coming towards him, and he put out his hand and rested it on Peter's shoulder.

"We shall be leaving shortly, Peter, and I do want to thank you for coming."

"Of course. I'm very pleased for you, but if you don't mind I believe I'll try to make the coach back to Woodbridge. I left a great deal undone and I should like to get on with it."

William's face wore a puzzled expression. It wasn't like Peter to be so preoccupied, not when there was an abundance of wine and pretty girls about.

"Oh, don't be worried about the work. A few more hours won't matter. You could stay the night at the inn and go back tomorrow," William suggested.

Peter shook his head and William could see by his face that he meant to leave.

"Very well, if you think you must."

Margaret was standing close to William during their conversation, but had not spoken. She was studying Peter's face. She had not realized that his eyes were so blue or that his mouth had a curve to it. He truly was unusually handsome, she thought.

Peter turned to Margaret as he spoke.

"I hope you will be really happy and I also hope you will like Woodbridge and Hawkes Nest as much as we do."

The expression on his face was warm and sincere.

"I'm certain I will, Peter," Margaret responded.

"Now, if you will both excuse me, I shall be on my way and I shall look forward to seeing you in approximately a week's time."

Peter bowed slightly to Margaret and took hold of William's hand for a brief moment. Then he left the room. Hetty Langley's eyes followed him to the door. Margaret also watched him until he disappeared into the corridor. Then she turned back towards her husband.

● 13 ●

Adam Barton's resentment and anger at Ellen Davis
had been festering like a stubborn sore. He saw her
almost every evening as he sat on the front stoop of his
cottage and watched her come down the road from
Hawkes Nest on her way home. It was always just at
dusk. She neither looked at him nor spoke. It was as if
he didn't exist. Sometimes Molly ran to meet Ellen, but
usually the child was busy helping her mother with
their supper. Ellen never acknowledged Adam's
presence.

This particular day he had come home earlier than
usual. Mrs. Barton questioned him about his early
arrival and he grunted some unintelligible response. His
mood seemed dark and brooding. He went into their
bedroom and shut the door. Amy Barton wondered if
he could be ill. However, Adam soon came out and sat
on the front stoop as he did every night. Amy spoke
loudly so he could hear her.

"This is William Hawke's wedding day. Soon they'll
be havin' a new lady up at Hawkes Nest," said Amy,
happily.

"They got a high 'n mighty one a'ready," muttered
her husband.

Amy turned and stared out at him, a puzzled look on
her face.

"You talkin' about Miss Davis?" she asked.

"That I am."

"But, Adam, she's only the housekeeper," Amy explained.

"Mebbe so, mebbe so. All the same she walks 'round here like she was so much better 'n us. The likes 'o her I can't abide."

"Oh, Adam, you're talkin' foolish. Miss Davis is a fine young girl and look how good she's been with Molly. Go wash up for supper."

Amy turned her back to him and went on with her duties in the kitchen, unaware that as she did so Adam left the front stoop and was walking down the road. He looked towards Ellen's cottage. It was almost dark now, but the lamp in the window was not yet lighted. He assumed Ellen must still be at Hawkes Nest.

With each step he took, Adam's thoughts were becoming more ugly. What right had Ellen Davis to treat him like he was dirt? Like he was nothin' at all. She was no more'n a housemaid herself. Walking past his place flippin' her skirts and never so much as a friendly word.

Adam walked faster and the perspiration began to bead on his face. He turned up the stone path towards the Hawke house and quickly darted among the thick trees and brush as he saw Ellen coming towards him. It had been a sultry day and she had unbuttoned the three top buttons of her dress so the cool evening air could reach her neck and throat. Her hair was damp and curly about her face.

As Adam Barton watched her approaching him, his palms became sweaty and he rubbed his hands along his breeches. He was breathing hard and the perspiration now was trickling down from his temples. The light was becoming so dim he could barely see Ellen's face, but he heard her steps. Just as she passed him he jumped behind her and put one strong, heavily muscled arm across her face and with the other he pinned her arms to her sides, holding her tightly against him.

Ellen struggled fiercely, kicking her foot back against his legs. As strong as she was, Ellen was no match for Adam Barton who had been a blacksmith for more than twenty years. His thick arms were solid muscle. He pulled back into the bushes and pushed her to the ground, pinning her arms under her back with his left arm.

"Ya think yer a lady? A fine lady? I'll fix ya so's nobody'll think yer a lady!"

His speech was slurred and raspy, but Ellen recognized his voice. She barely could see his face, sweaty and red-eyed, bending over her. She opened her mouth to scream, but he quickly forced his lips over her own. Ellen thought she surely would faint. He was tearing at the neck of her dress and she kicked her legs wildly. She heard the fabric tear apart and then his hand went inside between her breasts and he moved his rough fingers over the soft flesh. Ellen tried to kick him again and he hit her across the face. She could taste the blood at the corner of her lip.

He still held her arms in a vise-like grip. In the name of God, what was he going to do? He kept pulling at her dress with his free hand and it suddenly ripped open to her waist. Ellen was terrified and she tried with all her strength to push him away from her, but his body felt like an iron weight and she began pleading with him to let her go. As she struggled in the thick underbrush she felt something scratch her cheek. Then on her arms. Briars, of course. Oh God, oh God, she prayed, please help me! She felt his hand on her thigh and then he was ripping her underclothes. Ellen was certain he was going to kill her.

She tried again to free herself, but she was so exhausted now that she could not move. She felt his chest expand against her own as he breathed heavily. Ellen tried to twist her body free but the effort was futile. Then she felt his mouth on her right breast, then her left. And his teeth bit into the soft mound. She screamed with pain and he hit her again across the mouth. Ellen went limp and lay still. She felt his hand probing between her legs and she shuddered. And he forced himself, large and hard, inside her body, moving rhythmically against her, groaning in his ecstacy. Suddenly he raised up and was bending over her.

Ellen closed her eyes. She could not bear to look up at him. Her body began to shake and she felt the sobs deep in her throat. She heard him shuffle away and she lay quite still, her hands over her face as if to shut out the sight and memory of what had happened to her. She was shaking uncontrollably now and she clenched her fists trying to still her twitching muscles. The taste of blood still was in her mouth.

Slowly, Ellen sat up. She could see nothing in the darkness, but she knew her clothing was badly torn because she could feel the cool air on her exposed breasts. Pulling the torn garments across her chest, Ellen got to her feet. She felt so weak she thought she could not stand, but then she realized that she had to get home somehow without being seen. In the darkness Ellen went down the path to the road. There was no one in sight. The village was quiet. If she could run, she might make it to the cottage without anyone seeing or hearing her. Ellen was not sure she had the strength in her legs to carry her that distance. Just as she was about to start across she heard the heavy wheels and the horses of the coach. It was slowing to a stop. Ellen darted back into the bushes. In the light of the coach lamps she saw a man step down from the open door. He spoke to the driver as he reached for his traveling bag. It was Peter! He had come home from Bristol then, sooner than expected.

Holding her breath, Ellen did not make a move as he walked past her towards the house. Tears were streaming down her cheeks now. What was she to do? She felt utterly alone. There was no one she could go to for help. After she heard Peter close the door to the house, Ellen peered out to the road again. Now she must make a determined effort to reach her cottage.

Gathering her tattered clothes about her she ran as hard and fast as she could. Hurrying inside the cottage, Ellen closed the door behind her and leaned against it, gasping for breath. She was certain no one had seen her. She could not see herself in the dark room and she hesitated lighting the lamp. However, she realized she would have to take care of the cuts and bruises on her face and arms.

As soon as she could breathe more easily she lighted a candle and went to the mirror. When Ellen saw her reflection she cried out in anguish. A mad woman looked back at her. Quite mad. Her hair was in complete disarray, her mouth was cut at the corner, and her face was scratched and dirty and swollen. Ellen shuddered as she recalled the horror of Adam Barton's mouth pressed greedily against her own and his rough hands pawing over her body.

She wanted to wash off as quickly as possible and rather than start a fire in the stove and wait for water to heat, she reached into the pail of cold water near the stove and poured some into a basin. Her hands still were shaking, but the cool water was comforting to her scratched and swollen face.

Going into the tiny bedroom she got out of her clothes. As she reached for her cotton nightdress, Ellen began to sob again, deep racking sobs. She lay down on the bed, her face buried in the pillow, her body shaking from fear and shock.

Ellen did not know how long she lay like that, but she must finally have slept because she opened her eyes to find that morning had come. The sun was streaming through the curtains at the window next to her bed. As she started to get up, her entire body felt sore and she moaned from the pain. Ellen looked in the mirror again. Her hair still was matted and tangled, but her face was the worst. The cut lip had swollen enormously and her cheeks were black and blue where Adam had struck her. How could she leave the cottage? How could she return to Hawkes Nest and face Peter? Whatever was she going to do? Tears returned to her already red and puffy eyes, but she brushed them off. No good would come of that she decided. Ellen reached for the hairbrush and began trying to smooth out her hair.

When Adam Barton returned to his own cottage that night his wife was standing on the stoop listening for his footsteps.

"Adam, where on earth have you been? We've been waitin' supper ever so long."

"There was somethin' I had to do," he replied, not looking at her, but going straight to his chair at the small table in the kitchen.

As Amy began to put the food on his place, she could see by the dim light of the candles that his hands had deep scratches on the knuckles and his clothes were covered with dirt and briars.

"What's happened?" she asked. "You look a sight. You get in a fight with somebody?"

"Yeh, I got in a fight," he replied, stuffing his mouth with food.

"Adam, what have you done?" Amy asked, anxiously.

"Jes' you shut up 'n leave me alone. It's none of yer knowin' anyhow, woman." Adam's voice was harsh and angry.

Amy Barton lay awake for hours that night, listening to the heavy breathing of her husband beside her and wondering if her suspicions could possibly be true. She remembered Adam talking about Ellen Davis just before he disappeared from the house. Why did he dislike her so? She supposed it was because of the night Ellen had come to the cottage at Molly's urging to break up his attack on her with his belt. Could he possibly have mistreated Ellen? Amy thought of the many times Adam had forced himself on her with his incredibly strong arms and hands. Finally, just before dawn, she fell asleep.

With determined brushing and pulling, Ellen's hair was almost back to normal. There was precious little she could do about her face, however. She would just have to stay hidden for a few days until the swelling around her mouth subsided. Possibly the bruises could be covered with something from the kitchen, but the deep scratches on her hands were another matter. How could she explain it all? What would Peter Hawke think when Ellen did not appear at Hawkes Nest on time as she always had? And her body still was so sore she scarcely could move without pain.

No, she would just have to pretend to be ill and let no one into the cottage. Suddenly she realized she was very hungry, having had no supper and no breakfast. Spreading some butter and jam on bread, Ellen ate rapidly. The hot tea was pure bliss going down her throat. She was about to pour her third cupful when she heard a knock and then someone called her name. It was Molly Barton. Ellen made no sound.

"Miss Davis, can we read today?" asked Molly.

Ellen knew that if she did not answer the child might become alarmed and go for help.

"I'm not feeling well, Molly. I can't see you for a few days. Then we'll read again."

Ellen spoke through the door and listened for Molly's

97

footsteps as she retreated from the cottage. She knew the little girl would tell her mother that Miss Davis was feeling ill and no doubt Mrs. Barton would come right away. Ellen needed to get word to Peter that she would not be at Hawkes Nest for a day or two. As she expected, in a matter of minutes Amy Barton was outside her door.

"Is there anything I can do, Miss Davis?" asked the woman.

"I'm all right, Mrs. Barton. I mean I'll be all right in a day or two, but could you go and tell Mr. Hawke that I am ill, that I have the congestion and won't be able to come to the house for a couple of days?" asked Ellen.

"Of course. I'll go right away."

Ellen was grateful that Amy Barton did not press her for an explanation of her illness, and she hoped the woman would not alarm Peter as to her condition. She stayed in her cottage for three days. Ben Hammond had come by and she told him through the door that she had been ill, but expected to be up and around in another day or two.

After the third day Ellen realized she would have to go to Hawkes Nest. William Hawke would be coming home soon with his bride and Ellen had promised him that she would have the house in order on his return.

The swelling around her mouth had been reduced by a cold water poultice, but there still was some discoloration on her cheeks and the scratches on her hands had not yet disappeared. However, she decided she would have to get on with her duties and make the best explanation she could.

When Ellen walked into the kitchen at Hawkes Nest, Peter was sitting at the table having his breakfast. His face had an astonished look when he saw her.

"Great heaven, Ellen, you look as if you'd tangled with a briar patch—or worse!"

Ellen smiled. Why hadn't she thought of that?

"What happened?" Peter continued.

"Well, Sir, you're exactly right. I went berry picking and I had a bad fall over a log," she explained, the words tumbling out rapidly. "Of course I've had the congestion too," she added, remembering what Amy Barton was to have told Peter.

"Well, I hope you are on the mend. William and Margaret will be arriving in two days and I know there must be much to do before they get here."

"Yes, Sir. What's she like, Sir?" Ellen asked, her eyes bright with expectation.

Peter hesitated a moment and then looked out the window. His voice was quiet and deliberate as he spoke.

"She's like springtime, Ellen. Very beautiful. You'll see."

Ellen noticed a thoughtful, far-away expression on his face, but then perhaps that was merely her imagination again.

Peter did not seem to want to talk further so she began to clear the table. She had much to do, having been away for three days from her usual chores. Ellen became aware that Peter was watching her closely. Could he suspect that she had not told the truth? Ellen's face flushed and she felt ashamed and embarrassed.

Peter was indeed puzzled by her appearance. She had the look of someone who had been beaten, yet he couldn't imagine Ellen being involved in any such encounter. If so, who could it have been? He suddenly felt a tenderness and sympathy towards the girl.

"You'd best not go berry picking again, Ellen," he said solemnly. "At least not without some assistance."

He got up from his chair and walked out of the room. Ellen did not see him again until late in the afternoon.

"Sir, would it be agreeable if I left a little earlier today? I'm still not feeling quite well."

"Of course, Ellen. I believe you should."

She wanted so much to reach her cottage before Adam Barton returned from his work. Ellen could not bear the thought of having to pass by him sitting in front of his house. She knew she would have to face him eventually, but she hoped not just yet. Also, she hoped to avoid Ben Hammond.

Walking down the path past the spot where Adam had forced her to the ground, Ellen felt the fear and shame all over again as she had upon arriving that morning. Her heart was heavy as she went on towards her cottage. She felt unclean, as if nothing could wash away the memory of that night.

Passing some of the villagers she spoke a greeting, and no one seemed to notice her face. At least nothing was said to her in that regard. Molly Barton saw her and came skipping up the road to meet her.

"Oh, Miss Davis, I'm so glad you're better. I've missed the stories." said the child, reaching for Ellen's hand. "Could we read today?" she continued.

"Molly, I'm still very tired. I just want to rest for a while. In a few days perhaps. You ask me in a few days."

Ellen could see the disappointment in the little girl's eyes and she almost changed her mind. Still, she really did not want any company. Once inside her cottage she thought she could shut out everyone and everything, but she found the same thoughts kept recurring to her. Adam Barton and Amy. And Peter. Dear Peter. Did he suspect her story was not fully true? What if someone had seen her that night after all? What if that person began to talk to others? What if Adam Barton should boast of his conquest of her some night at The Bell?

"Stop thinking about it! Stop worrying about something that hasn't happened yet! Stop, stop!" she admonished herself.

Ellen whispered to herself, "I really must believe no one will ever know. I must."

She put the kettle on to boil water for tea, picked up one of her books and sat down in the rocking chair to read.

• 14 •

William and Margaret sat in the Bristol coach surrounded by luggage. There were even more bags and boxes on top of the coach, and very little room for additional passengers. Margaret had so many clothes and bonnets.

Their wedding trip to Bath had been very pleasant. They had stayed at the finest hotel in that city and had dined at the best restaurants. They had walked about looking in the shops and enjoying the summer weather.

Knowing the innocence of his young bride, William had been very gentle with her. He did not feel that she shared his ecstacy in their lovemaking, but he hoped that would come in time. As for himself, he could hardly get enough of her. He still found it hard to believe that such a beautiful girl actually could be his wife. He was amused at her vast trousseau, teasing her about putting on and taking off so many clothes. Yet he delighted in watching her. The tiny waist, the soft rounded breasts, the narrow hips all were exciting to him. More than once when she had been sitting at the dressing table brushing her long dark hair, the soft silk of her nightdress clinging to her figure, he had lifted her in his arms and carried her to the bed where he could once more find the greatest pleasure in her warm, tender body.

As the coach rumbled along the road towards Woodbridge, William looked down at Margaret next to him and thought about the people in the village. They would be wide-eyed when they saw her, he was sure. Every man in Woodbridge would envy him. William wanted to do everything possible to make Margaret happy at Hawkes Nest.

"I think we shall have a gathering soon, my dear," he said, taking her small hand in his. "I want everyone to meet you as soon as possible. Besides, we haven't had a party at Hawkes Nest in a very long time. There hasn't been any reason to until now."

She smiled up at him, her eyes luminous and loving.

"That sounds lovely, dear. I adore parties. And which dress shall I wear?"

William laughed heartily and squeezed her hand.

"You can just reach out and pick any one. You look beautiful in everything," he replied. "Oh, I say, we're almost there," he added, leaning forward a little to peer out the window.

Margaret followed his gaze at the green and rolling farmland and the forest in the distance.

"Oh, William, are we?" she asked, excitedly.

As the coach slowed to a stop very near the entrance to his home, William became anxious. Would Margaret like it? Would she be as happy as he was in Woodbridge? Would she miss Bristol and her friends very much? He hoped Ellen had remembered about the flowers for their room.

As they stepped from the coach, the driver began handing down their luggage which William piled in a heap at the side of the road. He would have to get Peter to come and help him take it up to the house. Then he and Margaret started up the cobbled path through the trees to Hawkes Nest.

"Oh, William, it's beautiful," she said as the house came into view. "It's all you told me it was. How very lovely!" Her voice rose in her enthusiasm.

"I'm glad you think so, my dear. I want so much for

you to be happy here," William said, hugging her arm against his side as he spoke.

The door opened and Peter and Ellen came hurrying down to meet them. Ellen found it hard to keep from staring at Margaret. She never had seen anyone so lovely, and William's face was glowing with pride and happiness.

Peter took the bags from his brother and then William said they would have to go back down to the road for the rest. Ellen led Margaret into the house as the two men went for the remainder of the luggage.

"Would you like me to show you to your room, Ma'm?" asked Ellen.

"Oh no, thank you. I'll wait for William. What a lovely house. It really is," replied Margaret as she walked into the large sitting room, her eyes darting about, looking at everything.

"Yes, Ma'm," Ellen agreed.

"How long have you been with Mr. Hawke?" asked Margaret.

"About six months, Ma'm."

Peter and William came into the house, laughing and puffing under the load of bags.

"The desk and dowry chest are coming later. There simply wasn't another inch of space in the coach," said William glancing at Margaret, his eyes teasing. "Perhaps if we all help, we can get this up to our room at one time," he continued.

So the four of them carried the various pieces of luggage up the stairs to Henry Hawke's bedroom. William was visibly pleased when they entered the room. Ellen had bouquets of flowers on the bureau, the table by the bed and in the deep recesses of the windows. On the bed he saw a pair of white pillowcases to which Ellen had sewn a row of fine lace. Her wedding gift. William thanked her profusely, as did Margaret.

Ellen was relieved that William had noticed nothing unusual about her, but then her face now was almost back to normal and he had no occasion to look at her hands.

"Would you like some tea, Sir?" she asked. "I've made fresh scones."

"That sounds marvelous, Ellen. I think we'll need the strength to unpack all of this luggage."

He still was in a teasing mood to Margaret. She smiled at him condescendingly as she untied her bonnet and laid it on the bureau.

Peter had been leaning against the door watching the scene. What a bride, he thought. He felt envy towards his brother, an emotion which was rare for him.

As Margaret began to unbutton her coat and William moved towards her, Peter and Ellen decided as one that they should leave the room. Peter followed Ellen down the stairs and into the kitchen where he sat down at the table to watch her prepare the tea things.

"You're quite right, Sir," Ellen said, smiling at Peter. "She *is* like springtime. And Mr. William is so happy you can see it all over him."

Peter made no response as he reached for one of the buttered scones and began to spread it with strawberry jam. Several minutes passed before William and Margaret came into the room.

"Would you like the tea in the parlor, Sir?" asked Ellen.

She thought that perhaps now there was a mistress in the house the parlor would be a more likely spot for tea than the kitchen.

"No, I think not. This will do fine," William replied, matter-of-factly. "There's much to discuss and I want you here, Ellen.

As they seated themselves at the table William asked Ellen to bring another cup so she might join them. She felt a little strange sitting at the table, but since she had been asked there she guessed it was all right.

"Ellen's the best cook you could ever imagine, Margaret," said William as he poured the tea into the cups and handed them around.

"I think we should have a party so everyone can meet Margaret," he continued as he prepared a scone and put it on his wife's plate. "An afternoon affair, I should think."

"Fine idea, William," Peter remarked. "When did you think this might be?"

"How's Saturday, a week?" William replied. "And if it is as nice as this day we could have it in the garden."

"Oh, that sounds wonderful, Sir," said Ellen, excitedly. Her eyes were sparkling with anticipation. She never had been to a party.

Margaret had sat quietly drinking her tea, aware that Peter's eyes were upon her and trying to take no notice. She suddenly felt strangely uncomfortable and for the first time since her marriage she missed her home and her own routine. She found that she scarcely heard the conversation going on about her and she wondered how her father was getting along in the house in Bristol. He must be very lonely without her.

"How many are you planning to invite" Peter asked suddenly and Margaret turned quickly to look at William.

"Well, I hardly think we can leave anyone out," replied William.

Ellen's heart skipped a beat and she felt a chill run over her. That meant the Bartons too! Adam Barton in Hawkes Nest. It was hardly a pleasant thought. Still, she knew Amy would be more than delighted to come to a party.

"How do you plan to invite them?" asked Peter, leaning back in his chair.

"Well, I thought at the church on Sunday. Anyone

who isn't there can be asked afterwards," replied William.

Margaret's eyes widened in surprise. She would have thought written invitations would be delivered. However, she made no comment. This was not Bristol.

So it was settled. The party would be at three o'clock in the afternoon, a week from Saturday.

Ellen's first thought was for a new dress. She would stop in at Ben Hammond's shop on her way home and see about some fabric. Besides, she hadn't seen him since she had come out of her "illness." Of course he would be invited to the party too.

When they all had finished with the tea, William and Margaret returned to their room to try to find places to put Margaret's finery, and Peter went back to work. Ellen busied herself cleaning up the dishes. She had noticed that Margaret seemed very quiet during the discussion of the party, and Peter had kept his eyes on his new sister-in-law most of the time they were at the table. Probably the young bride felt somewhat strange the first day in her new home. And Ellen hardly could blame Peter for staring at Margaret. She had found it hard to keep from doing the same thing.

Later, after she had prepared their supper, she hurried to the village to get to Ben Hammond's shop before it was closed and shuttered. He seemed genuinely pleased to see her and she was grateful for that. Ellen looked over all the goods carefully and finally chose a soft pink cotton printed with small bouquets of forget-me-nots. That would look pretty under her white apron.

"This is for something very special, Ben. You'll hear about it in church on Sunday," she said, her eyes bright with excitement. She had been unable to keep from telling him something about the party.

"You make me very curious, Ellen. Shall we have tea again after church?" asked Ben, eagerly.

Ellen nodded her head and picked up her bundle.

Then she left the store without another word. A strange feeling had come over her as she was talking with Ben and she became anxious to leave. As she walked towards her cottage she was deeply puzzled by her thoughts. Looking at Ben as he had wrapped her purchase, Ellen became faintly nauseous, imagining Ben's hands on her as Adam's had been. What a sinful, wicked thought! Whatever had come over her? She only knew she had to get outside in the fresh air where she could breathe again. How could she even think such a thing about Ben Hammond? He had never touched her or kissed her, though she knew he had wanted to more than once.

Approaching her cottage, Ellen saw Adam sitting on his front stoop staring in her direction. She dared not look at him, nor did she intend to speak. She walked by quickly, knowing his eyes were upon her, knowing he was thinking about his power over her, perhaps reliving that night in the bushes at Hawkes Nest. Ellen loathed him with a passion stronger than any feeling she had ever had. As she passed him, he spoke directly to her.

"Good evenin', Miss Davis. Nice to see yer about agin."

How she hated him! She held her bundle tighter against her chest and hurried on. Ellen was most anxious to begin working on her dress for the party.

The next week was filled with activity in almost every house in the village. There was going to be a party at Hawkes Nest and there wasn't a feminine body in Woodbridge that wasn't going to be clothed in a new dress. Ben Hammond had done more business in three or four days than he had in the last three months. The ladies all were busy with needle and thread, making new summer frocks. Most of them had had a glimpse of the new Mrs. Hawke at the church on Sunday and quickly realized that they would have to look their very best to receive any notice at all. Children had been invited too. It was to be an affair for the whole of Woodbridge.

Ellen had been so busy at Hawkes Nest getting the house in order and doing the baking that she had found little time to work on her own dress. The night before the party she was up late, sewing by lamplight until well past midnight. Finishing the last stitch, she decided to try the dress on again to make certain it fit properly.

Ellen went into the bedroom and got out of her dress and slipped the new one over her head. She looked in the mirror. It fit perfectly. Just the right snugness over her breasts and the fitted waist gave her figure a very slender appearance. As she studied her reflection she felt that somehow she looked different. What was it? Her skin was glowing and her eyes seemed unusually bright. She decided she was just excited and eager about the party.

She took the dress off and laid it flat on the bed. By smoothing out the few wrinkles, it would be ready. Perhaps she could tie her hair back with a ribbon the day of the party, like Mrs. Hawke. She noticed that Margaret always had a ribbon in her hair. Maybe even a housekeeper should be allowed a whimsey on special occasions, she decided.

Saturday arrived, warm and sunny. Peter and William had moved the long dining table out to the garden and Ellen covered it with Mary Hawk's best linen cloth. There were two bowls of punch, platters of assorted biscuits, three kinds of cake and several bowls of raspberry trifle. Ellen had arranged roses in a large urn she found in one of the cabinets in the kitchen. The table looked festive and sumptuous.

Margaret and William were in their room dressing for the party. As William fastened the last button on his waistcoat, he turned to look at his wife. She stood in front of the large armoire trying to decide which dress she should wear. Margaret looked very desirable in her lacy undergarments, her soft rounded arms bare and graceful, her small breasts appearing deceptively fuller as they were pushed up provocatively by the tight girdle about her waist. Her dark hair was curled and tied back with a pale velvet ribbon. William moved behind her and put his arms about her waist, holding her close against him, his hands caressing her breasts.

"Looks as if I may have dressed too soon," he murmured, as he kissed one soft bare shoulder.

"I can't decide which dress to wear," she said, taking no notice of his show of affection.

He looked at the row of dresses and then reached for one of pale blue silk with lace edging the low wide neckline and the long flowing sleeves.

"I like this one, Margaret. You look especially lovely in blue."

As he handed her the dress she turned to him and she raised her face for his kiss. He held her tenderly, looking down into the dark, heavily fringed eyes.

"Do you have any idea at all how much I love you?" he asked, his voice husky.

When he released her he smiled and suggested that if he didn't leave and let her dress they might never get to the party.

Below stairs the first guests were arriving. Peter was at the open door, his face happy and welcoming. Ellen, looking unusually pretty in her new pink dress, her hair caught back with a silk ribbon, directed the early arrivals to the garden.

Ben Hammond was one of the first to come through the door. His admiration of Ellen was so noticeable that Peter remarked later to her, "Ben Hammond is quite obviously in love with you." She had blushed profusely and Peter apologized for having made so personal a remark. Looking at Ellen, he had to admit to himself that he never realized before today how really attractive she was.

More and more of the townspeople were coming up

the cobbled walk, all dressed in their very best. Crisp new dresses of every share, bright ribbons, frilly bonnets, plain dark coats and trousers, black silk cravats. Several of the young unmarried girls lingered by the door, cooing and preening before Peter like so many brightly plumaged birds. He was charming to them all, suggesting that they might like to try the refreshments in the garden.

Ellen now was at the table, serving the wine punch, and she was fascinated by the colorful finery displayed. One never would assume that so small a village as Woodbridge could turn out such a wide variety of people. Some folks she had seen in the shops and walking about on the road through the town now seemed totally different. Ellen decided that having a party was a very fine idea. At least it got everyone cleaned up!

Then she saw Molly Barton and her mother coming towards her. She did not see Adam with them and had the fervent hope that he might not be coming. Amy commented on Ellen's pink dress.

"That is certainly a becoming color on you, Miss Davis. Your cheeks are positively glowing."

And then Adam was at Ellen's elbow, holding his cup out in front of her.

"You gonna pour some o' that fer me?" he asked, sullenly.

Ellen made no reply as she ladled some of the liquid into his waiting cup. Her body trembled and she felt nauseous as she remembered his rough and clumsy hands. She found that she could not look at any of the Bartons. As Adam started away with his wife and Molly, he leaned very close to Ellen and whispered in her ear.

"Better be a little more friendly, Miss Davis, effen ya' don't want no more trouble."

Ellen was so startled she turned quickly and looked him full in the face. He made a knowing and suggestive smile and walked away. Ellen felt very faint and her legs were shaking. She caught a glimpse of Ben Hammond watching her. Lowering her eyes to the punch bowl, she tried not to think about Adam Barton.

All heads turned suddenly and the garden became quiet as William and Margaret came out of the house. William had her hand clasped tightly in his as he made his way around the group.

Peter stood watching from his place on the step, his face unusually solemn and thoughtful. Then he became amused as he noticed the expressions on the faces of the young ladies watching Margaret. Everything from envy and awe to delight and pleasure was evident. The prettiest of the girls seemed envious, the plainer ones merely astonished. The men, young and old alike, were as one in their admiration of William Hawke's young bride. The party took on a new excitement and voices were buzzing now. Everyone seemed to be chattering happily and William knew that the party was a success. Hawkes Nest had a new mistress and it was quite obvious that Woodbridge was welcoming her in the fullest measure.

It was almost dusk when the last guest was taking his leave. That guest was Ben Hammond. As he expressed his pleasure to William and Margaret and to Peter, he started down the path to the road. Ellen called to him from the side of the house, through the window.

"Ben, would you please wait and see me home?" she asked. "It will be dark before I'm quite finished and I really don't fancy going through the trees in the dark," she explained.

Ben smiled broadly. He was more pleased than Ellen ever would know. He still was hopeful that someday soon she would accept his offer of marriage. So he waited patiently while she finished her duties in the house.

Ellen was strangely quiet on the walk to her cottage. Ben assumed she was only tired from the party. She had had much to do and he realized she had every reason to be fatigued.

"Would you like me to come in and light the lamp for you?" he asked as they reached her door.

Ellen hesitated briefly and then replied.

"That would be very kind of you, Ben."

He lighted the oil lamp on the table and the room took on a soft glow. Ben turned to face Ellen and took hold of her hands.

"Ellen, you know I still want to marry you. I'm a patient man, but I wish you would give me some indication of your feelings toward me."

Ellen looked at him intently, her brown eyes thoughtful and concerned. Could she ever let any man touch her again? She was slow to answer Ben.

"Ben, I'm very fond of you. Truly, I am, but I just don't know yet how I feel about getting married. You are very kind and good and I may be foolish not to decide at once, but please give me a little more time. Please?"

He looked at her with a steady gaze. Then very quickly he leaned forward and kissed her on the mouth.

"Goodnight, my dear," he said, gently. He turned then and went out the door.

Ellen put her hand to her lips. Strange. She had felt no emotion. Neither revulsion, as she had feared, nor excitement. Nothing. Wasn't she supposed to feel something? Something exciting and wonderful? Ben loved her. That was evident. Why couldn't she feel towards him as she did Peter? She could not expect Ben to wait indefinitely for her decision. There were other women who would accept him without any hesitation. He had a secure business and was a kind man.

When she finally lay down on her bed she was unable to sleep. She wondered if Adam Barton really meant to harm her again, or if he were only trying to frighten her. And then there was Peter. She realized her love for Peter was a hopeless situation, and her real problem was her unwillingness to face that truth. Somehow, she kept telling herself, she belonged at Hawkes Nest and someday she would be mistress there.

A light breeze was stirring the thin curtains at her bedroom window. Moonlight streamed through the tree branches at the side of the cottage, making intricate patterns on the walls of the room. Ellen's thoughts turned to William and Margaret Hawke. She wondered what it must be like to be as beautiful as Margaret and to be so loved. Ellen turned her head and looked at her new pink dress hanging on the hook next to the bureau. It was barely discernible in the pale light of the room. She remembered that Peter had noticed the dress and had told her she looked very pretty. Perhaps she would wear it to church tomorrow. Her thoughts were crowding over one another until finally she became drowsy and soon was asleep.

● 15 ●

When William and Peter were at their work, which was for long hours each day, Margaret found that time passed very slowly. There seemed to be nothing for her to do. Occasionally she went into the garden and brought flowers in for the house. Sometimes she walked to the village to look at the shops, but after having scoured the stores in Bristol with their great variety of goods, Margaret found nothing in Woodbridge she either wanted or needed. So she was spending more and more time at her desk writing letters to her father and to Hetty Langley and to some of her other friends in Bristol. Margaret went to great length to describe Hawkes Nest and Woodbridge, but found nothing especially interesting to relate about the people she had met.

Margaret did not mention to Hetty that in the two months she had been at Hawkes Nest there had been only the party William had given to introduce her to his friends and neighbors. And there had been no dancing at all. Margaret sighed to herself. She knew she would have to find something to do to occupy her time. Embroidery work was boring, and reading became tiresome after an hour or two.

"I regret having so little time to spend with you," William had remarked this very morning, "but Peter and I already are far behind. I'm sure you miss the activities in Bristol, darling, and in a few more weeks I shall try to make up for that."

"Don't be concerned about me, William. I'm quite content," Margaret had replied, politely.

However, she thought later, she *was* bored and she *did* miss her friends and Bristol.

Peter was spending most of his evenings at The Bell. Immediately after supper he would go out and William and Margaret seldom saw him again until morning. Peter was finding it difficult to be around his brother and Margaret, assuming that they very probably would like to be alone in the house. On the contrary, William missed his long conversations with Peter at the end of the day. They usually were quiet when at work, so the evenings had been pleasant interludes for both of them.

Peter offered to take the next journey to Salisbury and William readily accepted, being not at all anxious to leave his bride so soon, particularly when this next trip would be longer than usual since stops were to be made in Bath and Wells.

The night before he was to leave, Peter was sitting in the inn talking and laughing with some of his friends. Suddenly the conversation quickly changed.

"What's it like to have that beautiful woman in the house? Wish you'd got there first, Peter?"

Peter stared at John Robbins who had asked the question. He made no comment, but got to his feet.

"I'm leaving early tomorrow, so I bid you good night," he remarked.

Walking back to Hawkes Nest, Peter admitted to himself that he was finding it increasingly difficult to be near Margaret. She had been in the house only two months, although it seemed much longer to Peter. He had become aware of her every gesture and expression.

The last two afternoons he had gone riding, returning just before supper.

"Is it really pleasant to ride, Peter?" Margaret had asked while they were finishing their meal. "I've never been on a horse, you know."

"I enjoy it very much. Particularly since the weather has been so fair," Peter replied.

"Perhaps you could teach me sometime," Margaret suggested.

Peter glanced at William before he answered.

"If you like. What do you think, William?"

"A fine idea. If you think you'd like riding, my dear, by all means you should learn."

"I think I'd like it very much," Margaret responded, looking directly at Peter.

He pushed his chair back from the table and stood up.

"Very well. When I return from Salisbury we'll give it a try. Now, if you will excuse me."

Margaret's eyes followed his tall, rangy figure until he was out of sight.

"My dear," William began, "Reverend Thomas has asked us for tea on Sunday. I believe we should accept."

"Of course, William. Whatever you say."

Now Margaret had two new things to think about. Learning to ride a horse and what to wear to Reverend Thomas's house on Sunday.

● 16 ●

Ellen Davis was pregnant with Adam Barton's child. Feeling ill in the early hours of the day, she was puzzled by her condition. She could think of no reason why she should be nauseous and weak. Suddenly realizing what had happened, she clutched at her stomach.

"Oh no, oh no!"

Ellen's voice was a moan. She began to retch, over and over, until her throat was burning. Then she was sobbing, her hands covering her face. What was she going to do? Where could she go for help. There really was no one to whom she could turn. Ellen suddenly wished she never had come to Woodbridge. All she had hoped for was crashing down on her.

When her spasms of crying finally stopped, Ellen washed her face and rinsed her mouth with water. Looking in the mirror she studied her reflection. She didn't look any different. Maybe it wasn't really true. Maybe she wasn't carrying a baby. Perhaps there was some other reason for her nausea, some other reason for being "late."

Ellen sat down on the edge of her bed, her hands folded tightly in her lap. She would have to come to a decision soon. There was no time to waste if she really were pregnant. As she thought about her problem, there seemed to be only one thing she could do. She could marry Ben Hammond immediately. Of course Ellen knew that would be a wicked thing to do to him, but if they married within the next few weeks he never need know the baby was not his.

When she finished her duties at Hawkes Nest that evening she went straight to Ben Hammond's shop, hoping to arrive there before the place was tightly shut for the night. However, she found the shop closed and no sign of Ben. She most certainly could not go in search of him, so she would just have to wait for tomorrow and hope to see him then.

Ellen had not yet decided how to tell Ben she was willing to accept his offer of marriage. It had been such a short time since she had asked him to wait a while longer for her decision. No doubt he would wonder what had caused her to change her mind in a matter of weeks. Thank goodness men did not expect women to know their own minds!

She really did not want to marry Ben. She was not in love with him and the thought of Ben, or anyone else, touching her intimately made her feel faint and nauseous again. Perhaps Amy Barton would know how to get rid of a baby. But that idea made Ellen cringe. Amy was the last person she could to go for help.

As she twisted her hands together they felt damp with perspiration. There seemed to be no answer except to marry Ben and as soon as possible. She would have to think about Peter and Hawkes Nest some other time.

The following evening Ellen again arrived at Ben Hammond's shop, this time just as he was closing the shutters on the windows.

"Well, to what do I owe this pleasure?" he asked, smiling broadly.

"I want a bit of muslin, Ben."

Ellen spent so much time looking at the goods that it was almost dark when she decided upon her purchase. It now was the middle of September and the long summer twilights had given way to early dusk. Starting out the door of the shop, Ellen paused and turned back towards Ben.

"Oh, I didn't know I had stayed so long. It's almost dark. Could you possibly walk to the cottage with me? I'd be most grateful."

"I say, you do seem to have a fear of the dark, don't you?" Ben laughed. "Do you stay awake all night?" he teased.

He quickly closed the door of the shop and the two of them walked towards Ellen's cottage.

"Such a change in the weather," Ellen remarked. "It's right cold, wouldn't you say?"

She tucked her arm inside his as if for warmth.

Ben agreed that the evening was indeed quite cool.

"Would you like to come in and light the lamp for me and have a cup of tea?" Ellen asked as they reached the cottage.

Ben seemed delighted at the invitation. He appeared in no way curious of Ellen's asking him into her house. While Ben lighted the lamp, Ellen put her coat and hat in the bedroom. She glanced at herself in the small mirror, fluffing her hair about her face and moistening her lips. Her glowing cheeks seemed never to need pinching to bring out the color. She smoothed the taut bodice of her dress and walked back to the small sitting room where Ben was standing by the round table. Ellen moved beside him and her voice was soft as she spoke.

"Oh, thank you, Ben. I always have such a time getting the lamp lighted. It can be such a bother."

Actually she never had had any difficulty at all with the lamp, but she saw no harm in a little feminine deception. The glow of the lamp was shining on Ellen's face and hair as Ben looked at her. His eyes roamed approvingly from her wide brown eyes to her nose to her soft full mouth. Ellen never changed her gaze as she faced him. All the time she was thinking, "Why doesn't he say something? Why doesn't he?"

And then Ben was leaning towards her, pressing his lips against her own. He put his arms around her and held her close to his thin chest. Ellen was somewhat surprised at the hardness of his arms. Her body stiffened suddenly and she drew away from him.

"Ellen, what is it? You're trembling."

"I'm sorry, Ben. I don't mean to—"

Ben's pale grey eyes were suddenly dark.

"Will you marry me, Ellen?" he asked, earnestly.

She studied his face, her heart pounding with anxiety. She mustn't seem overly anxious though. That wouldn't do at all. Ellen slowly nodded and dropped her eyes, fearing to look at him, fearing to speak.

"Oh, my dear." Ben's voice was low and he kissed her again, gently.

Afterwards, when he was gone, Ellen sat on the settee for a long time, staring into space. Well, it was done. She felt relieved and unhappy at the same time. The child would have a proper father and she a husband, but what of her hopes and plans involving Hawkes Nest and Peter. Ellen's throat and chest ached when she thought of Peter. Marrying Ben, her dreams would be forever lost. Once Ben's wife, there would be no turning back.

When Ben left Ellen's cottage he was happier than he had ever thought possible. His pulse was racing and his blood felt warm as it coursed through his body. Ellen Davis was going to be his wife.

The young women in the village had paid Ben scant attention, he supposed because of his frail appearance. Now as he walked the road he felt six feet tall. He decided to stop in at The Bell and have an ale to celebrate his good fortune. Ben wanted very much to share his news with somebody.

The first person he saw as he entered the tavern was the blacksmith, Norman Arthur, and next to him was Adam Barton who worked as Mr. Arthur's assistant.

They looked up as Ben approached the bar counter and they nodded a greeting.

"Well, yer sort of a stranger 'round here, Mr. Hammond," said Polly Andrews, the barmaid, but her smile was warm and friendly.

Ben looked about the room. Everyone seemed to be deeply engrossed in his own conversation. He turned back to Polly. He had to tell someone. It might as well be her.

"I'm getting married in two weeks."

"Are you now? Who's the lucky lady?" asked Polly.

"Ellen Davis," Ben said proudly.

Adam Barton raised his head and stared at Ben when he heard Ellen's name mentioned.

"Yer marryin' Ellen Davis?" he questioned, his voice and manner surly.

"Indeed I am. In two weeks." Ben was enjoying the sudden attention.

"Well, I'm damned!" said Adam, leering at Ben. "She'll be a bit much fer ya', I'll wager, an' that's a fact. That un's overripe."

Ben felt the blood rush to his face and he became embarrassed as all eyes focused on him. The room had turned silent. What did Adam mean? What could he possibly mean? His implication was quite clear and Ben wanted only to leave as quickly as possible. The happy glow he had felt was gone. He finished his ale with one gulp and set the tankard on the counter. Without a word he left the tavern. Ben was deeply puzzled by Adam's remarks. Maybe the man was drunk, although he hadn't seemed so. Maybe it was just idle gossip, nonetheless nasty and unfair.

As Ben walked towards his house he decided he would go to Adam tomorrow and ask for an explanation. Ellen seemed so sweet and gentle that Ben could not imagine her having any contact at all with Adam Barton. Still, he knew he was going to spend a sleepless night.

The next morning before he opened his shop, Ben went to the blacksmith's to see Adam. Finding that he had not yet arrived, Ben went on to his own place, planning to see Adam later in the day. Perhaps the incident should be ignored entirely, for Ellen's sake. He thought that might be the most sensible thing to do. Ben's thoughts were interrupted as the door to his shop opened and Reverend Thomas's wife and daughter swept in.

"My, the wind is chill this morning. I do believe we're in for an early winter," said Evangeline Thomas, trying to rearrange her wind-blown hair under the heavy rose-trimmed bonnet.

Ben agreed with her that it did seem to be unusually crisp for September.

"How can I help you this morning?" he added.

Mrs. Thomas turned to look at her daughter as she spoke.

"Well, Frances needs a new wool dress for the winter and I thought we might as well get started with it."

Frances Thomas smiled meekly at Ben, but made no comment. He could sympathize with her shyness and made an effort to draw her out.

"What color do you like, Miss Thomas?" he asked, looking directly at her.

Before she could answer, Mrs. Thomas spoke up in her high-pitched, squeaky voice.

"I think grey is always so practical."

She was fingering some of the fabric on the shelves.

Ben secretly thought grey would make Frances look like a field mouse.

"Yes, it is, Mrs. Thomas, but dark blue is very attractive. So is this deep rose and it would be a nice shade on Miss Frances. Actually, I don't believe I have enough of that particular grey for you."

Ben was doing his best to steer Mrs. Thomas away from the dull color which he felt would be very

123

detrimental to Frances Thomas's already rather plain and dowdy appearance. She could be almost pretty, he thought later, if she were allowed to do something with herself. The charcoal coat and black bonnet she was wearing did nothing but accentuate the stiffly braided hair and the thin face and figure. Yet her eyes were a lovely dark blue and she had a rather sweetly curved mouth.

"You think the dark rose?" asked Mrs. Thomas, running her fingers back and forth on the woolen cloth.

"I think it would be most charming on Miss Frances," Ben replied, hoping his exaggerated tone would convince the girl's mother to take the rose wool. Which it did, and Ben was pleased to see the happy smile and bright look of pleasure on the girl's face.

"Oh, thank you, Mr. Hammond. I do so like that one," Frances said, smiling at him.

She was well aware of what he had done and wanted him to know she appreciated his efforts.

"Is there something else, Mrs. Thomas?" Ben asked, directing his attention to Frances's mother who was looking at some heavier woolen cloth used for coats and gentlemen's wear.

"No, I think not. That's all we can afford, really."

Frances blushed pink. She wished her mother would not refer to their meager finances in public. Ministers were notoriously a poor lot, but still there was one's pride, she thought, as she broke into the conversation.

"Mummy, do let's go."

Mrs. Thomas looked at her daughter in surprise. Frances was becoming more embarrassed. She was most grateful when other ladies entered the shop. This would distract her mother's attention from her. And of course it did. As the minister's wife, Evangeline Thomas knew all the members of the congregation by name, as well as the few people in Woodbridge who never seemed to at-

124

tend church. So the little shop began to buzz with the sound of female voices.

Ben looked from one to another, an amused expression on his face. He smiled knowingly at Frances as she caught his eye. Then she stepped towards him to pick up her package. She took hold of her mother's arm, urging her to be on their way. As mother and daughter walked along through the village towards the church, Mrs. Thomas remarked that Ben Hammond seemed quite interested in Frances.

"Oh no, Mummy, I don't think so," Frances was quick to reply. "He was only being polite and neighborly."

"Perhaps, but I think we should invite him to Sunday supper soon."

Evangeline Thomas had three sons at home, but Frances was an only daughter. Naturally, Mrs. Thomas was anxious for her to marry a man of some means. Married to a man who devoted his life to being of service to others, Evangeline Thomas had learned well how to make do with what little they had. She hoped Frances would have an easier life.

"Can we start the dress right away, Mummy?" asked Frances.

"It all depends on your father's plans for this afternoon. Old Mrs. Rollins has been taken quite ill and your father said we should stop by her place later today. We'll decide after we get home and talk with him. I do hope he doesn't object to that shade of cloth."

"Oh, Mummy, he couldn't, could he? I mean, it's really not at all bright." Frances's voice rose shrilly.

"Well, you know you your father feels about his womenfolk being conspicuous," replied Mrs. Thomas. "We'll see, Frances. Now don't concern yourself. We'll soon see."

Frances held the package of cloth tighter under her

arm. Never had she had a dress of such a pretty color and she wanted very much to keep it.

"Oh look, Mummy, there's Mrs. Hawkes. Isn't she beautiful?"

Margaret Hawke was walking towards them. She was wearing the blue velvet cloak and bonnet which were so becoming, and her arms were holding several packages. Mrs. Thomas and Frances nodded to her and since she merely nodded back and continued on her way there was no attempt at conversation.

She's not very friendly, is she, Mummy?"

Frances's tone of voice expressed her disappointment that Margaret Hawke had not stopped to speak with them.

"She may just be shy, dear. After all, she's been in Woodbridge only a short time," Mrs. Thomas responded matter-of-factly. "Give her a little longer," she added.

Even as she spoke she wondered why Margaret Hawke showed so little interest in the people of Woodbridge, especially since they had welcomed her so clearly at the party at Hawkes Nest.

"Well, now we must see to your father," she said as she and Frances reached the door of their house.

126

17

Peter stopped in Bristol on his way home from Salisbury for the sole purpose of meeting with Lowell Howard and learning something about the shipping business. He had decided that he might find he was more interested than he previously had thought. Lately, Peter was having doubts about staying on in Hawkes Nest with William and Margaret. He was feeling more and more like an intruder. Also, he was bothered most by the fact that he was becoming strongly aware of Margaret's **every move and gesture. He found he was thinking of** her far more than he should.

As he walked up the steps to Seagull's Point, Peter remembered the only other visit he had made to the house, the day of William's wedding. It was now nearly one o'clock and he hoped he would not be intruding upon Mr. Howard, if indeed the man was even at home.

The door to the house swung open just as Peter reached for the knocker, and Lowell Howard stood in front of him wearing a dark cloak and a tall grey hat, the same clothes he had worn on the dock the first time Peter saw Margaret when she stepped out of the black carriage. It now seemed long ago.

"Well, Mr. Hawke. This is a pleasant surprise. I was just on my way to my place of business so your coming could not have been more timely."

The old man seemed genuinely pleased to see Peter.

"We'll take the carriage, Mr. Hawke," he continued.

"I find the walk a bit too much for me now."

The Lowell Howard Trading Company occupied a small wooden building in the center of the docks area. There were two men seated at large desks, surrounded by books and papers. Mr. Howard introduced one, a Mr. Barnes, as his bookkeeper, and the other, a Mr. Walder, as his booking agent.

Peter was most interested in the cargo lists and their destinations. Everything was to be sent to Boston where Mr. Howard had a dispatching office, but once there the goods went to many different businesses and individuals.

"Now, if you'd like to come with me, Mr. Hawke, we'll go and see the *Bristol Cloud*. She's getting ready to sail at dusk and I think you'll find the sight most interesting," said Mr. Howard with obvious pride.

The *Bristol Cloud* was a sleek, black packet, three-masted, carrying a great wash of sail. Peter's heart leaped with excitement as they approached the ship, the older man quoting statistics as they walked along.

The afternoon was bright and sunny, crisp with the biting coolness of the autumn breeze off the harbor. Seagulls were swooping and diving about the ships, their shrill screeches piercing the already noise-filled air.

"Now, I'm thinking of buying two more of these for New York. That's why I'd like to open an office there, Mr. Hawke. That's where you might fit in. I've got Yancey Hamilton in Boston, but I need someone equally capable in New York," Lowell Howard continued his monologue.

Peter was too fascinated to say anything at all. Then he suddenly spoke as if in answer to a question.

"Yes, I think I could be ready to go in about four or five months."

"Could you now?" Mr. Howard was chuckling. "It will take me almost that long to complete negotiations in New York," he added.

"Well, I would have to work everything out with William in regard to our own business, but I think it can be managed," Peter explained hastily.

"Fine. You give it some thought and I'll get on with the matter in New York. In a month or two I should know something more definite."

As the two men boarded the ship, Peter could scarcely contain his excitement. He never had been on a ship before and the deck felt hard and firm beneath his boots. He glanced up at the top of the mainmast and was astonished at its height. Crewmen were climbing all over the rigging, shouting instructions at each other, most of which was unintelligible to Peter, but he marvelled at their agility.

Mr. Howard introduced Peter to the ship's captain and then walked about the deck, pointing out the various boxes and barrels of cargo which had not yet been taken to the hold. After seeing as much of the ship as was possible with all the necessary activity taking place, Peter and Lowell Howard walked back to the little building which housed the business office.

"I really must not take up any more of your day," said Peter, almost apologetically.

"Nonsense! It's almost time for a spot of tea and I thought we'd go over to the Imperial. Come along now," retorted the older man.

The two of them got inside the big black carriage Peter remembered so well and headed for the Imperial Hotel. As they entered the lounge where tea was being served and found a small table in a corner, a high-pitched voice addressed itself to Mr. Howard. It was Hetty Langley. She was seated with two women friends.

"Mr. Howard, how nice to see you! I've just had a letter from Margaret."

Hetty glanced at Peter as she spoke and nodded her head in recognition.

"Have you, my dear? Did she have any special

129

news?'' asked Margaret's father, depositing his hat and gloves in a chair next to him.

"No, nothing special really, but she does seem to think Hawkes Nest is uncommonly fine. That's your home too, is it not, Mr. Hawke?'' Hetty's gaze was steady and direct.

"Yes, indeed,'' replied Peter.

Hetty quickly introduced her friends to Peter and Mr. Howard and she was quite aware that the ladies were much taken with Peter's handsome features and his tall, lean figure.

"I do hope Margaret will come back to Bristol soon for a visit,'' Hetty said, looking at Peter. "Tell her we miss her, will you?''

"Of course.''

Peter sat down opposite Mr. Howard, and the girls turned again to their own tea. There was no further conversation between the two tables and soon Hetty and her friends got up to leave. Mr. Howard and Peter stood to bid them good afternoon and then the young women rustled away, whispering and giggling among themselves.

By the time Peter and Mr. Howard were ready to leave the hotel, it was too late for Peter to take the coach to Woodbridge so he decided to spend the night at the Falcon Inn. He had only a small travelling bag with him which he had left at the coach stop so he had just to go there and redeem it. Peter was grateful that Mr. Howard did not invite him to spend the night at Seagull's Point because he really wanted to be alone for a while. There was much to think about and he needed time to himself.

Peter thanked the old man for the afternoon he had given him and then bid him goodbye on the steps of the hotel. Peter watched as Mr. Howard got into the carriage and it rumbled off down the street. Then he started on his own way towards the coach stop to pick up his bag and proceed to the inn for the night. Tomorrow he would return to Woodbridge and perhaps then he would tell William of his plans.

Margaret was curled up by the window in the sitting room watching the raindrops run down the panes of glass. No two seemed to take the same path. She had been there for some time, quiet and pensive. The fire in the fireplace with its occasional crackling of burning wood was the only sound in the room. Margaret had not seen William since their mid-day meal, but she knew he was busy with his work. If only he would stop for a while and go for a walk with her. She wouldn't even mind the rain. Perhaps she could go and ask him. Seldom was he able to refuse her anything.

She started to move from the chair when she saw Peter coming up the walk. The windows were closed so tightly against the rain that she had not heard the coach. Margaret hurried to the door. Peter might have some exciting news from Bristol.

Peter was surprised when the door opened ahead of him and Margaret stood there smiling.

"Did you stop in Bristol?" she asked eagerly.

"As a matter of fact I did. Had a fine visit with your father and saw Hetty Langley. She wishes you would come for a visit soon," Peter replied, getting out of his cloak and hanging it on a nearby hook.

"Oh, do tell me about it. Come in here."

Margaret started into the sitting room and Peter followed, very conscious of the sweet smelling lavender sachet she kept in her clothes. He went straight to the fire and stood with his back close to the warmth of the flames. Margaret sat on the low footstool nearby, her hands clasped about her knees and looking up at Peter expectantly.

"How is my father?" she asked.

"He seems fine. We went to see the *Bristol Cloud* which was to set sail for Boston. Have you seen her?"

"Oh yes, but ships are smelly."

Peter laughed as she wrinkled her nose.

"Perhaps, but what a beauty!"

"Where did you see Hetty Langley?" asked Margaret, changing the subject abruptly.

"At the Imperial Hotel. She was having tea there with some friends. She had received your letter."

Peter noticed a sudden wistfulness about Margaret's face. Her dark eyes grew even larger as she looked up at him.

"She said you had much to say about Hawkes Nest," he continued.

"Well, of course. It's my home now."

"Do you miss Hetty and the others, Margaret?" Peter asked, his eyes searching her face.

"Yes, sometimes I do. But not much, really. Hetty can be an awful bore. I miss seeing Father though."

At that moment Ellen entered the room.

"Oh, you're home, Sir. I didn't notice the door," she said, brightly.

As Peter glanced at Ellen he thought she looked different, prettier than he had remembered. What was it that made her seem changed from one time to the next? Ellen's cheeks were always glowing, but somehow her eyes seemed bigger and brighter and her hair more golden. Peter studied her carefully as she spoke.

"Would you like some tea now, Sir?"

"That would be splendid. And why don't you tell William to come and join us?"

"Oh yes, Sir. I'll tell him."

Ellen's heart was pounding as she left the room and went back to the kitchen, unaware that Peter was watching her every step, taking full notice of her rounded, curving figure. She felt weak and her stomach was fluttering. She knew why and she did not want to admit to herself that seeing Peter again made her realize her feelings towards him had not changed. She still was deeply in love with him.

As Ellen put the cups and saucers on the tray, her eyes flooded with tears. Suddenly she wished he had not come back until after she had married Ben Hammond. However, he was back and there was nothing she could do to change that fact. She wiped her eyes quickly and went to tell William that Margaret and Peter wished him to join them in the sitting room.

Ellen had not yet told any of the Hawkes she was getting married in less than two weeks. She realized she must tell them and decided that tomorrow she would do so. Ellen had no way of knowing that tomorrow would be a disastrous day and one she never would forget.

18

Morning dawned bright and sunny, the rainclouds having moved on to the east. Ben Hammond closed the door to his cottage and started down the road towards the village and his shop. The walk took him past the blacksmith's. Since the night at The Bell when Adam Barton had made his strange and suggestive remarks about Ellen Davis, Ben had not seen him. Somehow Ben always was early in passing the blacksmith's and Adam was not about. This morning, however, Ben was later than usual because he had stopped to tie up some climbing roses which had drooped over in the rain. As he started to pass the blacksmith's, Adam's heavy voice boomed out at him.

"Still gonna have that weddin'?"

Ben stopped and looked at him inquisitively.

"And why should I not?" he asked.

His voice had a certain defiance, foreign to his nature, but Adam Barton seemed to invite antagonism and suspicion.

The blacksmith had the heavy bellows in his hand and he worked them over the fire, fanning the heat.

"She ain't no virgin, Mr. Hammond. She ain't."

Ben's face went scarlet and he moved quickly towards Adam, his fists clenched at his sides, his voice shrill with anger.

"How dare you speak such a lie? How do you dare?"

Adam grinned at the distraught man and worked the bellows faster.

"I know all right cuz I've had her. An' I've had her more'n once."

Ben lunged at the blacksmith and hit him in the mouth.

"You're a liar. You're a damn liar!" Ben shouted as he tried to hit the big man again.

Adam was surprised at the sudden movement and he gave Ben a shove, knocking him to the ground. As the smaller man got to his feet and started towards Adam again, the blacksmith raised his bellows up over his head in a threatening gesture.

Ben was livid with rage and his small frame shook with anger.

"You know it's a lie! I'll kill you for such a lie!" he cried.

Ben reached for the bellows but Adam jerked away.

"Jes' ask her, Hammond. Jes' ask her. She waitin' fer me up at the Hawkes. In the bushes, Hammond, ready 'n waitin'," Adam kept taunting Ben, eager for a fight.

The noise of the two men's voices had attracted some passersby and several people were approaching. There clearly was no match between the two men. Adam probably had three inches and more than thirty pounds on Ben Hammond.

"You're a liar!" Ben cried again, his anguish now more acute as he became aware of the townfolk.

"Jes' ask her, Hammond. I tell ya', jes' you ask her. Yer a fool, Hammond. Ask Ellen Davis effen I ain't her lover."

The words seared into Ben's brain and he realized that the people standing by had seen and heard the same as he. The whispering and gasping made him even more angry. Summoning every ounce of strength he had, he lunged towards Adam again. As he did so, Adam moved quickly and struck Ben with his bellows. In trying to escape the blow, Ben lost his balance and fell forward. There were cries of alarm from bystanders as his head hit the base of the forge and he lay still. Blood was spurting from a deep cut at his temple. He did not move. As Adam looked down at Ben no one spoke.

Then, "Better get Dr. Booth," someone remarked.

Adam still stared down at the lifeless form at his feet, uncomprehending. Why didn't Ben get up? What was the matter with him?

"It was an accident, Adam. It surely was an accident."

He could not remember later who had first said it was an accident. But it must have been. He had no intention of killing anybody. Besides, Ben Hammond was coming after him. They all saw that Ben Hammond was coming after him.

At the moment that Ben Hammond fell against the blacksmith's forge and hit his head with a fatal blow, Ellen Davis was busy in the kitchen of Hawkes Nest preparing breakfast. She planned to tell the Hawkes this morning of her coming marriage and she had been going over the words in her mind, repeating and repeating to herself what she planned to say.

"Ben Hammond and I are going to be married in a few days, but it will make no difference in my duties here. I will come at seven o'clock every morning just as I have done." Ellen whispered the words to herself again. "Good morning, Ellen," said Peter as he seated himself at the table.

"Good morning, Sir."

Looking at Ellen, Peter thought her face was rather pale which was most unusual for her.

And then William and Margaret arrived, Margaret shining in pink silk, her dark hair tied back from her lovely ivory face.

"Peter, this seems a fine day for my first riding lesson," she said, brightly.

Peter glanced at William and then at Margaret.

136

"If William will agree, I'd be happy to, Margaret," he said, his gaze turning back to his brother.

"Very well, Peter, but try to be back by eleven. We have a great deal to do today. I'm far behind on Mr. Howard's order and I shall have to turn over some other work to you so I can get on with it."

"Speaking of Mr. Howard," Peter began, "I had a talk with him about my going into the trading business. He thinks I might open a branch for him in New York soon after Christmas."

The plate Ellen was holding slipped from her hand and crashed on the floor, scattering into infinitesmal pieces. She burst into tears.

"Oh, I'm so sorry. I'm so sorry."

"Now, Ellen, don't be so concerned. There are more plates," said William calmly, as she bent down to gather up the tiny fragments of china.

All thoughts of telling the Hawkes about her forthcoming marriage left Ellen as the conversation continued at the table while she cleaned up the floor. How could she think about Ben Hammond when Peter was talking about leaving? New York! It was like the end of the world, thousands of miles away. She never would see Peter again. Ellen's throat felt tight and her heart was pounding so hard it seemed a wonder they couldn't hear the sound.

"That's only three months away, Peter," William remarked.

"Well, it might be January or February even, but I'm giving it some serious thought," Peter went on, handing his cup to Margaret for more tea.

"I went aboard the *Bristol Cloud,* William, and the idea intrigues me. Mr. Howard thinks I can do it. He thinks I can learn the trade and I'd really like to give it a try. He's negotiating now with a New York shipping company for another ship or maybe two."

Margaret had not spoken, but now she remarked,

"Besides, Peter, if you don't like New York, you can always come back here."

"Thank you, Margaret. That's a comforting thought."

Peter finished his tea and then pushed back his chair from the table.

"I'll saddle the horses, Margaret, and you'd better put on some heavy clothing. We can start in about twenty minutes," he said, looking down at Margaret's upturned face. Her eyes were bright and eager, almost like a small child.

"I'll be ready," she said, smiling at Peter.

Ellen was having difficulty in clearing the table, as her hands kept shaking.

"Ellen, are you not feeling well this morning?" asked William, as he noticed her trembling.

"I feel quite well, Sir. I really don't know what made me drop the plate."

"Never mind the plate," William said, dismissing the matter.

He turned to Margaret.

"My dear, you'd best wear your warmest cloak. I don't want you catching your death out in the wind. Riding can be a chilly business."

"Very well, dear, I'll go now and get ready."

Margaret rose from her chair and left the room. William poured another cup of tea.

Ellen decided she must speak to him about her marriage. She should not wait any longer.

"Mr. Hawke," she began, "Ben Hammond and I are going to be married on Wednesday next, but it will make no difference in my position here. I will still come at seven as always."

There, she had said it at last. She could not tell by William's expression whether he was surprised or annoyed. Then a smile broke across his face.

"Well, Ellen, that's great news. He's a fine man and he's most fortunate to have you for a wife. I've always said your talents were somewhat wasted on us. Of course I'm delighted you will stay on. Heaven knows, we can't manage without you. Mrs. Hawke would be at her wit's end with this entire household to care for. I can imagine what chaos we should be in."

He smiled broadly as he continued.

"Now I can understand the dropping of the plate and the shaking hands. Why were you so worried about telling us?"

"I don't know, Sir. You're always so kind, but I thought you might be angry that I hadn't mentioned it before now or that you might think I would be leaving."

"I was not aware that you had been seeing Ben Hammond."

"Mr. Peter knew, Sir."

"Did he now? Well, Peter must be more observant than I."

Ellen made no further comment.

"Do you wish me to tell Mrs. Hawke and Peter, or would you rather tell them yourself?" William asked as he stood up from the table.

Ellen hesitated before she answered.

"Perhaps it would be easier if you tell them, Sir."

"Very well, Ellen, and again I offer my congratulations."

"Thank you, Sir."

The confusion and excitement at the blacksmith's had increased with the arrival of Dr. Booth. There was, however, nothing he could do for Ben Hammond. As he asked for details, all the bystanders began talking at once. Some of them had witnessed the quarrel between Adam and Ben. Most had not. Facts became mixed with gossip and imagination. Each time the story was told it became more complicated. Dr. Booth finally raised his hands for silence.

"Will someone please help me get Mr. Hammond into my wagon and I will take him to his home. And the Reverend should be told."

"Who's going to tell Miss Davis?" asked Polly Andrews, the barmaid at The Bell.

"Miss Davis?" asked Dr. Booth. "Is she kin?"

"Oh, no, they were to be married in a matter of days."

There were more gasps of surprise and then a low moan went through the crowd.

"How sad. How sad," murmured Dr. Booth. Then he turned to Polly Andrews.

"Perhaps you should go and tell her," he suggested.

"All right. I can do that."

Polly turned and left the group and started towards Hawkes Nest. As she came to Adam Barton's house she wondered if Amy Barton knew about the accident. Probably not. She knocked on the door and it quickly was opened. Amy's face wore a puzzled look when she saw Polly Andrew's on her doorstep.

"Mrs. Barton, there's been an accident," Polly began.

"Adam? Is he hurt?" Amy's voice was anxious and her hands began tugging on the apron she wore over her plain brown dress.

"No, it's not Mr. Barton. It's Mr. Hammond. He's dead. He fell and hit his head against the forge."

"God in heaven! How did it happen?"

"They say Mr. Hammond and your husband were quarreling.

"It was something about Ellen Davis. Mr. Hammond was planning to marry her in a few days," Polly explained, openly.

Amy Barton's throat tightened and she felt suddenly

cold. Why should Adam quarrel about Ellen Davis? And why hadn't Ellen mentioned to Amy that she was planning to marry?

"I'm on my way now to Hawkes Nest to tell Miss Davis. It's so sad," Polly continued.

"Is my husband still at the forge?" asked Amy Barton. Her voice was flat and without emotion.

"I think so. I think he was helping Dr. Booth get Mr. Hammond to his home," Polly replied.

"I didn't see it happen, Mrs. Barton," she continued. "But don't blame your husband. It was an accident."

When Amy closed the door after Polly Andrews left, she felt limp and she barely could move to a chair. A man had been killed and Adam was part of it. And Ellen Davis was involved. What could that mean? Her earlier suspicions about her husband were returning to haunt her. What explanation would Adam make? Or would he say nothing to her?

She walked slowly to the bedroom and reached for her cloak as she decided she must go to see about Adam. It was her wifely duty and she would be expected there. Her two little sons had gone out with Molly so they would not miss her.

Amy walked with a heavy step as she started through **the village and then she heard excited voices and saw** people coming towards her. Suddenly she felt apprehensive and frightened.

"It was an accident, Amy. Adam didn't mean to hurt him. Ben fell and hit his head."

"They were fightin' about Ellen Davis."

"Ben was going to marry her soon."

"In just a few days it was."

"Adam said she was no virgin 'n Ben got furious."

"Shut up, you fool!"

"Well, that's wot started it all jes' the same."

Amy threw up her hands in a defensive gesture.

"Where is my husband?" she asked, her face pale and her voice sounding thin and hollow.

"At the forge, Mrs. Barton. He's still there," someone answered.

"It's not his fault, Mrs. Barton, it ain't. Ben fell. That's all there is to it. Ben fell."

The crowd of villagers stepped aside as Amy started to move forward. They became silent as she looked at them helplessly and walked slowly away in the direction of the blacksmith.

Ellen was upstairs changing the bed linen and did not hear the knock at the door when Polly Andrews arrived at Hawkes Nest. However, William Hawke was walking through the hallway on his way to the workroom when he heard the knock, so he quickly retraced his steps and swung the door open wide. He appeared somewhat startled to see the local barmaid on his doorstep, but realized at once that she must have good reason to be there.

"Is Ellen Davis here?" asked Polly immediately. Her voice had a sense of urgency to it.

"Why yes, she's upstairs, I think. Come in, won't you? Is something wrong?" asked William as Polly stepped inside and he shut the door behind her.

"I'm afraid so, Mr. Hawke. There's been an accident and Ben Hammond's dead. He fell and hit his head against the forge. He and Miss Davis were going to be married and—"

William and Polly heard a deep moan from the top of the stairs. They both looked up to see Ellen staring down at them, her face white and her eyes wide and frightened like a cornered animal. Then they saw her knees buckle and she pitched forward, tumbling down the stairway. She had fainted.

Polly and William leaped towards her in an effort to

break her fall, but she was almost to the bottom of the steps before they reached her. She lay at an awkward angle, her legs twisted under her and her head thrown back. Ellen's eyes were closed and her face was deathly white.

Polly Andrews was trembling herself, now, quite shaken with the events of the morning.

"Is she dead?" she asked, her voice barely audible.

"Of course she's not dead," replied William sternly as he took hold of Ellen's arm and felt her pulse.

He began to rub Ellen's hands and then patted her face, trying to rouse her. He and Polly straightened out her legs so that she was now flat on the floor. William put his arm under her back and raised her up so that she was resting against his chest. She uttered a low moan and her eyelids fluttered.

"She's comin' 'round, Sir," said Polly, excitedly.

Ellen's eyes opened and shut and opened again. She appeared bewildered as she looked first at Polly Andrews and then became aware that William had his arm about her and she felt his strong hard chest behind her back.

"Oh yes, I remember. It's about Ben, isn't it?" she murmured.

"There was an accident, Miss Davis," Polly said, patting Ellen's arm.

"Do you think you can stand, Ellen?" asked William. "I think you should get up to bed and we'll ask Dr. Booth to come and have a look at you. That was a very bad fall."

He and Polly helped Ellen get to her feet. There seemed to be no broken bones readily discernible, but her right ankle was very painful and it was difficult to put her weight on her right leg.

"Put your arm about my waist, Ellen," directed William, "and I'll help you upstairs. You can lie down

143

in my old room. Miss Andrews, could you please go for Dr. Booth?''

"Oh yes, Sir. I'll go right away.''

Polly never had felt so important before. She seemed to be needed everywhere this morning.

Ellen, with William's strong arm supporting her, had almost reached the top step when she cried out in pain and doubled up, clutching her stomach. What was happening to her? She almost dropped to her knees, but William picked her up in his arms and carried her to the bed in his former bedroom. She was moaning in pain as he laid her down.

"Oh, Mr. Hawke,'' she cried, "what's happening to me?''

Then William saw the dark red stain on her dress. She was bleeding profusely. She must be hemorrhaging. Now what was he to do? How long would it be before Dr. Booth arrived? William reached for a blanket out of the chest at the foot of the bed and covered Ellen. She was in considerable pain and obviously was very frightened. William was alarmed and did not know what to do for her.

It seemed an eternity before Dr. Booth came up the stairs, followed by Polly Andrews.

"She's bleeding heavily,'' said William, his eyes grave with concern.

Dr. Booth asked William and Polly to leave while he examined Ellen. It was some time before he came out of the room.

"She's had a miscarriage,'' he said, bluntly.

Polly looked quickly at William Hawke to see his reaction, but she could detect nothing unusual. He seemed to accept the doctor's diagnosis without emotion. Inwardly, William was somewhat disturbed. Ellen always had seemed so naive and innocent and he found it hard to imagine Ben Hammond taking advantage of a girl he wished to marry. Still, Dr. Booth must know.

"It must have been the fall. Fortunately, she was not too far along and she should have no trouble recovering. However, she will need to stay in bed for a few days. She will be very weak," the doctor continued. "I suggest she not be moved from here, if possible, Mr. Hawke, and she will need some fresh clothing."

Dr. Booth then turned to Polly.

"Do you think you could go to her cottage and find something?"

William spoke up before Polly could reply.

"That won't be necessary, Doctor. Mrs. Hawke will have some things for her."

"I'll be back in a day or two to look in on her," said the doctor as he and William started down the stairs.

"Very well. By the way, what really happened at the forge?" asked William.

"I'm not at all sure. So many conflicting statements, but it appears that Adam Barton and Mr. Hammond were quarreling. It does seem to have been an accident, however."

After Dr. Booth left, Polly Andrews decided she too must leave. William turned to her and his face was solemn.

"Miss Andrews, I think for all concerned nothing should be said about this. Can I count on you?" he asked.

"Yes, Sir. I'll not tell a soul. Poor Miss Davis. Poor miss."

But of course by nightfall Polly had told half the village what had happened at Hawkes Nest. How could William Hawke expect her to keep such a secret, she wondered?

Just as Polly was disappearing among the trees on her way to the village road, Peter and Margaret arrived.

Margaret's eyes were sparkling as she came running towards William.

"Oh, William, it was lovely. Riding is lovely and Peter says I shall do well," she said. Her voice was shrill with excitement.

But she at once detected the serious look on her husband's face, as did Peter when he soon followed Margaret into the house.

"What is it, William?" he asked, curiously.

William explained the events of the morning and when he told about Ellen both Peter and Margaret were aghast.

"Ellen? I can scarcely believe it. Ben Hammond taking advantage of a girl like Ellen?" said Peter. "Will she be all right?" he asked, obviously concerned.

Peter suddenly felt a very real anger towards Ben Hammond and sincere sympathy towards Ellen. The girl had no family but the Hawkes and they must take responsibility for her welfare.

William explained what the doctor had said regarding Ellen's recovery.

"Is there anything I can do, William?" asked Margaret.

"No, dear. She just needs rest for a few days. She will stay here for a while and I'm sure she'll be just as good as new. Ellen's strong and healthy," William remarked in his quiet voice.

"Oh yes, there is something you can do, Margaret," he went on. "Could you find one of your dressing gowns or sleeping gowns for her to wear?"

His wife looked dismayed.

"My things?" she asked, incredulously. The idea obviously was distasteful to her.

"You must have something, Margaret. Now please go up and help her out of her clothes. They will have to be disposed of." William directed.

"But William, I—"

"Margaret, please don't act like a child," William interrupted, impatiently. "Ellen has had a great tragedy happen to her and she has no family. She needs our help. Certainly neither Peter nor I can go up and care for her. She needs you. Now please do as I ask, will you?"

Margaret looked at him, her face angry and sullen, all the soft beauty gone. Her husband never had spoken to her in such a manner before. Now he was ordering her about as if she were his servant and Margaret was resentful. She stared at William, her dark eyes blazing. Then suddenly she turned and ran up the stairs without another word.

Ben Hammond was buried in the cemetery behind the stone church. The village folk who went to the funeral looked for Ellen Davis, some out of morbid curiosity, but there was no sign of her. Nor had anyone seen her since the day of the accident. The Hawke brothers were at the church, but not Margaret Hawke. The Reverend Thomas inquired after Mrs. Hawke.

"She's taking care of Ellen today," William replied simply.

"And how is the poor girl? Is there anything I or Mrs. Thomas can do for her?"

"No, I think not. She will be up and about in a day or two. It's been a dreadful shock. You knew they were to be married?" replied William.

"Yes, Mr. Hammond had talked to me about a week ago."

Adam and Amy Barton also were missing from the mourners at the funeral. Adam had refused to discuss the accident with Amy or anyone else. He seemed morose and withdrawn as he went from his cottage to the forge and back again. His moodiness increased and

147

he stayed to himself, not even going to The Bell as he always had done in the evenings. Adam was not unaware of the gossip which had gone through the village, that he had been Ellen's lover, that she had had a miscarriage, and that the quarrel had been caused by Ben's jealousy.

Adam hadn't really meant any harm to Ben Hammond, but the man was so smug, so sure of Ellen, and she always acting so righteous. He had been unable to hold his tongue. And now Ben was dead and Ellen Davis was sick up at the Hawke house. No one had seen her since the day Ben died.

Amy had decided that Molly should not spend any more time with Ellen Davis. The child was unconsolable when Amy said she was not to go to Ellen's house again. Her mother would make no explanation and this caused even more frustration to Molly.

"But, Mummy, why? Can't you say why?" she pleaded.

"Molly, I'll say no more'n I already said. I don't want you over there no more. She's brought trouble to us all. Now I don't want to hear any more about it."

Molly fell on her bed weeping and refused her supper. Ellen was her friend. How could Ellen hurt anybody?

"Can't you stop her makin' all that blubberin' noise?" asked Adam as he and Amy sat at the kitchen table.

"Adam, I think we should leave Woodbridge," Amy said, ignoring his question.

She was solemn as she looked directly at her husband. His face was without expression. She could not guess what he was thinking. Then he wiped his mouth on his shirtsleeve and leaned back in his chair.

"I've been thinkin' the same thing, Amy. I'm tired 'o this place. Why don't we go up to Liverpool where a man can earn a decent livin'?"

"Liverpool? Well, I hadn't thought of goin' quite so far. Maybe just to Bristol."

"All right. Bristol then."

Adam did not know how desperate Amy was to get away from Woodbridge and all that happened. He did not know it was mostly because she could not bear to see Ellen Davis. Amy was certain that Adam had forced himself on the girl and she felt that for Ellen's sake they should go away. Ellen would have to live with the gossip which already was swirling about the village following the circumstances of Ben's death. Such matters had a way of growing and entangling everyone involved.

Amy Barton felt in her own mind that Adam was to blame for the accident and the best thing she could do would be to leave with her husband and children for some other place where they would be strangers, where they could start over and there would be no suspicions or questions, and maybe things would be better all around.

So that very evening Amy and Adam began to sort out their few belongings. Adam would tell Mr. Arthur the next morning that they were leaving, and they could take the afternoon coach to Bristol. He didn't have any thought about where his family might stay until he found work, but he knew there would be someplace for them to go once they got to Bristol. No need to worry about that.

When Ellen was able to be up and about at Hawkes Nest, the Barton family already had left Woodbridge. She did not know this, however. She had not asked the details of Ben's death and none of the Hawkes had discussed the accident with her. She was not aware of the gossip making the rounds of the village either. Soon enough there would be questions.

This morning she awoke to the sun streaming through

the windows of her room. She sat up and wrapped her arms around her knees. Ellen became aware of the gown she was wearing, a soft white silk edged with lace about the neck and long sleeves. Margaret Hawke's of course. Suddenly she shivered and slid back down under the blankets. They must all know about the baby. And Peter. Most of all, what did Peter think? And what about Ben? They would think it was his baby, of course. They must all believe she was wanton.

Ellen remembered Margaret Hawke's coolness when she had come into the room with Ellen's tray the previous mornings. No doubt Margaret never had had to do for anyone but herself and she obviously resented Ellen's intrusion into her way of life, particularly when she thought of Ellen as a tarnished person, a girl involved in a fatal quarrel between men, and a girl carrying an illegitimate baby. When Ellen thanked Margaret for the use of the silk nightdress, Margaret had replied haughtily.

"You may keep it. I certainly will have no further use of it now."

A knock on the bedroom door interrupted Ellen's thoughts and she sat up in bed.

"Yes?"

"It's William. I've brought your breakfast. May I come in?"

"Yes, of course, Sir."

William entered the room with the tray and put it on the table next to the bed. Then he looked at Ellen.

"You're looking quite fit this morning," he remarked.

The questioning look on her face made him realize that she was wondering why he had come with the tray instead of Margaret.

"I hope you don't mind that I brought your breakfast. Mrs. Hawke is having another riding lesson with Peter this morning. I do say she's beginning to be quite the horsewoman. Wants to ride all the time.''

"It's a lovely morning for it, I'm sure," Ellen responded. "The doctor says I can go home now," she added.

"Yes, he told me, but are you sure you're feeling well enough?" asked William.

"Oh yes. And I can start my work again tomorrow morning. I know this must have been a great inconvenience to Mrs. Hawke and I'm truly sorry.''

"We've managed fairly well, although I must say we've missed your cooking.''

"If someone would just go to my cottage and bring some of my clothes and my coat, I'd be—''

William interrupted Ellen almost at once.

"Of course. I'll go.''

"You're so kind, Mr. Hawke. You are all so kind. I don't know how to thank you.''

"No need, Ellen. We are all sorry about Ben, and the baby. Did he know about that?''

Ellen dropped her eyes. She could not look at William as she felt her cheeks burning. She she replied in a soft, tremulous voice, her head still bent, "No, Sir. The baby was not his.''

There was a long silence and she felt William's eyes upon her. Finally he spoke.

"Do you just go around getting into bed with—''

"Oh no, Sir. I was forced. I mean I was—''

Ellen covered her face with her hands as her eyes filled with tears. She felt so ashamed and embarrassed in front of William.

He put his hand on her shoulder as he spoke.

"Never mind, Ellen. It's really none of my business, but we are concerned about you.''

Several moments passed and neither spoke. Then William asked.

"Do you mean someone forced you against your will?"

Ellen nodded, her face still shielded by her hands.

"Do you want to tell me, Ellen?"

"No, Sir. I'd rather not."

"Very well. I'll go for your things," said William and he started for the door. As he was about to leave the room he turned again to face Ellen.

"Don't you think Peter and Mrs. Hawke should be told the truth?" he asked.

Ellen raised her head to look at him, her face now tear-stained and pale.

"If you think so, Mr. Hawke. At least Ben should not be blamed. But I can't tell them, Sir. I really never could."

"All right. I'll explain and then the matter will be dropped. We'll say no more about it. However, Ellen, if the scoundrel should come around again I think you had best tell us."

"Oh, thank you, Sir. I'm sorry I've made such a muddle of things."

"Nonsense. Eat your breakfast," said William quickly. "I'll go fetch your things."

Ellen listened to his footsteps on the stairs. She wiped her eyes on the sleeve of Margaret Hawke's silk night-dress and turned to pour herself a cup of tea. She was just finished breakfast when she heard Margaret and Peter outside. She went to the window and looked down.

They were laughing as they brought their horses to a halt. Peter dismounted and came about to help Margaret down from her horse. He touched her only briefly and then took the bridle to lead the horse away with his own to the barn. Ellen watched as Margaret stared after him. She seemed to be waiting for something. Then Margaret turned suddenly and started for the house, slapping her riding crop against the side of her leg.

At that instant Ellen remembered the conversation about Peter going to New York and she wondered what had happened in that regard. So much had occurred in her own life the past few days that she momentarily had forgotten about the possibility of Peter's leaving. Now she felt restless and eager to be up and about, to find out what was going on in the Hawke family.

Ellen heard Margaret come into the house and come up the stairs. Then she heard the door close to William and Margaret's room. She supposed Margaret was changing out of her riding clothes. Such was not the case. Young Mrs. Hawke was standing by the window looking down at Peter as he started back to the house from the barn. His reddish blonde hair shone brightly in the sunlight and his easy gait was pleasant to watch. His long legs took great strides and his body moved gracefully. Margaret found herself fascinated by his movements.

Suddenly she trembled and felt cold. Why was she standing there watching Peter when she should be looking after her husband? This was the first time she had come in from riding that she had not gone straight to William to tell him about the ride. She hadn't even thought about William, she realized now.

Margaret flung open the door and hurried down the stairs. She went quickly to where William usually was working and found the place empty. Strange. Where could he be? She started through the kitchen just as Peter came in the side door and they collided.

"Margaret, I'm sorry! Did I hurt you?"

"Oh no, Peter. I was just looking for William. Have you seen him?"

"No, but he can't be very far," Peter replied. "Did you look in here?" he continued as he peered into the workroom and then stepped back into the kitchen.

"Well, I'm sure that wherever he is he'll return soon," Peter went on. "Margaret, you're shaking. Are you cold? Perhaps we stayed out too long this morning. Here, you sit down and I'll fix you something hot to drink."

Peter took Margaret's arm and led her to the rocking chair where she sat down like a dutiful child. Her eyes never left him as he took a cup from the cabinet and partially filled it with hot water from the kettle on the stove. She continued to watch as he put some sugar and spices in the cup and then added something from a bottle. He brought the cup to her and she took it with both hands.

"This will make you feel better, I'm sure," said Peter, smiling down at her.

He had to admit that she surely did not look ill in any way. The morning's exercise was still showing in her pink cheeks, and her eyes were sparkling. Soft curly tendrils of her black hair had escaped from under her riding hat and Peter thought she looked utterly charming.

"It's very good, Peter, whatever it is," Margaret remarked as she sipped the hot beverage. "Why don't you have some too?"

"You're the one who's cold," he replied, laughing. "Besides, I have to get out of these clothes and get to work. The morning is half gone."

They heard the front door close and both turned their heads toward the hallway. It must be William.

"William?" Margaret called.

"Yes, dear. Where are you?"

"In the kitchen. Where have you been?"

William walked into the room, his arms full of clothing. He bent down and kissed Margaret on the cheek.

"What on earth is that? Where have you been?" Margaret asked again.

"I went to Ellen's cottage to get some of her clothing. She's able to be up and about now," William replied, matter-of-factly.

"Well, I should hope so," Margaret muttered, with a hint of sarcasm. "Oh, William, do put those things down. You look so foolish," she continued.

"I'll take them up to Ellen. She's anxious to get back to work and heaven knows we need her," William remarked.

Margaret's eyes flashed as she looked up at him.

"Oh, my dear, I didn't mean—" William began quickly. "But you know you've never had to do these things before and I'm sure it's been very trying."

Margaret got up out of her chair, set the empty cup on the table and reached for the articles in William's arms.

"I'll take them," she said simply.

"If you wish."

As Peter stood watching the scene he wondered why Margaret seemed to show such antagonism towards Ellen. This was the second time she had been harsh with William regarding Ellen. Perhaps she resented a hired girl receiving so much attention. Still, Margaret must know how important Ellen was to the household and how much they all needed her.

When Margaret left the room William threw up his hands in a gesture of bewilderment and then shook his head.

"I'm afraid I'll never understand the ways of women," he said with a wry grin.

"Who does? Who ever does?" Peter responded.

"Never mind," he added. "It will all be forgotten by the time she comes back downstairs."

"I hope so," said William, walking towards the workroom.

Margaret burst into Ellen's bedroom without knocking.

"My husband brought you some clothes," she said, dropping the garments quickly into the chair next to the window.

"That was very kind of him," Ellen remarked, getting out of bed. "You've been very thoughtful also, Mrs. Hawke," she added, "loaning me this nightdress and everything."

Margaret stared at Ellen. The girl appeared smaller than Margaret had remembered and she looked prettier, or perhaps it was merely because Margaret never had taken much notice of her at all.

"Well, no matter. You may keep it."

"Oh, thank you, Ma'm. You must be very tired with all you've had to do so I shall get right on with things now."

"I've managed," Margaret's voice was flat. "The breakfast dishes are not yet done," she added as she started towards the door. Suddenly she stopped, turned and looked directly at Ellen.

"By the way," she began, "did you know that Adam Barton has left Woodbridge? Gone to Bristol, they say."

Ellen's face paled, but she made no response.

"I wonder if he really *did* kill Ben Hammond and if all those things Adam said *were* true," Margaret continued as she left the room and pulled the door shut behind her.

Ellen's heart was beating fast as she began to dress. She wished she had not eaten the breakfast after all for now her stomach felt queasy. What things had Adam said? What was Margaret talking about? Did everyone in Woodbridge know about the baby? Ellen wondered how she was going to face the village folk, and Reverend Thomas.

19

William received a letter from Lowell Howard reminding him that Margaret's eighteenth birthday was only three weeks away.

"Will the cab be ready in time?" he had asked.

William replied by return post that it would indeed be finished and inquired if Mr. Howard might wish to come to Woodbridge "for a visit so you could present the gift to her yourself." However, the old man felt a thirty mile trip in a coach on a rough road was a bit more than he could manage. And besides it was then thirty miles back to Bristol! At the close of his letter he added a postscript to Peter.

"I have had a response from New York and I would like to meet with you in that regard in the near future."

Even though the weather had turned bone-chilling and damp, Peter and Margaret continued with the riding lessons. William marvelled at his wife's stamina. He could hardly imagine so tiny a figure having such physical energy. However, now that Ellen was again managing the household, riding was the one thing that seemed to give Margaret great pleasure.

"Well, darling, how did it go?" William had asked when Peter and Margaret returned this morning.

"Splendid, William. I can go as fast as Peter now," Margaret replied, drawing off her gloves.

"But aren't you chilled to the bone? It's so bitter out."

"Yes, it's a bit nasty with the wind, but I'll soon warm up," Margaret replied. "Peter's going to fix another of those hot drinks he makes," she added.

"Perhaps you shouldn't ride for a few days while it's so cold," suggested William. "I don't want you becoming ill. Don't you agree, Peter?"

"You may be right," Peter responded, glancing at Margaret.

Her eyes were bright and luminous. She wrinkled her nose at him.

"You're just afraid I'll pass you up," she teased. "Let's go tomorrow anyway, Peter. The weather may change."

"Not likely. It will only get worse from now on," William remarked, knowingly.

"Just the same, Peter promised to take me across the valley to the river tomorrow and I want to go," Margaret argued.

"That's a very long ride, Margaret, and you could be extremely chilled before you got back. Why don't you wait for a while?" asked William.

Margaret stomped her small foot angrily.

"Don't you be such a fuddy-duddy! I'm going and you can't stop me!"

William turned to look at her, startled at her outburst.

"Of course, my dear, if it's that important to you. I didn't mean to upset you. Now come here and give me a kiss."

Peter filled the cups with the hot drink as Margaret walked towards William, her soft, full lips in a deep pout. When William kissed her he felt her cold cheeks and then her icy hands.

"You'd best have that hot whatever-it-is at once. You're like an icicle."

Margaret laughed and went back towards Peter and the waiting cup.

"And then you go upstairs immediately and get into some warm clothes," William continued. "Ask Ellen to bring you some hot water. I think she's up there now, changing the linen."

Margaret made no reply. She seemed to ignore William as she finished the cup of hot liquid and then left the room.

William was deeply puzzled by her behaviour. Lately she seemed so distant, so preoccupied. She scarcely spoke at supper and she would retire early, not telling him she was going up, so that when he got into bed beside her she would be sleeping soundly. Margaret seemed to avoid him physically as much as possible. When he questioned her about not feeling well, she merely said she was tired. William even wondered if she might be pregnant, but that was not the case. Perhaps the dreary winter was depressing to her, although he felt the weather in Bristol could hardly be much different. Yet he couldn't help but notice how bright and cheerful Margaret became whenever she and Peter went riding. Maybe she was alone too much. She didn't seem to take to the women of the village, never entertained at tea or went to visit anyone.

Thinking back, William could not recall whether she had many young women friends in Bristol. There was Hetty Langley and one or two others he remembered, but Margaret had seemed to spend most of her time with her father. Perhaps she missed him more than William had realized.

William was keenly aware that Margaret never had experienced the satisfaction that he did from their lovemaking. Lately she was remote and unresponsive. This night when they retired he took her in his arms and held her close against him. He could feel her heartbeat as she curled her body next to his.

"I love you, Margaret," he whispered against her soft hair.

She made no reply. Was she pretending sleep? The fragrance of lavender from her nightdress filled his nostrils. Desire for her welled up in his body and he put his hand under the folds of her silken gown and caressed her breasts and felt the smoothness of her soft thighs. She responded slowly as he pressed his mouth against her own.

"Darling," he murmured, "Darling, I adore you."

She did not speak as she moved against him. Why did she not express her love, he wondered. He could not tell if her response to him was pretended or real. Was she only being a dutiful wife? Had she ever wanted him as a lover more than a husband? If only he could be sure she loved him.

William removed the silk gown from her body and felt the soft warm flesh against his own. She put her arms around him, running her fingers up and down his back as he buried his face between her warm breasts. Then she opened her lips as his mouth touched her own and he spent himself within her. As William lay back on his pillow and Margaret reached for her gown she thought to herself, "Am I supposed to feel as he does? Am I supposed to feel ecstacy? Is there something wrong with me? Am I not a whole woman?"

And so the two of them lay there, each thinking about the other and their possible inadequacies, saying nothing, each wondering if the other was aware of the lack of understanding between them and wondering if their relationship always would be so and nothing more. Neither spoke and it was some time before they finally slept.

The next morning when Margaret and Peter returned from their ride, William noticed that they both were strangely silent. When he asked how the ride went, Margaret replied only that she was very cold and wanted to go and change at once.

"Was the ride too long for her?" William asked of Peter.

"It may have been. At any rate we won't be going out for a while. I've decided to go to Bristol tomorrow and see Mr. Howard."

"Oh, fine. I'm sure he's rather anxious to talk with you."

Peter made no response. Then he too left the room to change out of his riding clothes.

At tea that afternoon Margaret was so quiet and looked so pale that William was certain she must be ill.

"Are you not feeling well, Margaret?" he asked.

"I'm feeling fine, William. Don't be so worrisome," she replied impatiently.

"You know, dear, I haven't mentioned it, but I have to go up to London for about a week. Perhaps you would like to come along."

Margaret looked up, expectantly.

"To London?" she asked. "Oh, I think not. It's such a long journey and I don't know a soul there."

"It might be a nice change for you, Margaret," suggested Peter. "Besides, with William away and I shall be going to Bristol, you will be quite alone here, with just Ellen."

"You're going to Bristol?" Margaret asked, brightly. Then she turned quickly to her husband.

"Oh, William, couldn't I go along and visit with father and my friends while you are in London, and then Peter can bring me back?"

"Of course, darling. How stupid of me not to think of that. It's a perfect opportunity for you to be with your father for a visit. Peter can look after you and see that you return here without any difficulty," William replied.

Margaret got out of her chair and rushed to William. She put her arms about his neck and kissed him soundly. He had not felt such a show of emotion for some weeks. Margaret's heart was beating rapidly as the plans were discussed, and she wondered if William could tell how excited she was.

She would be alone with Peter! It was enough to set her mind whirling. Ever since this morning when Peter had taken her riding across the valley to the river and had helped her down from the big mare, her body had quivered with remembering that event. He had reached up and put his hands about her waist and as she slid down off the horse her body moved along his to the ground. Peter lowered her slowly and her firm small breasts pressed against the hardness of his chest and then her legs felt the muscles in his thighs as he set her on the ground.

Peter had held her so briefly and yet she had caught her breath from the physical impact of his body. Could he have noticed it too? He had looked at her so strangely, quiet and unsmiling. The ride back home had been so different from their other rides. Usually they were laughing and chasing each other at a gallop. This time they returned at a slow trot, not speaking at all.

Margaret dared not look at Peter now for fear she would give herself away. She was rubbing the back of William's neck with her hand as they talked.

"Mr. Howard may want you to stay at Seagull's Point, Peter," said William.

"Oh, I think it would be better if I stayed at the inn," Peter responded. "Margaret will be busy with her father and her friends and I should just be in the way. I can meet with Mr. Howard at his place of business for our discussions."

Peter noticed that Margaret avoided looking at him, yet he found it difficult to keep from watching her. He, too, was remembering the morning. Holding her soft young body in his arms, if only for a brief moment, had made a very real impact on him. Peter had held other

162

girls close to him, even made love to a few, but the feeling which had come over him when he held Margaret next to his body was something he never had experienced before. Looking at his brother he wondered if it was like that between Margaret and William.

Something would have to be done, Peter thought. His relationship with his brother and Margaret had come to a dangerous point. He knew he wanted his brother's **wife. Wanted her desperately. Yet he knew that was** beyond thinking about. He must break away somehow. Perhaps Lowell Howard had the answer. Perhaps it was time for him to leave and go to America for Margaret's father.

William's voice broke into his thoughts.

"Well, my dear, if you're going to Bristol for a week, you must have considerable packing to do. I can imagine you'll want to take half the things you own. Perhaps Ellen can help you."

"Yes, darling, I'll get on with it," Margaret said, happily.

She kissed him quickly on the forehead and hurried out of the room.

"I'll swear, sometimes she's like a child," said William, smiling at Peter with an amused expression.

The coach ride the next afternoon seemed unduly long and uncomfortable. A heavy rain was falling and the inside of the coach was cold and it smelled musty. Margaret had a heavy woolen robe over her legs and still was shaking with cold. She was wedged between Peter and another gentleman who had boarded some distance ahead of them. In the seat across from them sat two very portly men with a young girl. Probably the daughter of one, Margaret surmised. At any rate, all three of them kept staring at Margaret which she found quite annoying at such close quarters.

Peter was simply amused. He had become used to

Margaret's beauty and no longer needed to stare. In any event, there was no chance for conversation, which probably was just as well. Finally, Peter did lean towards Margaret to speak.

"This will be a pleasant surprise for your father, I'm sure."

"Yes, it will," she replied, and her teeth were chattering.

"Blast!" Peter exclaimed. "You're freezing. If I take you back with a cold William will be at my throat. Here, let me put my cloak about your shoulders."

He took off his grey cloak and wrapped it tightly about Margaret.

"Is that better?" he asked.

"Yes, but now you shall be cold."

"No, I'll be fine. Never mind about me."

They rode on, mile after mile, jostling against each other, both totally aware of the physical reaction of their bodies, but both knowing they must show restraint, whatever the cost to each other.

20

Margaret's surprise visit to Bristol turned into a week of constant tea parties and dinners once the word was passed that she was at Seagull's Point. Yet she was bitterly disappointed because she scarcely had seen Peter since the day she arrived at her father's house. Peter was very gracious in declining Lowell Howard's invitation to stay in his home, saying he had business to attend to and his hours might conflict with the schedule of the household. He would stay at the inn until time to return to Woodbridge.

So Margaret's plan to be alone with Peter had failed. She was certain he wanted to be with her too, and she was just as certain that his loyalty to William was holding him away.

Hetty Langley had invited Peter to her dinner party, but he had declined. Margaret pressed her father for information as to Peter's whereabouts.

"My dear," replied Lowell Howard, patiently, "we have had much to discuss. The young man wants to learn the shipping business. He's very busy all day and I'm sure he has no trouble in finding companionship in the evenings. Don't be so concerned about him. He's quite capable of taking care of himself."

All of which Margaret did not want to hear. She wanted to know where Peter was, who he was with and what he was doing, but she dared not keep asking.

So the last day of her visit she planned a dinner party for all of her friends who had entertained for her.

"Father, will you please go to the inn where Peter is staying and insist that he come to my dinner party this evening?" she asked.

"Very well, dear, I'll stop by with the invitation and tell him you are in no mood to be refused."

Her father was teasing her, but Margaret was unresponsive.

Later in the afternoon when Mr. Howard returned home he said that Peter had accepted the invitation and would join them at seven o'clock.

Margaret made sure that Peter was seated next to her at the dinner table, with Hetty Langley down next to her father. Hetty had mentioned to Margaret during the sherry in the parlor that she hoped Peter would be her dinner partner, at which Margaret merely smiled and turned to speak to someone else, dismissing the subject. During dinner she noticed Hetty staring at her and then at Peter. Hetty was such a bore!

Peter was polite to Margaret, almost too polite, as if she were a stranger. He seemed overly attentive to Rebecca Whitley who was seated on his right. Rebecca wasn't even pretty, Margaret thought to herself, and the color of her satin dress was a drab green which only made her skin look sallow. Nonetheless, Peter was turning his charm in Rebecca's direction at every opportunity. She, of course, found him very engaging.

Margaret kept asking him about the shipping business and what he was learning, but Peter made only short replies, merely to be courteous she thought, and went on to some other subject to bring Rebecca into the conversation.

"My brother is in Boston," said Rebecca, directly to Peter. "He says it can be hideously cold in winter and sticky hot in summer. Sounds awful to me."

Peter laughed at her remark, but made no comment.

"He says there are compensations, however,"

Rebecca continued. "Most anyone can find work and he's been greatly surprised to find the place so civilized. He says it's not at all what he expected. I understand some of the houses are beautifully furnished, with things from England, of course, and France."

"I expect to be seeing a good deal of Boston in a few months," Peter remarked, "so what you say sounds encouraging."

"Oh yes, Peter will be in my father's business, Rebecca," Margaret spoke up, causing him to turn in her direction.

The candlelight shining on her ivory face and shoulders rising from the silken sheen of her gown made Peter's heart quicken its beat as he looked at her. My God, how he wanted her!

The dinner ended with the ladies retiring to the parlor and the gentlemen remaining for port and cigars, a custom which Margaret abhorred. Just when the conversation was becoming interesting she always had to leave!

When Peter bid goodnight to Margaret and her father he outlined the plans for the return journey to Woodbridge.

"We should be ready to leave here at two in order to board the coach for Woodbridge, Margaret, so I shall arrive in plenty of time to help with your luggage," Peter explained.

The long ride to Woodbridge the next afternoon seemed even more uncomfortable and tedious than it was in coming to Bristol. Particularly so, because Peter chose to sit opposite Margaret rather than next to her. Margaret watched him closely but he kept his gaze mostly out the window, so they rode along in silence, all of which added to Margaret's increasing frustration.

Arriving at Hawkes Nest just before dark they noticed there were lamps lighted in the house.

"Ellen must have waited for us," said Peter. "I'll wager she will have some hot tea ready," he added, cheerfully.

And so she did, although she appeared ready to leave for the day, having already tied her bonnet on under her chin. Now she quickly removed the bonnet and her coat.

"I thought you might be chilled and a good hot cup of tea would be welcome," Ellen remarked. "I'll get the tea things for you."

"You're always so thoughtful, Ellen," said Peter, thinking just then how glad he was to see the girl. One thing about Ellen, he thought later, she was always the same. Cheerful and pleasant and always concerned about someone else.

"Could you stay long enough to unpack my things?" asked Margaret, looking at Ellen. "I'm really too exhausted to do it myself."

"Of course, Mrs. Hawke," Ellen replied.

After they had drunk the tea, Peter carried the luggage up the stairs, followed by Ellen and Margaret.

"Did you enjoy your visit, Ma'm?" Ellen asked Margaret.

"Very much indeed," Margaret replied, but made no further comment.

Peter went to his room and shut the door.

While Ellen was putting Margaret's clothes away and removing the luggage from the room, Margaret got out of her travelling clothes and into a dressing gown. Then she sat down at the dressing table and began to brush her hair.

"Is there anything further, Ma'm?" asked Ellen, returning to the room.

"No, thank you, Ellen. You may go now."

Shortly after Margaret heard Ellen close the door downstairs she went out into the hall. She saw the light coming from beneath the door to Peter's room. She felt desperate. William would be home tomorrow from London, and she felt she must talk with Peter. He had been so quiet on the drive back from Bristol, making only polite conversation about her father and what she had done all week. Margaret felt sure that Peter must be as miserable as she, that his longing for her must be as great as hers was for him.

She went down to the kitchen and poured two glasses of cider and put them on a small salver with some biscuits. Then she climbed the stairs and knocked lightly on his door.

"I thought you might like some cider. It seems too early to go to bed. Could we talk for a while?"

The words tumbled out in rapid succession as he opened the door.

"Of course," Peter replied. "Come in and sit down."

He took the tray from her and set it down on the bureau and directed her to the one large chair in the room. Peter sat on the blanket chest at the foot of his bed. There was a rather awkward silence as they sipped the cider.

Peter had removed his jacket and cravat, and the white shirt he was wearing was partially unbuttoned. Margaret was very conscious of his long legs stretched out in front of him and of the thick reddish brown hair showing through at the neck of his open shirt. Like William, she thought idly.

Peter put his empty glass on the floor beside him and looked at Margaret. She was so beautiful in the lamplight. She had removed the pins and ribbons from her hair which now hung thick and shiny about her face and shoulders. Her dressing gown was a pale blue silk with a fine ivory lace collar, one of the many presents William was always bringing her, he supposed, and it was fastened with pearl buttons to the waist. There she had tied a sash about her tiny waist and the skirt fell in long folds to the floor. She smelled faintly of lavender. He had noticed it when she had handed him the cider and moved to the chair.

"When are you going to take me riding again, Peter?" Margaret asked boldly.

Peter stared at her for a few seconds, studying her face, before he spoke.

"Are you sure you want to, Margaret?"

She smiled and almost in a whisper she asked, "Don't you, Peter?"

Her face flushed pink. They both stood up and Margaret set her glass back on the tray. Still neither spoke. Then Peter moved towards her. Her fragrance, the softness of her gown, the shining hair made him ache to hold her. Suddenly her arms went around his neck and he clasped her close to his chest. His lips came down on hers and as she parted them his tongue moved inside her mouth. Her body trembled and he lifted his head.

"Margaret, Margaret," he murmured into her hair.

She clung tightly to him and he could feel the warmth of her body along his thighs and into his groin. Her breasts were firm against his chest. Then he found her mouth again.

Peter bent down and lifted her in his arms and carried her to the bed. Her fingers helped him unfasten the buttons of her gown and he pulled it away from her body. Margaret put her hands inside his shirt and moved them softly across his chest. He kissed her again and then he pressed his lips against the soft mounds of her breasts.

"Oh, my love, my love," she murmured and she moved gently against him. As he brought his weight down upon her she moved her hands against the small of his back, pressing him towards her. The thick hair on his chest felt soft against her skin. Slowly he moved into her, back and forth, back and forth, gently, gently. She uttered a soft moan and their union was complete.

"Oh, my darling, I love you," she whispered.

"Margaret, oh my God, Margaret!"

Margaret woke from a deep sleep and turned towards Peter. He was awake and lay staring at the ceiling. The early light of day was turning the sky a soft pink. It was Sunday and William would be home before nightfall.

"Peter, darling." Her voice was a soft whisper.

She put her arm across his naked chest and he turned his face towards her.

"Margaret, forgive me. I'm sorry."

"Sorry? Oh, Peter, don't say that. Don't," she pleaded. "You know we belong together."

"But, Margaret, you know nothing can come of this. It's impossible," Peter remarked, bluntly.

Margaret sat up quickly, pulling the covers about her. The pale silk dressing gown was lying in a heap on the floor. Before she could speak, Peter went on.

"I shall have to leave here."

"Leave? But Peter, I love you. I love you."

"I love you too, Margaret. I wish to God I didn't. But you're William's wife! My brother. Do you realize what we've done?"

Peter's voice rose as he got out of bed and reached for his shirt.

"He must never know about us, Margaret. That's why I must leave," Peter continued. "I could never stay on here in the same house with you and still keep my hands off you, Margaret. That's asking too much."

Her shoulders sagged as she sat in the bed looking at him, not believing what she was hearing. How could he deny her? How could he leave when he loved her?

"Peter, I want to be with you wherever you go."

"Margaret, you know that's not possible. It's got to stop right here. Now." Peter's voice cracked.

Margaret reached for the silk gown and wrapped it about her as she got out of bed. She walked towards Peter, her black hair touseled and her cheeks flushed. She reached up to put her arms about his neck and he grasped them both.

"No, Margaret, I mean it. We cannot do this. William will be home tonight and I will tell him that I want to go. He really doesn't need me. Besides, your father has offered me a position, you know about that."

"But, Peter, I'll die without you."

"No, Margaret, you won't die. We'll both get over it in time, but not if I stay here. That can only cause real grief for all of us. Please believe me, I wanted you. I still do, but you're not my wife. You never can be."

Margaret's face grew pale and she felt weak.

"Peter, kiss me," she whispered.

"No, I can't."

"Please, Peter."

He looked down at her pale face, her eyes glistening with tears. His heart skipped and the blood felt hot running through his veins. Peter bent his head and his lips touched her mouth. Her lips were velvet soft. He cupped her face in his hands and kissed the wet cheeks and the closed eyelids.

"I love you, Margaret. I think I've always loved you since the day I first saw you in Bristol. But promise me, Margaret, promise me that William never will know about us."

Margaret walked blindly back to her room and fell on the bed, exhausted and drained of emotion. She felt hollow inside. Too spent even to weep, she lay with her face buried in the pillows. The house was so quiet. The village had not yet stirred on this Sabbath day. A dog barked in the distance and a rooster crowed. Then it was quiet again.

Margaret turned and lay on her side looking at the large mahogany highboy placed against the wall across the room. It had come from her bedroom in her father's house in Bristol. A fine piece that he wanted her to have. William was so proud of it since he readily recognized the fine cabinetwork and the beautiful wood. She sighed. How could this have happened? How could it? She thought she was in love with William when she married him, but she never had felt like she did with Peter. Margaret trembled as she remembered their passion together.

William was so considerate and thoughtful of her. How could she do such a wicked thing to him? She loved him, she guessed, but it was in a different way. How else could she have agreed to marry him?

Margaret's mind was a jumble of thoughts, racing one after another. William would be home in a few hours and no doubt would bring her some lovely presents from London. He always brought presents. And he would be so anxious to be alone with her. He always laughed and said, "Come on up, Margaret, while I change and you can open your presents." As she opened the boxes he would remove his coat and then the cravat, the waistcoat and the shirt and the heavy boots. And he would want to make love to her.

"Next time you simply will have to come with me," he would say. "I can't bear to be away from you for so long." Then later he would decide the trip would be too tiresome.

When they went to bed he would hold her close against his chest and stroke her soft shining hair with his big hand. He always had been so gentle with Margaret, almost as if she were a child. Her skin was so soft and her slim body so warm where it curved against him. William felt complete ecstacy in loving his wife, but he was never sure she felt as strongly towards him.

The slamming of the door downstairs roused Margaret from her thoughts and she raised up on one elbow. It must have been Peter. Then she heard the galloping hoofbeats as he rode off down the road.

Peter rode hard mile upon mile and stopped only when he realized his horse was sweating profusely and obviously was tired. He patted the animal gently as he dismounted, and then led the horse to the stream for water.

Lying on his back on the cool grass, Peter looked up at the autumn sky. Clouds were beginning to move along ahead of the swiftly rising breeze. There probably would be rain before nightfall. And William would be home from London. Peter felt such guilt towards his brother. It was an emotion he had not known before. He and William always had had a good relationship with one another, and up to now it had been honorable.

William loved Margaret so deeply that he probably never would suspect any indiscretion on her part. And certainly he never would expect his own brother to take another man's wife for a few moments of passion. Peter clenched his fist and pounded the grass beside him. There was no one to blame but himself. He had wanted Margaret from the beginning. Their coming together was inevitable. Now there was no alternative but for him to leave Woodbridge.

He would go to Bristol and wait for the next sailing of the *Bristol Cloud*. He hoped that would be soon. William might wonder about the sudden decision to leave, as Peter had planned to wait until after the Christmas holidays. Now that was no longer possible. Peter could not risk being at Hawkes Nest with William and Margaret. A passing glance or a touch might be too difficult for either Margaret or himself to hide.

When Margaret heard Peter ride away from the house, she glanced at the clock on the bureau. It still was early in the day. Yet she felt wholly exhausted. She did not know at what hour William would be home. The coach on Sunday never seemed to hold the same schedule for some unexplained reason.

She got up from the bed and went to the mirror of her dressing table. Her hair needed brushing and pinning, and her eyes were red and swollen from weeping. Perhaps she should lie down for a while and put a cold compress on her face. She did not want William to think she was ill and start asking questions.

When Margaret lay down on the bed and put the wet cloth over her eyes, her body trembled as she thought again of Peter's arms about her and his lips on her own. How could she pretend nothing had happened between them? How could she, when every breath she took made her ache with longing. Shivering from the cold in the room, she decided there was no use lying there. Might as well get up and dress.

Peter usually started the fires downstairs on Sundays since it was Ellen's day away, but he was not about and the house seemed very cold and damp. Margaret wrapped a heavy shawl about her shoulders over the blue wool dress and went down the stairs. She didn't know if she would be able to start the fire in the kitchen stove, but she would try.

After several unsuccessful attempts, the flames took hold. Margaret filled the kettle on the stove with water and went to the cupboard for the tin of tea. She was shaking from cold. A feeling of resentment towards Peter suddenly welled up in her. He should not have left the house without seeing to her comfort. Surely he would be returning soon.

Margaret moved the rocking chair as close to the stove as she could and she sat there waiting for the water to heat, listening to the sound of the clock on the wall and hoping Peter soon would come.

Minutes ticked by. Ten, twenty, half an hour. Then an hour. Two. Three. And Margaret heard the churchbell ringing for the Sunday service. Was Peter never coming back? Where could he have gone? He wouldn't just leave Hawkes Nest without seeing his brother or taking any of his belongings.

As William came into Margaret's thoughts she wondered how she would feel when her husband took her in his arms. She had promised Peter that she never would let William know there had been anything between them. Now she wondered if she would be able to keep that promise.

Margaret made some more tea. She had no appetite and could not eat, but the tea was helping to keep her warm.

It was nearly one o'clock when she heard the big oak door open at the front of the house.

"Margaret?"

It was William. She had not heard the noise of the coach on the road.

"Yes, William. I'm in the kitchen," she replied.

William came quickly into the room, still in his cloak and tall hat. When he saw Margaret huddled in the chair next to the stove he could not help but laugh.

"My dear, you look as poor as a churchmouse all bunched up in that shawl! Give me a hug."

He pulled Margaret to her feet and held her tightly against his chest. He could feel her small body trembling.

"Where's Peter? Why are you sitting here like this shaking with cold? Why didn't he start the fires?" William asked, his voice angry and impatient.

He kissed Margaret quickly before she could answer.

"I've missed you," he said, touching her mouth again.

"I'll have this fire roaring in a minute," William

commented as he took his hat off and got out of his cloak, both of which he laid on the chair where Margaret had been sitting.

He put a large amount of coal in the stove and poked the fire with a poker, stirring up the flames. Then he turned and took Margaret in his arms again.

"How was your holiday in Bristol?" he asked.

"Oh, it was fine. It was really fine. Father was so pleased and I saw many of my friends. There were lots of parties," Margaret explained, suddenly animated as she remembered the festivities in Bristol.

"Well, I'm sure you enjoyed that. Is your father well?" asked William.

"He seems so. A little rheumatic these days, but I guess that's just his age."

"Where is Peter anyway?"

"He went riding," Margaret replied.

"Riding? Well, I'm surprised you didn't go along."

"He left very early. I was still in bed," Margaret explained. "How was your journey?" she went on, changing the subject abruptly.

"Everything went well," William replied. "By the way, I have something for you in my bag. Come on up with me while I change and I'll show it to you."

"Oh, William, it's so cold upstairs. Couldn't we look at it here?" Margaret's voice was almost a wail.

She simply was not yet ready to go upstairs with William, to be made love to by him.

William laughed at her woeful expression.

"Of course, darling, I'll go get it."

He walked to the hallway where he had left his luggage. He soon returned to the kitchen with a large flat package which he handed to Margaret.

"Sit down here," he suggested, removing his cloak and hat from the rocking chair. He held the garments in his arms as he watched her open the package.

"Oh, William, how beautiful!" Margaret exclaimed as she pulled a deep red velvet gown from the wrappings. The dress was trimmed with black satin braid and she knew that would be stunning with her black hair. She stood up quickly, holding the dress in front of her for William to see.

"I thought you might enjoy it during the holidays," he said, smiling down at her.

"I will, William, oh indeed I will."

Margaret stood on tiptoe to kiss her husband quickly on the mouth.

"Come now, I want more than that," William said, pulling her closer to him, the dress crumpled between them.

He kissed her long and hard. When he released her he laughed.

"Well, there's only one thing for it. I've got to get this house warmed up before I can hope for anything else!"

Darkness had fallen and William and Margaret were at their supper when Peter finally arrived.

"It's beginning to rain," he said as he walked into the room, pulling at his riding gloves.

"How was London?" Peter continued, speaking directly to William.

"Very well indeed. Crowded and dirty, of course, but I did well for us," William replied. "Ready for some supper?" he asked of Peter.

"Some hot tea would be most welcome," Peter remarked. "The cheese looks good," he added as he pulled out his chair from the table and took his place.

"Margaret tells me you went riding early today. Have you been out all this time?" William asked.

"Yes, I've been riding almost all day. Riding and thinking."

Margaret's eyes darted towards Peter, her expression curious.

"Thinking?" asked William. "What about?"

Peter gulped the hot tea and set his cup down.

"Well, I had a most informative visit with Mr. Howard while we were in Bristol last week and I'm anxious to get started in the shipping business. I have decided to leave for Boston on the next sailing of the *Bristol Cloud*."

William looked rather startled as Peter spoke.

"But I thought you were going to wait until January," said William.

"I was until I learned that the sea can be especially bitter at that time and apt to be unusually stormy. Also, sometimes the harbor at Boston is full of ice. I shouldn't relish that," Peter explained. "Besides, you are doing so well you hardly need me," he continued.

"Well, I can't say I don't need you, Peter," William remarked, "But I must say I'm a bit taken aback that you have decided so suddenly to leave."

Margaret said not a word. She kept her eyes on her husband and could see the look of curiosity on his face.

"Does Mr. Howard know of these plans?" asked William.

"Not yet, but he will be pleased, I know. I thought I would leave here on Wednesday for Bristol. That will give me two days to get all my things in order," Peter explained. "I shall stay at the inn there until the next sailing," he continued.

Margaret finally spoke up.

"But that won't be for weeks, Peter. The *Bristol Cloud* sailed just last week, you know."

The room was silent for a few moments before Peter responded.

"Yes, I realize that, but I have much to learn and now I will have time to delve into the business with your father. I'm sure he would feel better about my having all the knowledge and instruction I can get. Don't you agree, William?"

"There is no doubt whatever that you both would benefit. I'm just not quite ready to see you go, Peter. You have given me a bit of a shock," William replied. "Boston seems terribly far away."

Margaret's face turned pale as she looked from William to Peter. She pulled the wool shawl closer about her shoulders.

"Are you still cold, love?" asked William, noticing her movement.

"No, just getting comfortable."

She managed a faint smile in her husband's direction.

"It's not the end of the world, William. Look how many have left England already for America. And very few have returned, which indicates there must be **something in its favor. I want to have a go at it, in any** event, and if it doesn't work out I'll surely come home," Peter explained in a matter-of-fact voice.

"If only that were true," he thought to himself, as the words "come home" stuck in his mind.

He still had barely noticed Margaret, purposefully. She lifted the teapot and offered him more tea, at which time he had to look at her.

"Thank you, I will," he responded, his eyes meeting hers across the table. But he said nothing further.

"Well, you shall need money for the passage, and some additional clothing, I'm sure," suggested William. "I doubt that Mr. Howard can give you free sailing for such a journey."

"I should not expect that," Peter said quickly. "I would certainly like to use father's trunk though, if I may?" he added.

"By all means. Of course you should take it," William remarked, now caught up in his brother's plans.

180

21

So Peter was leaving. The day Ellen had dreaded and tried to put out of her mind had come with unexpected suddenness. She learned of his plans upon arriving at Hawkes Nest at her usual hour on Monday morning. A large trunk sat in the middle of the hallway and there were numerous unrelated articles piled about on the floor. Boots, a stack of ledger paper, several books, cravats unfolded and lying in a heap, some quilled pens, and a pair of riding gloves.

At first sight Ellen thought the trunk and items must have been put there by William Hawke when he returned from London, but a further glance reminded her that Mr. Hawke never travelled with a trunk.

She went into the kitchen to start breakfast and found that Peter already was there and the fire in the stove was burning briskly.

"Good morning, Ellen."

"Good morning, Sir."

Ellen's heart was pounding so hard as she looked at him that she quickly turned away, fearing that he would notice her reaction.

"I'm going to Boston, Ellen."

"Indeed, Sir. When do you leave?" Ellen asked, wondering at that moment if she would be able to avoid tears.

"I'm going to Bristol on Wednesday and see Mr. Howard and then I shall wait for the *Bristol Cloud*," Peter replied.

He was leaning against one of the china cabinets, his arms folded across his chest, his blue eyes bright with enthusiasm.

"It will be a very long voyage," he went on. "Takes almost five weeks."

"Do you have no fear of storms at sea?" asked Ellen. I have heard such tales that—" her voice dwindled away.

Her heart ached with a longing she could not will away. A lump like a stone seemed caught in her throat.

"Oh, I don't imagine a storm at sea can be very pleasant, but the *Bristol Cloud* is a very stout ship. After all, she has made many crossings without a mishap of any kind. Mr. Howard is very proud of her," Peter explained. "Of course if the *Bristol Star* were ready to sail I could board her, but that ship had some damage on its recent run to Boston and is being repaired. However, it's a smaller packet anyway and I think I'd prefer to go on the *Bristol Cloud*. I've been aboard her and she's beautiful."

Ellen knew nothing at all about ships and could think of nothing more to say so she busied herself putting the breakfast things on the table. As she did so she noticed that her hands were icy cold. How she would miss Peter! He never would know of her dreams and plans, nor of her deep love and affection for him. If only there had been more time and their circumstances had been different.

Now he was leaving and very likely would not come back. No doubt in Boston he would meet someone to marry. He was so handsome and charming that he was sure to have many invitations to social affairs in no time at all. Ellen felt a deep envy and resentment towards the young ladies in America.

"Is there some way I can help you with the packing, Sir?" Ellen asked, finally.

"That's very kind of you, but I think I can manage. If you will just see to my shirts and stockings and any other things you find lying about, that would be of great assistance," Peter replied.

"Of course, Sir."

There was no further conversation as Peter sat down at the table and proceeded with his morning meal. He wanted to finish before Margaret and William arrived. When he was through eating he hurried up the stairs to his room and closed the door. There were some people in the village he must see before he left for Bristol—The Reverend Thomas, Dr. Booth, the shopkeepers whose places he had frequented, Polly Andrews at The Bell, and he had a few letters to write. Strange. Now that he was leaving Woodbridge he suddenly felt a longing to see all of the townspeople he seldom thought about. They just always had been there. Shy little Frances Thomas. He wondered what might be her future. She probably would end up a spinster or married to a widower from one of the outlying farms. Yes, he could see her doing that all right. Making a "good marriage," so to speak.

And what about Ellen? Now that Ben Hammond was gone she seemed to keep to her cottage almost like a recluse when she wasn't at Hawkes Nest. She even had stopped going to the church. Peter mentioned to William that perhaps they should talk to Ellen and try to get her with the village folk again, but William said she must have time to do what she thought best and in her own way.

Still, Peter felt a concern for Ellen which puzzled him. Why should he care what became of her? She had a good position and William would always see to it that she was not in serious need. However, Peter knew she must be lonely. She probably would be happier in a large town like Bristol or Bath, but he never would suggest such a move because she was so necessary to Hawkes Nest.

Thinking of Ellen, Peter suddenly realized he was going to miss seeing her. He would miss hearing her singing as she worked about the house, and he most certainly was going to miss her cooking. He smiled to himself. She probably would not find that particularly flattering.

Peter heard William and Margaret descending the stairs for breakfast. He knew that if he opened his bedroom door he would smell the lavender fragrance which was so much a part of Margaret. Now he remembered the softness of the silk gown she had worn the night she came to his room. The warmth of her body and the silkiness of her black hair were haunting to him and he wondered if he ever would be able to put Margaret out of his mind and heart.

The night before Peter was to leave for Bristol, a rainstorm blew in such as Woodbridge had not seen for many years. Trees were bending and snapping in the gale-force wind, their leaves having long since blown away. Rain drummed incessantly against the windowpanes and now and then a tree branch banged against the side of the house.

In the sitting room Wiliam and Margaret and Peter had gathered before the blazing logs in the fireplace. The brothers were having brandy while Margaret took a small glass of sherry. Ellen had served a very special dinner, all the things of which Peter was most fond.

"Ellen, believe me, I shall not forget your thoughtfulness. I'm sure there will be many a time I'll wish I could be here again at this table," Peter had said, speaking directly to Ellen, his blue eyes friendly and sincere.

"It was nothing, Sir. Just wanted to get you started off right."

Ellen had a wide smile on her face as she spoke,

obviously pleased that Peter had taken notice of her efforts.

When Ellen brought the tray with coffee into the sitting room Peter watched her intently. She was a pleasant person to have around, he thought, seeming always to be content with what she was doing and so eager to please. Getting Ellen into Hawkes Nest had been a great stroke of luck. He had not noticed until now that she was wearing the flowered pink dress he had admired the day of the party for Margaret.

"She must be cold in that thin cotton," he thought to himself.

How long ago that July day seemed now. So much had happened in just over four months. Ben Hammond was dead, Ellen had lost a baby, Margaret and Peter had fallen in love, and now Peter was going away to a new land and a new life.

"I hope this storm is not a bad omen, Peter," William remarked suddenly.

"I should hope not, too," Peter responded, putting his empty glass on the table next to him.

"More brandy?" asked William.

"No, I think not."

Margaret seemed unusually quiet and distant. She scarcely had spoken during dinner and only toyed with her food. Now her gaze was fixed on the burning logs.

"Are you not feeling quite well, Margaret?" William asked.

She looked up quickly.

"I feel very well, thank you. I was just wondering what Boston might be like," she replied, which was not at all what had been on her mind.

Gazing at the burning wood she had had the daring thought of going with Peter, of stowing away on the *Bristol Cloud* until it had cleared the harbor and was well out to sea. Of course she quickly realized she never could do such a rash thing. It would be impossible. Margaret tried to guess what Peter would think if he knew her thoughts. He hardly had noticed her since the day they had been together. Now that time, only three days ago, seemed almost like a dream, as if it never had happened. Yet when Margaret looked at him she felt her heart quicken its beat and the memory became all too real.

The storm outside continued its fury against the house with unabated shrieking wind and pelting rain.

"I don't believe Ellen should attempt to go home tonight," said Peter.

"You're quite right," William agreed.

When Ellen returned for the coffee tray, William spoke up immediately.

"Ellen, you had best not leave here tonight. The storm is really too strong. You can use the spare room," he suggested.

"Thank you, Sir. That's very kind of you."

And so Ellen Davis once more was bedded down under the thatched roof of Hawkes Nest. Lying in the same bed where she had been after Ben's accident she listened to the sounds of the storm outside and suddenly she felt a bleak loneliness and mounting despair. Her whole being ached as she thought of Peter. Was this all life would ever be for her? No home of her own, no family, no one to love or to love her?

Ellen tossed restlessly in the bed. Perhaps something would happen to make Peter stay. It seemed unlikely now that he would be able to leave for Bristol in the morning. The roads probably were impassable due to the heavy rain, and even if they were not, the coach surely would be delayed. Ellen cherished every minute that kept Peter in Hawkes Nest. She didn't care if the storm should last for days.

William and Margaret had retired early to their room

and as William began to undress he watched Margaret brushing her hair at the dressing table.

"I'm going to miss Peter very much," he remarked, soberly.

"Yes, it will seem quite lonely without him," Margaret stated, her voice calm and without emotion.

"The house will be almost empty and it will be strange working alone," William went on. "Ever since we were boys we've been together in that room."

The glow of the lamp on the dressing table turned Margaret's face and hair to a satin softness as William looked at her. He bent and kissed her on the shoulder. She put the brush down and looked up at him.

"Margaret, we should have a baby," he said, simply.

"But, William, God has not seen fit to—"

William lifted her up from the chair and held her close against him.

"We must try again."

Margaret pretended a passion she did not feel. Her thoughts were of Peter. How she wished it were Peter making love to her. Tears streamed down her cheeks.

"Oh, my love, what is it?" William asked, anxiously.

Margaret only shook her head, unable to speak.

In Peter's bedroom he was busy packing his travelling bag with the things he would need in Bristol. The trunk downstairs was filled and ready to be taken to await the *Bristol Cloud*. As his eyes scanned the room looking for anything he might have missed, Peter seemed to see Margaret everywhere—in the armchair, standing by the door with the cider glasses in her hand, lying on his bed in her blue silk gown, her hair black and glossy on the pillow. Would he be able to forget their passion for each other? Would he ever love someone else with the same intense feelings? Peter shook his head as if to answer his own questions. The noise of the storm prevented him from hearing the clock in the hallway strike the eleventh hour, but he knew when he finally got into bed that it must be getting late.

Peter felt tired and more than a little uncertain about his future. Nevertheless, the decision had been made and tomorrow he would be leaving Hawkes Nest and Woodbridge. He wondered now what was ahead of him. Time alone could answer.

Part Two.

● 1 ●

It was a dreary December day. Rain and sleet were falling intermittently. The wind was increasing in velocity, whistling through the rigging, and the *Bristol Cloud* lay over at a sharp angle, her decks wet and slippery. Somewhere through the rain and sleet was Boston. The ship was due to arrive there before day's end.

Peter's eyes burned from the strain as he searched for some sign of land. The oilskin he wore over his grey cape kept him only partially dry. Still, he preferred to be on deck rather than down inside the ship which after more than five weeks had become stifling and odorous.

Peter long since had lost his appetite for the meager fare on board and found that his clothes no longer fit properly. He must have lost considerable weight, he surmised. How he would love some of Ellen's scones with a pot of really hot tea. As Ellen came into his thoughts he remembered how her eyes had filled with tears the day he bade her goodbye.

"Are those tears for me, Ellen?" he had asked, smiling down at her.

As he had clasped her hand she managed a smile and she had wished him well.

Ellen was sweet and gentle and he suddenly realized how much a part of his home she had become. No use dwelling on that, however. He quite possibly never would see her again. Peter was determined that whatever his life was going to be he would find it in America. There would be no turning back.

Hoarse shouting came from the watch in the crow's nest. Land had been sighted! The ship soon would be in Boston harbor. Peter felt the excitement and anticipation of a new experience as he clung tightly to the rail, waiting for his first glimpse of America. He had become unmindful of the cold now, so eager was he to put his boots on land again.

The *Bristol Cloud* slowed as it left the open sea and entered the channel. The other passengers on board had come topside and now were lined up along the bulwarks, shivering with cold but nonetheless anxious to see what Boston looked like.

As the ship moved closer and closer, Peter realized that harbors are much alike. Ships of all sizes rocked at anchor, water slapping against their hulls. He heard the sound of bells ringing and smelled tar, fish and tobacco. Men's voices, raucous and profane, shouted at each other on the long quay with its warehouses and offices now coming into view.

The rain and sleet had turned to a soft snowfall which melted as soon as it hit the water. One or two gulls flew about aimlessly, looking for shelter. As the *Bristol Cloud* was anchored and tied, Peter saw several people on the dock, edging close to the ship. No doubt they were awaiting packages and mail or had family on board. The darkness of the day made the hour seem much later than it actually was so that everything Peter looked at appeared sombre and grey. Just like Bristol in the dead of winter, he thought, only much colder.

The suddenness of Peter's decision to come to Boston had left Lowell Howard no time to contact his associate at the Boston office, Yancey Hamilton, so he had merely given Peter a letter of introduction outlining his plans for a New York branch. Peter carried the unopened letter in his travelling bag. It now was up to him to locate the Lowell Howard Trading Company and find Mr. Hamilton. In Bristol Mr. Howard referred to his business as a shipping company, here it was a trading company. Peter did not know why the difference in names.

Lamps were coming on behind the windows of the buildings along the quay. Peter caught a sudden whiff of molasses and rum. It was some time before he could get off the ship due to the necessary regulations and papers involving a foreign vessel. When finally he walked down the ramp, darkness had fallen and the snowfall was increasing. Perhaps he should find an inn for the night and pursue Mr. Hamilton in the morning. In all the confusion of arrival he looked about trying to decide in which direction he should start.

"Are you looking for someone?" inquired a strange voice.

Peter turned around to face a large man wearing a heavy black cloak and a flat grey hat whose brim was dusted with snow. The man's face bore deep pox marks which were clearly visible even in the dim light of the lamps on the wharf. Peter noticed the breadth of the man's shoulders and the barrel chest straining against the buttons of his cloak.

"Not exactly," Peter replied. "However, I should like to find shelter for the night. Is there an inn nearby?"

"Aye, an Englishman, is it?" The man smiled, showing tobacco-stained teeth. "Well, there's an inn not four rows away. Come. I'll take you there. What are you called?"

"Peter Hawke. I'm from Woodbridge, England. That's not far from Bristol. And what is your name, Sir?"

"Nathaniel Crowe, but I'm always called Nat. Born

here in Boston and never left. Don't intend to. Is that all your luggage?'' asked the man, looking at Peter's travelling bag.

"No, I have a trunk still to come off the ship. I was hoping to store it somewhere until I get settled,'' Peter explained.

"Don't pay to leave things lyin' about on the dock. We'll put it in my wagon and take it along to the inn.''

At that moment Peter wondered if he should go with a stranger to some unknown destination with everything he owned. What if Nat Crowe was planning to rob him? Peter looked at Nat inquisitively and apparently the man realized his apprehension because his face broke into a wide grin.

"It's all right, Mr. Hawke. I mean you no harm. I don't need your money. I'm a sailmaker. Come along. Let's find the trunk.''

Peter was taken to an inn with the rather startling name of Oliver Cromwell's Head, which made him chuckle to himself. The barroom had a large fireplace, blackened by smoke and soot, and the low ceiling was heavily beamed, much like the inns of England, Peter observed. He doubted the ale would be comparable, however, and then found to his pleasure that the drink was quite tasty, very reminiscent of a good English ale. The barmaids appeared comely also. Perhaps the place wasn't so uncivilized after all!

Nat explained to the innkeeper, a Mr. Shipley, that Peter had just come in off the *Bristol Cloud* and needed a room.

"How long will you be stayin'?'' asked Mr. Shipley, eyeing Peter curiously.

"I don't really know. I have to contact a certain gentleman at Lowell Howard Trading Company. Several days I should think, until I know just where I'll settle,'' Peter replied.

"Howard Trading Company is close by," said Nat. "You must be lookin' for Yancey Hamilton," he added.

"I am. Do you know him?" Peter asked.

"Everybody knows him," Nat replied, but made no further comment. Then "The food's good here," he continued, preparing to leave.

And off he went, leaving Peter somewhat astonished at his sudden departure. Peter then went into the small dining room for some supper. The food was indeed delicious, or perhaps it was merely a welcome change from what he had been having on the *Bristol Cloud*. In any event, he relished every bite.

Glancing about the room Peter realized that he was alone except for two young men seated by the window. They were deeply engrossed in their own conversation and paid no attention to him. Finishing supper he went to find his room.

A young chambermaid, rosy-cheeked and with bright red hair showing beneath her cap, took him along a dimly lighted corridor and up some narrow stairs to a small room overlooking the street and facing the harbor. Looking out the window he could see that the snowfall had stopped.

"Ye'll be needin' a warmer for the bed, Sir," remarked the girl, lighting an oil lamp on the small table next to the bed.

Irish, thought Peter, turning from the window to look at her.

"I'll fetch ye one," she continued as she left the room.

Peter suddenly knew deep loneliness, a feeling strange to him. His eyes took in the small room, its corners in darkness as the one small lamp cast a meager light. He realized in that moment how much he missed the warmth and comfort of Hawkes Nest. Now he was truly alone. There was no William to turn to for advice or encouragement. No Ellen with her bright smile and her quiet efficiency. Most of all, there was no Margaret.

Peter's heart felt like a stone in his chest as he thought of Margaret and her alabaster skin, her lavender fragrance, the black cascading hair and her warm softness.

The chambermaid returned with the warming pan and slipped it between the covers of the bed.

"This'll fix it up fine, Sir," she said, happily.

"Thank you very much," Peter responded.

When the girl disappeared he opened his travelling bag and took out some writing paper. He must get something off to William and to Mr. Howard so that by the time the *Bristol Cloud* was ready to start her return voyage to England he would have letters on board.

The light from the lamp proved so dim that Peter decided to wait until the morrow. Besides, after he had seen Mr. Hamilton and walked about Boston he should have considerably more information to pass on to William.

Peter found that sleeping in a bed again without the motion of the ship took some getting used to. He tossed about fitfully at first and then relaxed into a deep sleep. He slept so soundly that it was past nine o'clock when the chambermaid wakened him as she came bursting through the door.

"Oh, my soul, Sir! I thought ye was already up and about. Do forgive me. I came to tidy up the room, but I'll come back later."

Before Peter could say a word, she had scurried away. Past nine. Yancey Hamilton would surely think him a laggard if he knew, thought Peter. However, Mr. Hamilton knew nothing whatever about Peter Hawke and would not until Peter presented the letter from Lowell Howard.

Peter did not know the contents of the letter and could only guess that it outlined the plans for a New York office and Peter's place with the Lowell Howard Trading Company.

After a hearty breakfast of porridge with bread and tea, Peter asked Mr. Shipley for directions to the Howard Trading Company.

The air outside was bitter cold with an icy wind off the sea and the sky so heavy with dark clouds that Peter was certain there would be more snow before the day's end. He was astonished at the severity of the weather. He never had experienced such cold. Woodbridge had many raw, damp days and occasionally there would be snow, but the winter at home could not compare with what he already was experiencing in Boston.

Peter walked along the street past a gunsmith shop, a blacksmith's, a sailmaker and across the street he noticed the sign of a silversmith. The roadways were narrow and mostly of brick, although there were some of cobblestones.

He turned at the corner and started for the wharf. Now the wind was blowing directly into his face and every breath he took seemed to freeze in his chest. He quickly spotted the Howard Trading Company and hurried along the street and through the door of the office. A thin, bespectacled man seated at a large oak desk looked up as Peter entered the room.

"Good morning," said Peter, with a broad smile.

"Good morning, Sir," replied the man behind the desk.

He neither smiled nor frowned, only looked at Peter inquisitively.

"Is Mr. Hamilton about?" asked Peter.

"Yes, Sir. What is your business?"

"I'm Peter Hawke, just off the *Bristol Cloud,* and I have a letter from Lowell Howard for Mr. Hamilton," Peter explained.

The man put his pen down and got out of the chair. "Come this way, Sir."

Peter followed him towards the back of the room to a panelled door. The man knocked and then opened the door.

"A Mr. Hawke, Sir, with a letter from Lowell Howard."

"Come in, come in. You must have arrived on the *Bristol Cloud.*"

Peter looked towards the husky voice speaking to him and faced a man who surely must be the fattest, most grotesque looking creature he ever had set eyes upon. So this was Yancey Hamilton. No wonder Nat had said that everyone knew him. He couldn't be missed! His jowls hung in folds over his high collar and his chest and stomach were one vast expanse from his neck to below his waist.

As Yancey Hamilton came forward to clasp Peter's hand in greeting, Peter suddenly wondered how the man got in and out of his boots! His hands were unusually large with pudgy fingers and his clothes were straining at every seam. He smiled as he spoke to Peter, showing yellow-stained teeth. No doubt he indulged in great quantities of tobacco, Peter thought, along with everything else. In spite of his appearance Peter thought the man must be a competent businessman or Lowell Howard surely would not be associated with him.

"What did you say your name was?" asked Yancey.

"Peter Hawke. I have brought a letter from Lowell Howard. It will explain, I'm sure, why I'm here," Peter replied and he handed the letter to Yancey Hamilton.

"Please sit down, Mr. Hawke. May I offer you a bit of wine?"

"No, thank you. It's a little early in the day I think."

Mr. Hamilton laughed.

"Perhaps it is," he agreed, sitting down behind his desk.

Peter watched as the man intently read the letter. When Mr. Hamilton finished reading, he folded the letter and put it back in the envelope. Then he looked up at Peter.

"Do you know the contents of this letter?" he asked.

"No, Sir."

"Well, Mr. Howard speaks highly of you and says I am to help you set up an office in New York. I had not realized he would be ready so soon although I knew he was negotiating for two more packets. Those will be working out of New York, according to his instructions. This is quite an opportunity, Mr. Hawke. How old are you?"

"Twenty-one, Sir."

"I see."

The fat man's eyes narrowed as he studied Peter's face. Secretly he wondered if so handsome a man could have any business sense at all.

"The *Bristol Cloud* will be sailing for England in three days. I suggest we have a plan to forward to Mr. Howard and put it aboard ship at that time. You realize, of course, that Christmas is a mere eight days away. I hardly think we can journey to New York and back with any degree of satisfaction in that length of time. I suggest we plan to make the trip right after Christmas," Yancey Hamilton spoke precisely.

"Very well," Peter responded.

He had no idea of the distance to New York, but assumed that Mr. Hamilton must know what the journey entailed.

"Where are you staying?" asked the fat man.

"At Oliver Cromwell's just a few streets away," Peter replied.

"Well, I suppose that will do until we can find you better quarters. At least it's close by. Now I want you to come with me to the *Bristol Cloud* and we'll check the cargo being loaded. This can be a very important matter, Mr. Hawke. We must be certain there are no empty barrels stowed or anything not listed on the cargo sheets.''

Yancey Hamilton's enormous bulk increased as he fastened a heavy black cloak about his shoulders and drew on some black leather gloves over his big hands. Peter thought the man appeared almost comical as he added a tall grey hat to his attire. At any rate, the two of them went out into the snowy street and started towards the ship, a most unlikely looking pair.

It was mid-afternoon before they left the *Bristol Cloud* and Peter was ravenous, as well as being chilled to the bone.

"Come along," said Yancey. "I know just the place for some hot spiced rum and the best oysters you've ever tasted."

It was during their meal that Peter learned something more of Yancey Hamilton besides his unusual appearance. The man had been born in Boston of English parents. His father fought against the king in the Revolution and was killed. His mother also was dead, but he had two sisters, both of whom lived in Boston, one being a widow with a daughter, the other never having married. Yancey had a wife, Charlotte, but no children.

"Tell me why you wanted to leave England, Mr. Hawke," said Mr. Hamilton, quickly changing the subject away from himself.

"I have wanted to see America for some time, Sir. My brother, William, is married to Lowell Howard's daughter and so my connection with the shipping business came about quite by accident, or by marriage, you might say. My brother and I are wagon and coach-makers by trade, as was our father, but I've been anxious to do something else. When Mr. Howard offered me the chance to come here and start in shipping, I felt it was an opportunity I could not refuse,'' Peter explained.

"Indeed not.''

"I'm not certain I can survive the winter, however,'' Peter added, smiling broadly.

Yancey Hamilton's face moved in ripples as he laughed, all the time attacking the oysters on the platter.

Peter was fascinated by the man's gluttony. He never had seen anyone eat so much, nor so fast.

"You must come and have Christmas dinner with us, Mr. Hawke. I assure it will be far better than staying at the inn,'' said Yancey, between bites.

"I should be honored. That's very thoughtful of you.''

Peter never had been away from Hawkes Nest at Christmas until now, and at the very mention of the holiday he suddenly felt a melancholy and a deep longing for home.

Yancey noticed the expression on the young man's face.

"You homesick?'' he asked, bluntly.

Peter looked startled, then smiled.

"Not really. I suppose one always thinks of home at Christmastime. It will pass.''

Yancey did not pursue the subject as he wiped his fat fingers with the napkin.

"Meet me at the office at nine tomorrow and we shall lay out our plans for Mr. Howard,'' he directed later.

"Very well. At nine o'clock. I'll be there,'' said Peter.

"Can you find your way back to the inn?''

"Yes, I'm sure I can. Thank you.''

As Peter headed back to Oliver Cromwell's he felt that his first day in Boston made his future look promising. Mr. Hamiliton had indicated his willingness to be helpful as well as friendly and Peter was anxious to get everything written down to William.

"My dear brother:

The *Bristol Cloud* arrived in Boston in fine condition although I must admit the voyage seemed interminable. I could not believe the distance so great across the Atlantic.

What I have seen of Boston so far indicates there is considerable business of a lucrative nature as well as an unusual amount of ingenuity. There are gunsmiths and silversmiths with goods that appear of quality and there are many coffee houses and saloons. I have seen some fine leather boots. Also places where meat pies are sold. But nothing like Ellen's, I'll wager.

Most of the streets are of brick, as well as many of the buildings. You would not believe how cold it is. Snow is piled up everywhere.

You also would not believe Yancey Hamilton. How I wish you could see him! He's the strangest looking man I've seen in my life. However, he is treating me well and I have an invitation for Christmas dinner at his home. This will be my first Christmas away from Hawkes Nest and that will indeed be strange."

Peter's letter was lengthy. There was so much he wanted to say. The Christmas holiday would be long past by the time the *Bristol Cloud* reached England and then he knew it would be at least six weeks or more beyond that before he could expect to hear from William. He had ended his letter with kind regards to Margaret and to Ellen.

When Peter watched the *Bristol Cloud* move out of Boston harbor two days later on its return voyage to England, he knew that the last link with his home had been broken. His eyes followed the ship until it was out of sight. He turned then and started up the narrow street towards the sailmaker's. This was where he would find Nat Crowe.

Peter had seen Nat only once since the night he arrived in Boston and Nat had taken him to Oliver Cromwell's. When Peter and Yancey Hamilton went to board the *Bristol Cloud* they had passed Nat's shop and Nat had been at the window. He gestured a greeting but there had been no time for conversation.

Now Peter wanted to see the man who had first shown him kindness. He opened the door to the shop and went inside. Nat looked up from where he was working at a long table beside a roll of canvas.

"Well, Mr. Hawke, I take it you have settled your business with Yancey Hamilton."

"Not settled really. Just getting started. But I must admit he's being most helpful and cooperative," said Peter.

"And well he should. Yancey Hamilton has reaped much from the Howard Trading Company. Have you seen his house yet?"

"No, but he has invited me for Christmas dinner and I'm looking forward to that."

"Well, almost everyone gets to Yancey's at least once. He's very proud of that house, I can tell you. It's right fancy. I don't think Mrs. Hamilton likes it as much as he does. She's so quiet and shy. Don't ever seem to have much to say. But then I guess Yancey pretty well controls everything wherever he is."

Nat chuckled as if suddenly recalling an incident involving Yancey, but he said nothing further.

"I was wondering if you would have supper with me at the inn," said Peter.

"My wife and children are expectin' me, Mr. Hawke, but I would have an ale with you and then you come along home with me for supper," Nat suggested.

Peter shook his head.

"I don't wish to impose myself on your wife, Mr. Crowe."

He was embarrassed. For some reason he had not pictured Nat with a family.

"My wife has people in England and she'd be well pleased to meet someone recently come in from there. Besides, we don't have folks around much. I'd like you to come," Nat explained.

"Very well. That's very kind of you."

Looking at Nat's deeply pocked face with its coarse features and at his heavy muscular body, Peter wondered what kind of woman might have married him. He was pleasantly surprised when he saw Rachel Crowe. Almost as tall as Nat, Rachel had large hazel eyes, dark blonde hair she wore in a braid down her back, and deep dimples which appeared whenever she smiled. Certainly she was the most attractive woman Peter had seen since arriving in Boston.

Nat's house was small, made of brick, and it appeared very tidy and clean. Peter was reminded of Ellen when he noticed the white curtains at the windows. Nat's two children were boys of three and six years.

"Nat tells me you have family in England, Mrs. Crowe," said Peter as they sat down at the table to begin supper.

"I have an uncle and a cousin in Bath," Rachel explained. "However, I have not heard from them in almost two years."

"Was Bath your home?" Peter asked.

"No, we lived in the country, but I was quite young when my father and mother decided to come to America. They are both dead now."

"Do you think about going back to England sometime?" Peter asked.

"No, I have no reason to. My uncle, my mother's brother, never forgave my father for bringing us here. Mother died soon after we arrived and my uncle felt the voyage and the hardships of making a new home had been too much for her. That may not be true. I only remember that she became very ill and weak and nothing seemed to help. She died when I was twelve."

"I'm sorry to hear that, Mrs. Crowe," said Peter.

Rachel Crowe looked at him intently, almost curiously. She never had seen so handsome a man.

"Do you have a family, Mr. Hawake?" she asked.

"I am not married, Mrs. Crowe, but I have a brother in Woodbridge, England. That's near Bristol. My parents and my sister are dead," Peter replied.

"Mr. Hawke's goin' to Yancey Hamilton's on Christmas Day, Rachel," Nat Crowe spoke up, and his face broke into a wide grin.

Rachel clapped her hands together and smiled, her dimples deepening.

"Oh, that will be a day all right, Mr. Hawke. And you'll meet his two sisters and his niece and of course Mrs. Hamilton."

Rachel's voice rose with animation.

"Are you going to work with Mr. Hamilton?" she continued, leaning across the table to fill Peter's cup with more tea.

"I was sent here by Lowell Howard to open a New York office. Mr. Hamilton is going to help me with that. We shall be going to New York soon after Christmas," Peter explained.

"Oh, then you won't be staying in Boston?" said Rachel, with obvious disappointment in her voice.

Nat turned and looked thoughtfully at his wife. She was facing Peter Hawke, the teapot still in her hands.

"No, I'm afraid not," Peter replied. "I'm rather sorry too, because so far I like what I've seen. But tell me, will it be as cold in New York?"

Rachel and Nat both laughed, exchanging glances.

"We haven't been there, Mr. Hawke," said Rachel, smiling at Peter.

The three of them sat at the table for some time,

talking and laughing. It was after ten o'clock when Peter took his leave and started back to the inn.

● 2 ●

Christmas Day dawned bright and very cold. The snow sparkled and shimmered in the sunlight. Peter awakened to the sound of churchbells and he was reminded of his family and Woodbridge and Hawkes Nest. It would be Margaret's first Christmas at the house and he wondered if there would be candles and greenery in all the rooms again, now that Hawkes Nest once more had a mistress. William would no doubt see to the festivities and Ellen would be there to help. It would be a happy day. Peter wondered too if he would be missed.

Looking out the window of his small room he saw that the street below was empty. There were no carts or wagons being moved about, no men's voices shouting at each other. Only a white stillness in the bright sun. Peter could see the masts of ships in the harbor, some of whose rigging still was ice-crusted.

The quiet was such that Peter wondered if he might be alone in the inn. The chambermaid had not yet appeared with the water for washing. Perhaps she would not come today. Peter cursed the cold as he began to dress and he suddenly remembered the warm fires in Hawkes Nest. Funny, the things one took for granted that seemed so important in different circumstances.

Peter pulled his boots on and stood up just as a knock sounded at the door, followed by the sprightly entrance of the chambermaid.

"A merry Christmas, Sir," she said, happily. "I've brought your tea up this mornin'."

"Thank you so much. And a merry Christmas to you. I thought you might not be here today."

"Not be here! Oh, Sir, I'm always here. I have nowhere else to be."

"You mean you live here at the inn?" asked Peter, pouring some tea into a blue flowered cup.

"Yes, Sir. Next the kitchen. It's quite the warmest place to be."

The girl's eyes twinkled as she spoke and then she turned and left the room as quickly as she had arrived.

Peter guessed she must have no family and had come alone from Ireland. The thought occurred to him that she seemed very young to be in a strange place with no one to look after her.

The hot tea warmed Peter's insides and he went downstairs to breakfast and then planned to take a walk about the town. Yancey Hamilton's carriage was to come for him at a quarter past two so there was plenty of time.

The narrow streets were shadowed by the buildings on either side while the open spaces appeared bright and clean in the sunlight. Trees around the Common were bare of leaves except for the few evergreens whose branches were drooping with fresh snow.

As Peter walked about Beacon Hill he noticed the fine looking houses, mostly of brick, and three stories tall. He wondered then if this might be where Yancey Hamilton lived.

Some of the people he passed on the street nodded to him in greeting and spoke, "Merry Christmas." Others ignored him, going on their way for whatever purpose. Peter walked for a long time, looking in the shop windows and the coffee houses and wending his way back towards the inn and the wharf. He was hungry

208

now, but decided not to spoil the dinner at Yancey Hamilton's. From the looks of the man he obviously ate richly and in great quantity! So Peter decided to ignore his hunger pangs and wait for the Christmas dinner he now was eagerly anticipating.

The Hamilton house was even more opulent than Peter had been led to believe. On a piece of land Peter estimated at close to three acres, the house was three stories high and built of brick. There were palladian windows on either side of the double door with large brass fixtures. Green boughs tied with red ribbon hung in profusion above the pediment.

Peter was welcomed into the large foyer by Yancey Hamilton, resplendent in a silk brocade vest under his dark brown coat.

"Your promptness is a virtue, Mr. Hawke," said Yancey, a wide smile crossing his pudgy face.

"Let me take your coat and hat," he continued, as a young boy appeared at his side to take Peter's belongings.

"My family is waiting in the parlor. I have prepared a special drink for us today," Yancey went on.

"I'm admiring your home, Mr. Hamilton," said Peter as his eyes took in the crystal chandelier with its drops of colored glass, and the fine Chippendale furnishings placed along the walls.

"Ah yes. Everyone does," Yancey acknowledged. He spoke with pride as he led Peter to the large parlor.

Three women seated on a sofa rose in unison at the sight of the two men and came forward to be introduced. The contrast between Peter and Yancey must have been startling.

"My wife, Charlotte Hamilton; my sister, Mrs. Jonathan Wood; my sister, Rebecca Hamilton. This is Peter Hawke," said Yancey. "He's just in from England, came on the *Bristol Cloud*," he added.

Peter graciously acknowledged the introduction, quite aware that all three ladies were staring at him.

"Do sit down, Mr. Hawke," said Charlotte Hamilton, finally.

She was small and frail in appearance, almost bird-like, Peter thought as he watched her move back towards the sofa, followed by Yancey's two sisters. The three of them sat side by side, hands folded in their laps.

"This is a most beautiful house, Mrs. Hamilton," said Peter to Yancey's wife.

"Thank you, Mr. Hawke. Mr. Hamilton planned it all," said Charlotte Hamilton. Her face was expressionless.

Peter had noticed the carved mantel and the lavishly gilded mirror over the fireplace. The chandelier in the center of the ceiling had etched glass globes, much like the ones at Seagull's Point. He wondered at that instant what Lowell Howard would think if he could see this house. No doubt he would feel that either he was paying Yancey Hamilton too much or else the man was cheating him. Peter wondered about that too.

The dark red velvet draperies and brilliantly patterned carpet accentuated the opulence of the room. Peter's eyes fell on the long-case clock standing against one wall.

"You have an admirable looking clock," he remarked. "Did you order that from England?"

"No, Mr. Hawke. We have some fine craftsmen here, you know. It was made in Salem," Yancey replied.

"Now I want you to try some of my special punch," he went on, ladling liquid from a large china bowl.

He served each of the ladies a small glassful and then handed Peter a larger glass filled to the brim.

"A merry Christmas to you all," said Peter.

"And to you, Sir," said Yancey.

At that moment a young girl entered the room, still in bonnet and cloak.

210

"Forgive me for being late, Uncle," she said, bestowing a kiss on Yancey's ruddy cheek. And then she saw Peter.

"Mr. Hawke, this is my niece, Dora Jane Wood," said Yancey, proudly.

The girl curtsied slightly and smiled at Peter.

"My pleasure, Miss Wood," he acknowledged.

She was not pretty, Peter thought, nor was she unduly plain. Her grey eyes were large and inquisitive as she looked at him.

The young boy who had relieved Peter of his hat and cape appeared at Dora Jane's side to take her bonnet and cloak. The girl smoothed her brown hair and took a chair near the fire.

"It's very cold out today," she stated.

"This will warm you up," said Yancey, handing her a glass of his brandy punch.

"Will you be staying in Boston, Mr. Hawke?" asked the girl, turning towards Peter.

"I'm afraid not," Peter replied.

"Mr. Hawke will be going to New York," Yancey began. "He's to open an office there for Lowell Howard."

"Oh, I see. Then you will be in the same business as Uncle Yancey," the girl observed.

"Yes, and I'm eager to get started," Peter remarked.

The three ladies on the sofa continued to stare at Peter, making no attempt at conversation. Finally, a servant girl appeared and announced that dinner was ready to be served, much to Peter's relief. His stomach already was making anguished sounds.

Having seen the manner in which Yancey Hamilton lived, Peter found he was not astonished at the sight of the man's dining table. He merely wished William and Margaret and Ellen could see the beauty and the elegance of the silver, crystal and china on the Irish linen and lace cloth stretching the length of the long table. Funny, he thought, how he always seemed to include Ellen when his home and family came to mind. At any rate, she would have been overwhelmed at the sight. So might Lowell Howard, Peter surmised. He could not help but wonder if Yancey Hamilton might not be cheating his employer.

The large bunches of holly placed about the room reminded Peter of his mother. And the table was aglow with candles. He was seated next to Yancey with Dora Jane Wood opposite. Somehow now she seemed more attractive. Perhaps it was the soft light of the candles.

Never had Peter seen so much food at one time and his host was excitedly urging him to try everything. Turkey, roast beef, ham, venison, wild duck, oyster stuffing, corn pudding, cranberries, jellies, brandied figs, squash.

"You know, Mr. Hamilton, for almost six weeks on the *Bristol Cloud* I had rather simple fare. I'm not sure I can fully master all this," Peter explained, looking at his heaping plate.

"It'll do you good, Mr. Hawke. Here, have some more wine," said Yancey, brushing aside Peter's remark.

"It must be frightening being at sea such a long time," said Dora Jane, turning to face Peter. "I seriously doubt I could ever make such a voyage."

"It was more tiresome than frightening," said Peter. "However, I should not like to do it again any time soon," he added.

Yancey laughed heartily.

"Once you get settled in New York you will be so occupied that you might wish for a few quiet days at sea."

"Perhaps," said Peter. "Nonetheless, I'm anxious to begin."

The dinner went on for some length of time because

of the endless array of desserts put on the sideboard. Finally, the ladies excused themselves and Yancey and Peter continued to sit at the table, enjoying the wine.

Peter's curiosity soon got the better of him and he inquired of Yancey regarding his home.

"I had not imagined one could accumulate such beauty in America as you have here, Mr. Hamilton. Could I possibly have so much to look forward to?"

"Indeed, Mr. Hawke, in time. However, I must tell you that my wife came into a considerable sum of money at her father's death and I was asked to manage it for her. Much of what you see here came from that source, and you can judge that I have done rather well," Yancey explained, his eyes narrowing as he leaned back in his chair.

Peter was considerably relieved. He had had an uncomfortable suspicion about Yancey and Lowell Howard and he did not want to be put in the position of a spy or informer.

"There is a tremendous market in this country for goods of all kinds, Mr. Hawke," Yancey continued. "One seems to be able to sell most anything."

Peter laughed.

"That should make my task easier, should it not?"

"Indeed. You will find Lowell Howard a shrewd businessman, but he knows well what he's doing and has profited handsomely by his relations with others in the trade. Too bad he had no son, really. Perhaps he has you in mind to fill that void."

Peter's face appeared startled at Yancey's suggestion.

"Well, you surely can't expect his daughter to carry on his business," Yancey continued, sounding somewhat exasperated.

"I hadn't thought about it, Mr. Hamilton."

Peter did not want to get into any discussion concerning Margaret or her father.

"Forgive me. I should not have mentioned so personal a matter. Shall we join the ladies?" said Yancey.

"Of course."

Peter was eager to move about after the heavy meal. In fact, he felt that the long walk back to the inn would be most beneficial, but of course he realized it was far too soon for him to take his leave.

Dora Jane was playing a tune on the harpsichord in the parlor and Mrs. Hamilton sat watching her, very quiet and almost trance-like. Yancey's two sisters were listening with rapt attention, hands again folded in their laps. All four women looked towards Peter as he and Yancey appeared in the room. Peter smiled and walked over to the harpsichord.

"You play very well, Miss Wood," he said, resting his hand on the instrument.

"Thank you. Do you play also?"

"I have no musical ability whatsoever," Peter replied, laughing. "Hardly can carry a tune, but I'm very fond of music all the same."

"Oh, I find music very comforting as well as diverting," said Dora Jane, her voice bright with enthusiasm. "It is many things, really."

"Do play some more, dear," said Yancey, settling into a large chair near the fire, his huge bulk covering the piece of furniture.

Dora Jane knew from past experience that her uncle was about to take his after-dinner nap and her playing the harpsichord was merely to ease him into sleep that much sooner. She smiled at Yancey and began to play a soft and melodic tune.

"I shall have to apologize for my husband, Mr. Hawke," said Mrs. Hamilton as it became obvious that Yancey was going to sleep without further delay. "He never lets anything interfere with his nap after a heavy meal."

"No need to apologize, Mrs. Hamilton," said Peter, thinking that Yancey must do a considerable amount of napping! "If you will forgive me, I should be on my way back to the inn. I have a number of letters to write before I leave for New York."

"If you wish, Mr. Hawke. Let me send for the carriage."

"No, if you don't mind, I should enjoy the walk. After so sumptuous a feast, I need the exercise."

Peter now was eager to be on his way.

Mrs. Hamilton rang for the houseboy to bring Peter's hat and cloak.

"I hope we may see you again, Mr. Hawke," said Dora Jane, still seated at the harpsichord.

"It shall be my pleasure, Miss Wood. And to all of you ladies, I thank you for a most memorable Christmas Day. Please express my gratitude to Mr. Hamilton when he wakes, will you?" Peter directed this last to Mrs. Hamilton.

"Of course, Mr. Hawke, and do come again."

"Thank you," said Peter, bowing slightly as he turned and left the room.

The sky was bright with stars in the cold, still night and Peter walked briskly, the chill air blowing against his face. The day had been pleasant enough, but he was glad to be out of Yancey Hamilton's overstuffed, over-furnished, over-elaborate house. The small room at the inn would seem a welcome relief, he thought, as he hurried along the street heading back towards the center of Boston. In a day or two he would be leaving for New York.

"I wonder what it will be like?" he said aloud.

● 3 ●

Yancey and Peter set up a small office in one of the brick warehouse buildings along the New York wharf in the center of the shipping activity. A wooden sign with bright yellow lettering signified that this was the Lowell Howard Trading Company of Bristol, England, with offices now in Boston and New York, and Peter Hawke was the New York manager.

Competition invites curiosity and Peter was not long in meeting the other traders and merchants. He found shelter in a nearby rooming house but the noisy, smelly neighborhood caused him to move some distance away to an inn. Peter wanted to be close enough to the wharf for an easy walk to his place of business, but soon realized that this was not possible since the area of New York was so much bigger than that of Boston. He had to reconcile himself to a much longer walk, or else find some means of transportation.

Peter had been in New York almost five weeks when he received his first letter from William. The *Bristol Star* had taken it to Boston and Yancey Hamilton forwarded the mail on to the New York office. There was a communication from Lowell Howard also.

William's letter appeared lengthy and Peter was eager to get into it. Now he sat at his desk with the letter in front of him.

"My dear brother," William began. "We were more than delighted to receive your long and informative letter. We were, in fact, greatly re-

216

lieved to know you had arrived safely in Boston. The voyage sounded exhausting. The winter in Woodbridge has been about the same as always with considerable amounts of rain and gusty winds. There has been only a mere dusting of snow, however. Nothing to compare with what you speak of. Business remains steady and there is a generous backlog of orders.

And now, Peter, for the really important news. Margaret is expecting a child. Sometime in July, we think. I have asked Ellen to move into the house, temporarily at least, because while Margaret is feeling fine now, I do not want her to be alone when I have to be away. Of course Ellen is being most cooperative. She is a gem, I must say. We simply couldn't manage without her. She seems to anticipate every need around here for both of us.

We miss you, Peter. The house seems strangely quiet now, but I do hope you are happy in your new surroundings.

Margaret sends her best regards and Ellen also wishes you well. We all pray you will find what you are looking for.''

Peter held the letter limply in his hand. Margaret was having a baby. In July, William said. A baby that could be his own, he thought suddenly. Could Margaret be wondering too? Beloved, beautiful Margaret. Peter sank lower in the chair, quite shaken at the thought of Margaret carrying his child. Then he realized there was no way of knowing for sure. The baby could just as easily be William's, and rightly so. But he knew that from this moment on there would be wonder and doubt in his mind, and probably in Margaret's. Now he realized their love for each other had brought them only anxiety and regret.

For the first time since Christmas day, Peter felt a

very real longing for Hawkes Nest and the quiet village he had always known as home. Would he ever be totally free of Woodbridge and all that it meant to him?

Weeks turned into months and Peter was busier than he ever had expected to be. There seemed to be no end of goods coming and going from Europe, England and the West Indies.

He had been invited to many dinner parties and dances, all of which he enjoyed to the fullest. The abundance of delicious food and the great variety of wines continued to astonish him. It did not take long for Peter to gain back the weight he had lost on the *Bristol Cloud* and along with it he had acquired a new maturity and self-confidence which only added to his already unusually handsome appearance.

Mothers of marriageable daughters were constantly inviting him to various social gatherings. He found many of the young ladies most attractive and charming, but he seemed not inclined towards marriage. This was most exasperating to the ladies involved, but his attitude tended to make him all the more irresistable. The girls whispered about his blue eyes, his reddish gold mustache and his tall, graceful physique. If Peter had known how much he was discussed in New York drawing rooms, he would have indeed been surprised as well as flattered. Instead, he accepted all invitations as a sign of great hospitality towards a stranger. Also, such events kept him from being lonely and of dwelling too much on Margaret and the child she was carrying.

Peter was counting the weeks and the months and knew it would be some time before he would hear about the child. William had written twice since his first letter, saying that all was well at home. So Peter could only wait with anxiety.

• 4 •

Spring in Woodbridge had been unusually fair and the gardens at Hawkes Nest were bursting with bloom. The yellow rose by the oak door at the front of the house was laden with buds, promising a bright and fragrant summer.

Ellen and Margaret were seated at the side garden just off the kitchen, Margaret doing some embroidery on a cradle cover and Ellen stringing beans for supper. There was no conversation between them. Had there been, they would have been discussing the same subject—Peter.

Ellen was remembering the day she and Peter had had a picnic in the garden, the only time they had ever been alone together. She remembered how he spoke then of going to America, and how he had helped her return the dishes to the kitchen. It soon would be a year since that day. She wondered if Peter ever thought of her at all.

Margaret, on the other hand, was remembering the night she had spent in Peter's room, loving and being loved. The baby that moved inside her might be Peter's. She could not help but wonder if it were, because their passion together had been so consuming. If only she could be certain. Perhaps the baby would have Peter's blue eyes. Well, no matter, Margaret thought to herself. She felt the baby was Peter's and that was all that really mattered. She was very happy about the child coming. It was as if Peter were close again.

"Have you decided on a name for the child, Mrs. Hawke?" asked Ellen suddenly, breaking the silence between them.

"Well, if it is a son, I think we will name him after our fathers. Henry Lowell, or Lowell Henry. William thinks that would be nice. What do you think, Ellen?"

"Oh, that would be a most gracious gesture. And if it's a girl?"

"I rather like Elizabeth," said Margaret. "Sounds queenly, don't you think?"

The two of them laughed heartily at Margaret's little joke.

"It will be lovely having a little one, Mrs. Hawke. I envy you, truly," said Ellen wistfully.

Margaret put her embroidery down and looked at Ellen.

"I am sorry about your loss, Ellen. However, you really should get about more. There are other young men in the valley, you know, and you are quite pretty. Don't stay about the house so much. You are very capable and you should have a home and family of your own. Isn't that what you really want?"

"I'm happy here, Mrs. Hawke," Ellen replied. "You and Mr. Hawke have been so kind. But I've been wondering, Ma'm, why does it hurt so inside when someone you care very much for is gone? I feel so hollow sometimes," Ellen continued.

Margaret assumed the girl was referring to Ben Hammond and she had often wondered what had attracted Ellen to pathetic, scrawny little Ben in the first place. Nonetheless, she could sympathize with her because Margaret felt the same gnawing pain when she thought of Peter.

"That's a bit difficult to explain, Ellen, but I suppose one could say it's part of being in love," Margaret replied, bending her head closer to her sewing.

220

Their conversation ended as William appeared. The post had arrived and there was a letter from Lowell Howard.

"Here's a letter from your father, dear," said William, giving Margaret a light kiss on the cheek.

She smiled up at him as she took the letter from his hand. Then she quickly opened the envelope.

"Oh, dear, he has been ill and he has a heavy cough. However, he said between Mary and the doctor he's been well cared for. And, William, he says Peter's doing an admirable job in New York."

"Ah, that's good. I'm glad he's pleased," said William proudly.

"He hopes I'm taking good care of myself and his grandson," Margaret continued, laughing. "He already thinks it will be a boy."

William smiled broadly, his eyes warm and loving as he looked at Margaret.

"Well, I must leave you two enjoying the sunshine. I have work to finish," he said, disappearing into the house.

Margaret folded the letter carefully back into the envelope and tucked it into her embroidery basket.

"Ellen, would you mind fixing the tea a little early today? I feel the need of something," she said, turning towards her housekeeper.

"Of course, Ma'm. I'll see to it right away."

When Ellen had gone into the kitchen, Margaret took the letter out again and re-read it, particularly the part about Peter.

"Mr. Hawke is doing an admirable job in New York. I am more than pleased. In fact, I am considering making him a partner in the near future. Yancey Hamilton says Peter has the intensity and self-confidence to make himself successful in whatever he chooses to do."

"Whatever he chooses to do," Margaret whispered to herself. If only she could share his life. She folded the letter and again put it in her embroidery basket. Dreaming, dreaming, always.

Ellen soon appeared with the tea tray.

"Mr. Hawke will be with you in a few minutes."

"Oh, fine. Thank you, Ellen."

When William joined her at the small table, Margaret handed him a cup of tea.

"It's a bit early for tea, isn't it?" he asked, his voice teasing.

"Perhaps, but I seem to be hungry all the time."

"The child becomes you, Margaret. You are even more beautiful," said William.

"Thank you, William. That's very kind of you. I've always thought pregnant women were rather grotesque."

William laughed heartily.

"You, my dear, certainly are not. Tell me, did your father have any other news?"

"Oh, he said he was thinking of taking Peter in as a partner."

"Did he now? Well, that should make Peter happy. Chances are he never will come back to Woodbridge."

"Oh, I hope he does," Margaret said. "I mean, I miss him, don't you?" she added, quickly.

"Yes, I really do," said William, setting his cup down. Then he got to his feet.

"Do you feel like a short walk? Dr. Booth said you should go for a walk every day, dear."

"Oh, bother, what does *he* know? He doesn't have to waddle around with all this inside him. I'm too tired to go for a walk," Margaret replied, irritably.

"Very well, if you really don't feel like it, I'll go back to my work."

"I think I'll go up and take a short nap."

"Do you want me to help you up the stairs?" asked William.

"Oh, William, for goodness sake. I'm not an invalid."

Margaret spoke with exasperation as she gathered up her embroidery basket and started into the house.

William caught her by the arm and pulled her close to him.

"You're my love, you know that, don't you?"

He smiled down at her, then quickly kissed her on the mouth.

"Now run along. I'll wake you before supper."

He gave her a pat on the bottom.

"William, whatever is the matter with you!" said Margaret as she hurried away.

His laughter rang in her ears until she reached their room and closed the door.

● 5 ●

The May days passed into June and the summer continued fair. This particular morning Margaret had been lying awake for some time. Daylight was just appearing through the windows. She felt feverish and her back was aching.

William was sleeping soundly next to her. She turned her head and looked at him. The strong line of his chin and jaw were silhouetted by the morning light. His thick reddish brown hair was touseled and his mustache suddenly appeared darker than she thought it was. My imagination, she whispered to herself.

Margaret continued to study his face, listening to his rhythmic breathing. She gasped out loud as a sharp pain took hold of her body. William stirred and opened his eyes.

"Margaret? Are you all right, dear?" he asked, drowsily.

"Yes, I think so," she replied. "I just had a sharp pain, but it's gone now."

William raised up on one elbow, looking at her.

"A pain? Do you think it's the baby?"

She shook her head.

"It's not due for another two weeks, William. I guess it's nothing, really."

He lay back again, his eyes focused on the ceiling. He had wondered the past few months if Margaret really was happy about the baby coming. Sometimes she seemed like an excited child when she was sewing on baby clothes and folding the tiny garments and the soft blankets. Other times she was so pensive and quiet that she seemed far away from him. He had heard that most women were moody and sometimes difficult to live with during pregnancy, so William supposed that Margaret could be having the same symptoms.

With Ellen's help, Margaret had converted the spare bedroom into a nursery. William had brought home a lovely cradle from his last trip to London, along with a tiny pillow and embroidered case and a blanket cover to match. Margaret had teased him about expecting a daughter because no boy could sleep in such a fancy bed. Nonetheless, she was delighted with the cradle.

Margaret cried out as pain gripped her again. William sat up quickly. Her large brown eyes were wide with fear and her face was ghostly pale.

"I think I should go for Dr. Booth," said William as he got out of bed and reached for his trousers hanging over the back of the chair.

"Oh no, William, don't leave me," she pleaded.

"But, darling, if it's the baby—"

"Just wait a little longer," she interrupted, managing a faint smile. "There now, it's stopped."

Wiliam looked out the window and then at the clock on the bureau. Almost six. He continued dressing.

Margaret was quiet now and she had closed her eyes. First babies often were long in coming, he thought, or so he had been told, and perhaps there was nothing Dr. Booth could do for several hours. Still—.

William stood by the bed and looked down at his wife. Her thick, glossy hair was even blacker against the white of the pillow case. The long lashes were fringe upon her pale cheeks. Her lips were pink and soft. The small hands rested on her distended stomach, the long ruffled sleeves of her nightdress limp on the bedcovers.

William felt a quiver run through him. Margaret's beauty never ceased to excite him. Sometimes he marvelled at the realization she was his wife.

Margaret seemed to know he was standing there looking at her because she opened her eyes and smiled up at him.

"I'm all right, William," she said, softly.

"Darling, I'll go down and see if Ellen has started the fire in the stove. She can fix you some breakfast."

William started for the door.

"Oh no, William. I don't want anything to eat. Nothing. Maybe just a cup of tea," Margaret smiled wanly.

He blew her a kiss and went out into the hall and she heard him descending the stairs. He was dear, he truly was dear, she thought drowsily.

Then the labor pains began to come with some regularity. William went for Dr. Booth and Ellen stayed by Margaret's side. With the intensity of each pain, Margaret became more terrified, adding to her ordeal. Ellen wiped the perspiration from Margaret's face and held her hand tightly each time her body was gripped with wracking pain and she twisted and turned, trying to get away from her torment.

William and Dr. Booth returned. William was most anxious when he saw the state of his wife and he turned quickly to the doctor.

"Is something very wrong?" he asked, in a quiet voice so Margaret could not hear him.

The doctor shook his head but did not speak. He then asked William to leave the room while he made his examination.

The sun rose higher and higher in the sky and Margaret's cries became more frightening to William. He held her hand tightly in his own, trying to will away her pain and suffering. He would not leave her side, even though Dr. Booth told him he would be much better off if he got some rest.

"There's nothing you can do, you know. These things are in God's hands," said the doctor. "It won't be much longer now."

Ellen came into the room with a basin of water and some clean towels at the doctor's request. She remained, also at his request.

Margaret now was delirious, uttering words, disconnected, with no meaning. Then she moaned, "Peter, oh Peter, don't go. Don't leave me. I love you, I love you, Peter."

Ellen felt a stab in her heart as she heard the words. Margaret and Peter? Surely not! Her own heartache subsided as she glanced across the bed at William Hawke. He looked startled, disbelieving. He still held tightly to Margaret's hand, but the color had drained out of his face and his big shoulders sagged. Could he have heard Margaret correctly? Could he? It was as if he had asked the question out loud. Ellen leaned across the bed and spoke softly.

"She's delirious, Mr. Hawke. Take no mind of it. Women say strange things when they're delirious."

William nodded his head slowly. Dr. Booth seemed to have been totally unaware of what had been said by any of them. Then, mercifully, the baby was born. It was a boy.

● 6 ●

Henry Lowell Hawke was three weeks old and William had not yet touched him. Margaret's words in her delirium had been so imbedded in her husband's mind that he seemed remote and silent. He looked at the child in Margaret's arms and no words would come.

"William, he won't break, you know. He's really quite a sturdy little fellow. Don't you want to hold your own son?" asked Margaret anxiously.

Your own son, William thought. Was the child really his?

"Not just yet, Margaret. Maybe later," he replied.

Margaret seemed delighted with the baby. She cuddled and kissed the child and hardly would put him down for sleep. Dr. Booth advised Margaret to stay in bed for at least ten days and during her convalescence William had slept in Peter's room. He had not yet moved back to his own bed with Margaret, and she had made no mention of the fact.

Lying in Peter's bed at night, William felt numb. Perhaps Ellen was right. He should take no mind to what Margaret had said the day the baby was born. There probably was nothing between his wife and his brother. Peter no doubt would be deeply offended if he knew the thoughts William was harboring. Still, when William remembered his brother's sudden departure occurring right after Peter had taken Margaret to Bristol to see her father, he couldn't help the suspicions clouding his mind. Did Peter leave Hawkes Nest because he was in love with Margaret? Or she with with him? Should he confront his wife with that question? Was the baby at Margaret's breast his own son, or Peter's son? The agonizing doubts were gnawing at William day and night. He found it hard to concentrate when he was at work and equally hard to pretend with Margaret that everything was the same between them.

Margaret seemed not to notice his sudden reserve. Perhaps she was so busy with the child. However, when Ellen entered the bedroom one day with a basin or warm water, Margaret spoke about William.

"Ellen, does it seem strange to you that Mr. Hawke pays so little attention to Henry? I mean, are all fathers like that when their children are small? He has hardly noticed his son."

Margaret seemed distressed and unhappy. Ellen did not look at her as she replied, but continued gathering up the soiled linen.

"I don't really know, Mrs. Hawke, but I'm sure it's only because the baby seems so fragile and tiny. Mr. Hawke is such a big man himself and he probably just finds it hard to—to—"

She was searching for the right words.

"He'll come 'round soon, I'm sure," Ellen continued, for lack of anything else to say.

At supper that evening Margaret asked William if he had written to Peter to tell him about Henry.

"No, I haven't. I thought perhaps you might like to," William replied.

"Good heavens, William, the child is already three weeks old! I should have thought you would have written your brother immediately."

Margaret's annoyance was quite evident as she spoke.

"I have been very busy, Margaret. I really was not aware that so much time had passed. I shall write this evening if that will make you happy."

"Make *me* happy! William, honestly, you seem so

sullen and unpleasant lately. Whatever is bothering you?"

Margaret's voice rose with her impatience.

William was slow to reply.

"I think you are imagining that, my dear."

A few weeks later Ellen moved back to her cottage. She convinced William Hawke that it would be better if she spent the nights in her own place now.

"I think it would be best for you and Mrs. Hawke," she said.

William looked at her so knowingly that her cheeks flushed pink.

"Do you think Henry is my son?" he asked, earnestly.

Ellen appeared shocked at so personal a question.

"Oh, Sir, please. Of course he is your son."

She felt most uncomfortable and wished to leave.

"You must forget about Mrs. Hawke's words that day. I'm sure there is nothing to it. Just delirium," she added.

The worried expression on her face caused William to smile.

"Don't look so concerned, Ellen. Perhaps you are right after all. At any rate, it is just between you and me, isn't it?"

"Yes, Sir."

William had great difficulty in writing to Peter, but eventually the words came. By the time the letter reached New York the child would be more than two months old.

Many of the village folk had come to see the baby. Reverend Thomas and his wife were among the first.

'Your first born, and a son," said Evangeline Thomas. "How happy you must be."

William nodded his head and Margaret's face was glowing with pride.

The baby seemed to thrive on Margaret's constant care and William soon found he was taking a greater interest in the child. He watched him sleeping in the cradle and finally he held the little boy in his arms, if only for a brief moment. The child looked up at William, a half smile on his tiny face. He had Mary Hawke's bright blue eyes, William thought, and Peter's.

● 7 ●

Early in October Margaret's father died. Lowell Howard suffered a massive stroke and passed away without ever having seen his only grandchild. Margaret was unconsolable and felt a deep remorse for not having visited her father with the baby.

William tried to comfort her, saying the child was much too young to risk travelling in a coach to Bristol.

"But I should have gone, I should have gone," Margaret sobbed.

Now she and William and the baby would make the journey to Bristol to take care of funeral arrangements and to speak with Mr. Howard's bookkeeper about the shipping company.

Lowell Howard's will left everything to Margaret, naming William as trustee in her behalf. By law all of Margaret's property would pass to her husband in any event, but Lowell Howard trusted William Hawke and knew he would take proper care of Margaret and of the property in the estate.

Mr. Barnes, the bookkeeper, gave William an unopened letter addressed to him. The letter contained his father-in-law's directions regarding the trading company, his house and personal possessions. William Hawke, his wife and child now would be wealthy beyond anything William had ever known.

"I should like to sell father's house, William. I couldn't bear to keep it without him," Margaret said, solemnly.

"We shall make provisions for Mary," she continued.

"My dear, let us not be hasty about this. Don't you think we should wait a few months? Mary can stay in the house to look after things. With all there is to do we will need a place to stay while in Bristol. And someday the business will be Henry's, perhaps, unless he decides to be a wagonmaker like me," William remarked.

Margaret did not seem to be listening. She sat motionless in her father's library, where William had first seen her.

"Do you still have the letter in which your father mentioned Peter's possible partnership?" William asked.

"I believe so. Why?"

"Well, there is no mention of it in the letter of instructions, but I know you said it was contained in one of his letter."

"Yes."

"Of course you can do whatever you like, dear," William suggested.

"Oh, William, I don't understand any of these things. Please don't ask me to make any such decisions."

"Very well, I'll ask Mr. Barnes to write to Peter and to Mr. Hamilton in Boston and tell them what has happened and to await further word."

"Can we go home soon?" Margaret asked, wearily.

"Of course, whenever you like."

The silent, tiresome ride in the coach back to Woodbridge reminded Margaret of her last trip to Bristol when she had spent a week with her father. Peter had sat across from her, quiet and distant. Almost a year had passed. She held her son close to her breast and now and then wiped a tear from her cheek. William patted her arm gently, offering what comfort he could.

When they arrived at Hawkes Nest it was nearly dark.

Ellen was waiting for them, the fire burning briskly in the sitting room.

"I'll have a nice cup of tea for you, Mrs. Hawke. You just sit down by the fire and rest," Ellen said, helping Margaret out of her cloak.

William took the sleeping baby up to the bedroom and put him in the cradle which he very slowly set to rocking. Then he went down to join his wife.

Margaret's grief at the loss of her father began to take its toll in the following weeks. She was unable to sleep and had no appetite. The baby became irritable and restless because she could not feed him properly. William consulted with Dr. Booth and Reverend Thomas, expressing his concern for her health and peace of mind.

"These things take time, Mr. Hawke. Your wife is strong and she will come out of it. You must be patient," said Dr. Booth.

"Perhaps if she spent more time with the ladies of the Church Guild," suggested Reverend Thomas. "They would be most happy to have her and there is much to do to take her mind off her sorrow."

"I could ask Evangeline to come and have a quiet talk with her, if you like," he continued. "Evangeline is very good at that sort of thing."

"I'm sure she is, Reverend Thomas. Let me speak with Mrs. Hawke and I shall let you know," William responded, although he thought later about Evangeline Thomas's shrill voice and wondered if she could talk quietly about anything at all.

However, this turned out to be Margaret's salvation. Never before had she shown so much interest in the townfolk. Now, at the urging of Evangeline Thomas, many of the ladies came to call on Margaret and to bring her small tokens of friendship and understanding. An embroidered handkerchief, small book of poems, some fresh cookies or jam. She responded to their sympathy and began to spend some time at the church every week. She helped arrange the flowers for the Sunday services and to repair the hymn books. Then there would be days when she would close the door the bedroom and William would hear her crying and she would not come down for hours.

In mid-November a long letter arrived from Peter. It was the first word they had had from him since Henry was born and since the death of Lowell Howard.

"Congratulations on the birth of your son. You must be very proud," the letter began.

Peter made no mention of Margaret's father, indicating he had not yet received the letter regarding Lowell Howard's death.

"I wish Peter were not so far away," said William, soberly. "It makes things difficult at best, this business of trying to communicate with weeks and weeks of waiting."

Does he make any mention of coming home?" asked Margaret, softly.

"No, he doesn't. You may read the letter, dear. It is intended for both of us," William replied.

"Oh, no, I don't need to read it. You just tell me what he has to say," Margaret's response was quick and decisive.

"Well, he mentions the bright red and yellow foliage of the trees in the country. Says they are much like some of our trees, only brighter and in greater quantity. There already has been considerable frost, but as yet no snow," said William.

"There are times," Peter wrote, "when I feel it is quite impossible there could be such a vast distance between us. Hawkes Nest seems very close, as if I could walk in at any time. Yet, when I see the ships sailing in and out of the harbor here I realize how far I have come."

William went on reading the letter aloud to Margaret:

"The shipping business continues to flourish and I can see no end to the demand for goods. I must admit that one can indeed make a fortune here."

Peter had closed the letter with his regards to Margaret and to Ellen, saying, "I have not yet tasted a scone like Ellen's."

William glanced towards Margaret as he finished the letter. She was leaning against the back of the chair, her eyes closed. Was she asleep, William wondered. Had she heard any of the letter? Margaret opened her eyes as he stopped speaking.

"Oh, I thought you might have dozed off," said William.

"Goodness no."

"Peter sounds happy, don't you think?" asked William.

"I expect so."

"Well, dear, if you will excuse me, I have some paper work to finish," said William, getting up from the chair.

Margaret watched him as he walked from the room and she suddenly realized that he had not kissed her for some time. Why would she think of that right now, she wondered. He had, in fact, not slept with her since before Henry was born. Margaret was surprised that she had not missed his attention all these weeks. Of course, with the new baby and her convalescence and then the death of her father, William probably was being merely kind and thoughtful of her, as indeed he always had. Still, he did not treat her as before, she thought idly.

Why had he not come back to their bed? William, who never had been able to keep from caressing her and who wanted her body with such gentleness.

Margaret sat forward in the chair then as she heard Henry cyring. In her haste to get to the baby, William left her thoughts.

In the ensuing weeks William spent endless hours in the workroom. Orders remained fairly constant and going over Lowell Howard's papers took a considerable amount of time. Correspondence with Mr. Barnes in Bristol was frequent.

William came to meals and then resumed working, retiring long after Margaret had gone to bed. His behaviour was becoming increasingly frustrating to her. He remained polite and considerate, but Margaret sensed something was very wrong. Yet she did not know how to approach him. Too proud to ask why he did not return to her, she missed the love and devotion he always had given to her. She missed having his arms about her as she went to sleep, his hand stroking her hair. She missed the warmth of his body next to hers.

What was she to do? How could she talk to him? How could she let him know she was worried and unhappy? Suddenly, Margaret knew. She would not wait for him to come to her. She would go to him, just as she had done with Peter.

Margaret lay quite still in the bed as she thought about her husband. The clock in the hall had just struck the eleventh hour. She had not yet heard William's step on the stairs, indicating he still was working late. He surely would be coming up soon.

Margaret looked at the baby in his cradle. He was sleeping soundly. Getting out of bed, she went to the bureau drawer and removed the green velvet dressing gown William had brought her from London. Fastening it about her waist, she moved to her dressing table, picked up the hairbrush and began brushing her hair until it fell lustrous and curling about her shoulders.

She heard William coming up the stairs. He went into Peter's room and closed the door. Margaret waited for a few minutes, glanced at herself in the mirror again, and went across the hall. She knocked lightly on the door.

"William?"

He opened the door and looked down at her.

"Is something the matter?" he asked.

Margaret's dark eyes searched his face, imploring him to understand. Then she reached up and put both arms about his neck and moved close to him.

"Yes, I want to be with you," she said simply.

When William left the workroom that night he did so without turning out the wick on the oil lamp, something he always was careful to do. A large pile of books and papers lay next to the lamp. It would never be known what caused those books to teeter and slide, knocking the lamp over on the table. Perhaps a draft from a half-open window, perhaps merely the uneven weight of the pile. In a matter of seconds the oil had ignited from the burning wick, then the papers, soon the curtain at the window behind the table.

William and Margaret were in a deep sleep. Their love-making had been passionate and fulfilling, to Margaret because she needed her husband's attention and devotion, to William because he adored his wife and never had had a surfeit of her body.

Margaret woke first. There was a strange noise, a crackling. What was it? Where was it coming from? She sat up quickly, listening.

William roused from sleep.

"What's the matter?" he asked.

"I don't know, William. I hear the strangest noise."

Then they smelled the smoke drifting up the stairway. William jumped from the bed.

"My God, it's a fire! We've got a fire, Margaret! Get Henry at once!" he shouted.

Margaret pulled the velvet robe over her thin nightdress and ran across the hall to the baby. The smoke was thick and acrid in odor, but the stairs still were visible.

"We must get outside, Margaret. Quickly!" William's voice was demanding.

They ran down the stairs and out the big oak door at the front of the house.

"Stay right here, Margaret. Don't move," William directed as they reached the cobbled walkway.

The fire was in the workroom and the kitchen at the back of the house. From where they stood they were unable to see the extent of the flames.

"I've got to get your father's papers and books, Margaret," said William starting back into the house.

"Oh no, William don't go! No, no, don't go in!" Margaret pleaded, tugging at his arm.

"Margaret, I've got to see how bad it is. We can't just let the whole house go!" said William, pulling away from her.

She held Henry tightly as she watched her husband disappear into the house. The noise of the fire was frightening and the baby began to cry. Margaret rocked him back and forth in her arms, trying to soothe him. She called to William, but he did not answer. Unable to wait any longer, she laid Henry on the grass well away from the house and ran back inside to find William.

"William, where are you? William, William!" she cried in alarm.

"I'm coming Margaret. Get out, get out, I tell you!"

Margaret had reached the kitchen which was aflame all along one wall. She could see William in the workroom, now burning furiously, and he was coming towards her, his arms carrying a metal box. Just as he neared the door one of the heavy oak beams across the

239

ceiling gave way and crashed down, knocking William to the floor.

Margaret screamed and ran towards him. Another beam fell, pinning her beneath it. Neither of them could reach the other.

"Margaret, Margaret, oh my God, what have we done!" William moaned, struggling to move the heavy beam from his legs. Margaret did not speak. She had lost consciousness. Soon the intensity of the heat and smoke overpowered William too and they were beyond help.

Ellen Davis woke from a restless sleep. She could smell smoke. Getting out of bed, she checked the stove in the tiny kitchen of her cottage. The fire had gone out there hours ago. Strange. Where could the smoke be coming from? She went to the window next to the cottage door. Pulling the curtain aside she looked out into the dark night. A bright glow lighted the sky above the hill. Ellen gasped and put her hand to her mouth. Hawkes Nest! It must be Hawkes Nest!

She ran to the bedroom, pulled her coat off the hook and hurried out the door. As she ran towards the house she cried out to the neighbors.

"Help, help! Fire, it's a fire!"

Her voice was shrill and breathless as she ran. Cottage doors flew open and soon she was followed by some of the townfolk.

"It's Hawkes Nest!" she screeched helplessly.

Ellen's throat was dry and tight as she ran up the cobbled pathway to the old house she loved. She stopped suddenly as she came through the trees. The baby was crying somewhere and then she saw him on the grass, kicking his legs out of the blanket. Ellen gathered the child close to her and pulled the blanket snugly around him. He stopped crying and looked up at her, his bright blue eyes anxious and bewildered. Ellen kissed him and felt the tears running down her cheeks. Tears of fright. Where was Mr. Hawke? And Margaret? What had happened to them? They must have brought Henry out of the house. Where had they gone?

Ellen looked up at the house. The roof had collapsed over the kitchen and workroom and oddly enough the heavy rain-soaked thatch was now smothering the flames into dense smoke. The sitting room and front part of the house appeared to have been relatively untouched by the fire.

"At least it's not a total loss," remarked one of the villagers, standing next to Ellen. "Where's the master and Mrs. Hawke?"

"I don't know," Ellen replied, looking on in disbelief. "I haven't seem then, but they must have brought the baby out. He was lying on the grass."

"I'll have a look 'round."

Two other men joined in the search and now the garden began to fill with neighbors and friends. William and Margaret were not found until the embers had cooled enough to be moved and searched.

Woodbridge was in a state of shock at the tragedy. Folks spoke in whispers. Hawkes Nest in ruins and William Hawke's son an orphan. From the position of the bodies, it appeared that Margaret Hawke had gone to her husband's aid and been caught by a fallen beam.

"Such a beautiful lady, she was," said Evangeline Thomas, sorrowfully. "I never saw a prettier one. And Mr. Hawke so big and strong. It don't seem possible."

For days there was talk of nothing but the fire and the Hawkes and the orphaned child.

"Well, the only kin he has is Peter Hawke in America. I guess he'll have to look after him.

"Ellen Davis is carin' for him right now. But what'll happen to her? She don't have no place to go either."

"Ellen Davis seems to have a right amount of trouble, don't she? Makes you wonder, I'll say it does."

Sitting in her small cottage with Henry on her lap, Ellen knew there was only one thing she could do. She would have to go to Bristol to Lowell Howard's house and stay there with the baby and Mary, the housekeeper, until Peter was notified and could, in turn, tell her what arrangements to make.

The day Ellen was to leave for Bristol she walked back up the path to Hawkes Nest, Henry in her arms. The house was dirty and smelled of smoke. Everything was covered with ashes. She was thankful then that none of the Hawkes could see it in such a state. She stepped around the broken and blackened china where the cabinets had fallen over as the beams and roof had crashed down. The rosewood clock which had belonged to Peter's mother was gone. Only a few of the workings remained.

The sitting room was fairly well intact although the odor of smoke was in everything, the curtains, the chairs, the settee. All the brass pieces were grimy with black soot.

Ellen felt desolate and her heart was heavy. Somehow the fire seemed unreal, as if it could not have happened. Beautiful, beautiful Hawkes Nest now black, dirty, ugly to behold. She turned and went back out the door and down the cobbled path. She did not look back.

• 8 •

Yancey Hamilton arrived unexpectedly in New York and with him was his niece, Miss Dora Jane Wood.

"Thought I'd give Dora Jane a little change of scenery," explained Yancey as he and the girl entered Peter's office.

Peter had not seen Dora Jane since Christmas Day at Yancey's home. Now as he looked at the girl he thought she seemed less plain than he had remembered. Her figure was trim and neat and her face under the flower-trimmed bonnet was smiling and friendly. Peter long ago had realized he must stop comparing with Margaret every woman he saw.

"I'm pleased to see you again, Mr. Hawke," said Dora Jane.

"My pleasure indeed," Peter responded, bowing slightly. "Won't you sit down?" he added, pulling out a chair from beside his desk.

"I do hope we're not intruding," the girl remarked as she seated herself in the chair "but Uncle Yancey was determined that we see you before we made any further plans."

"Join us for supper tonight, Peter," said Yancey "and tomorrow I want to go over the cargo charts with you."

"Very well," Peter agreed.

There seemed to be no other reply to make. In his usual brusque manner, Yancey had control of the situation and one simply did not refuse him.

The next few days Peter found he had very little time for business since Yancey had extensive plans for entertaining his niece and seemed to include Peter in all that they did. Peter realized, of course, that Yancey would like nothing better than to see Dora Jane married into the Lowell Howard Trading Company and it was becoming obvious that Yancey thought Peter was just the man for his niece.

"You really should be giving some thought to marriage, Mr. Hawke. A man in your position needs a wife and family," Yancey had remarked one evening as they were waiting for Dora Jane to appear for dinner.

"I'm sure you're right, Mr. Hamilton," Peter had responded. But he let the conversation end right there, amused at the look of frustration on Yancey Hamilton's face.

Peter did not find Dora Jane unattractive nor uninteresting. Perhaps she would make him a good wife. She was always pleasant, indicating an even temperament. She spoke softly and she appeared to have genuine interest in Peter's work. He realized that he could do much worse than Dora Jane Wood for a wife. Perhaps he should give marriage some serious thought.

Nevertheless, when Dora Jane and Yancey ended their visit and returned to Boston, Peter found he was somewhat relieved. Now he could get back to work.

Peter sat at his desk in the trading company office with Ellen's letter in his hand. He felt numb with shock. It was only a few weeks since word had come of Lowell Howard's death. Now he read Ellen's letter and then again, trying to grasp the truth of what had happened. His brother and Margaret dead. Hawkes Nest a shambles. He read and re-read the words, unable to believe what he saw on the pages.

Ellen and Reverend Thomas had seen to the funeral,

and William and Margaret were placed next to Peter's sister, Henrietta, in the churchyard at Woodbridge.

"There was much damage to the furnishings from smoke," Ellen had written, "but I moved what I could to the bedrooms upstairs and locked the doors. I don't know how much can be saved. Reverend Thomas told me he would look after things until he hears from you."

Peter decided to send word to Yancey Hamilton as soon as possible because he knew at once that he would have to return to Bristol. Yancey must come to New York to handle the company affairs until Peter reached a decision as to what was best for him to do regarding his position with the company, as well as his responsibility to William's son.

The child now was Lowell Howard's sole heir and Peter was the baby's only relative. Legal arrangements would have to be made with respect to the child, the house in Bristol, the trading company, and what remained of Hawkes Nest. Of course the land still had value and perhaps the house could be rebuilt.

Peter knew he would have to wait until Yancey's arrival in New York before he could hope to start the long voyage back to England. Since he would be unable to take the first ship leaving New York harbor, he put a letter aboard for Ellen, advising her of his plans. Peter's letter crossed the Atlantic and reached Ellen two weeks before he was due to arrive in Bristol.

Christmas was spent at sea and Peter found it a far cry from the previous Christmas Day at Yancey's Hamilton's in Boston. However, there was no joy in reminiscing. He would be only too glad when the day was over.

On January 7th the packet *Sea Witch* pulled into the

Bristol Channel and made its way into the harbor. The day was cold and shadowed by heavy black clouds, threatening rain at any moment. As the ship drew close to the dock, Peter saw Lowell Howard's black carriage with its pair of matched greys and he remembered Margaret stepping down in her blue velvet cloak and bonnet. The memory of that day had never left him. Now he realized it must be Ellen in the carriage come to meet him.

Peter felt an eagerness to see her. He was surprised that he had such a longing for Ellen's warmth and gentleness, though he realized she had been in his thoughts many times during the long voyage from New York. In fact, in thinking over the past, Peter remembered that whenever he had been most lonely it was Ellen who had come to his mind, even over his desire and passion for Margaret, probably because he knew Margaret never could be his wife and he must put her out of his mind.

Lines from the ship were caught and made fast. Soon he would disembark. Peter glanced toward the black carriage again and saw the door opening. Then Ellen appeared. She was all in black, mourning his family of course. He waved his hand, trying to gain her attention, and as she sighted him they hurried towards each other.

"Oh, Mr. Hawke!" cried Ellen, and she began to sob, causing inquiring glances from other passengers and people on the dock.

Peter put his arms about her, patting her gently on the back.

"Dear Ellen," he said softly.

She reached for a handkerchief in her small reticule and then raised her head to look at Peter.

"I'm sorry, Mr. Hawke. Forgive me. I surely must have embarrassed you."

"Nonsense. On the contrary, I appreciate your concern. Now please don't cry anymore," said Peter, reassuringly.

As they walked towards the carriage, each became very aware of the other. Ellen thought Peter seemed so much bigger, more filled out and more mature. Very much like William had been. Peter saw that Ellen had developed into a very pretty woman, one people looked at with admiration as they made their way through the crowd on the dock.

"Where's the child?" he asked, suddenly.

"At Mr. Howard's. With the housekeeper, Mary."

"Come along then, it's starting to rain. I see you have the carriage," Peter remarked.

"Yes, Sir. Mary said I must use it, especially since it was you arriving," Ellen explained.

The rain began coming down heavily as they rode towards Seagull's Point.

Mary was looking out the parlor window when they arrived. She hurried to the door so they would not get unduly wet waiting on the stoop.

"Oh, Mr. Hawke, it's a real pleasure to see you," said Mary, offering her hand for his hat and gloves.

"Come into the library and I'll have a nice cup of tea for you. That'll warm you up all right," she continued.

This was only the second time Peter had been in Seagull's Point since William and Margaret's wedding day. The house now seemed darker and quieter as if conscious of the sudden tragedies which had come to the family.

"Is Henry awake?" asked Ellen.

"Not yet, but I'll bring him in soon as you've had your tea," Mary replied.

Peter and Ellen went down the corridor to the library. Mary had lighted the lamps and a bright fire was burning in the grate. As Ellen seated herself near the fire Peter noticed her hair was the same bright gold he had remembered and her rosy cheeks still gave a glow to her face. The black silk dress she wore was most becoming to her fair skin.

She turned towards him, suddenly aware that he was looking at her. He smiled and Ellen's heart beat faster in her breast. Nothing had changed for her so far as Peter was concerned. She still was deeply in love with him. How could he not know, she wondered.

Mary appeared with the tea tray and set it down in front of Ellen.

"Oh, thank you, Mary. How nice."

Ellen handed Peter a cup of tea. He had not yet asked her anything about William or Margaret or the fire and she began to wonder if he did not want to discuss what had happened. She waited, but he remained silent. Finally, Ellen spoke.

"I think you might be pleased to know that Mr. Barnes kept duplicate records for Lowell Howard, so everything is in order regarding the shipping company and the other property," she said.

"That is a relief indeed," Peter responded quickly.

He looked at her long and intently. Why was he doing that, she asked herself as she felt her face flushing.

"How can I ever thank you, Ellen, for all you have done?"

"There's no need. I'm sure anyone would have done the same."

"I don't think so," Peter replied, thoughtfully.

"You know," he continued, "I thought a great deal about you while I was on the ship coming back here. I kept remembering the first day you came to Hawkes Nest. I answered the door and you said you had an appointment with William. You were so nervous, do you remember that?"

"Indeed I do," Ellen responded, similing faintly.

"Then when I offered you a ride back to Mr. Crowley's you seemed so afraid of me. Were you?"

"Oh no, Sir. I was—well, very shy I guess."

"Do you want to tell me about the fire?" Peter asked, suddenly changing the subject.

"If you want me to," Ellen replied.

Peter nodded, his face now sober and unsmiling.

"It seemed to have started in the workroom, from a lamp apparently. Mr. Hawke had been working late, I guess, and had forgotten to put out the wick. Doesn't seem like him though. Anyway, as near as anyone can tell, Mrs. Hawke went to find him after she left the baby out on the grass at the front of the house. Some beams fell from the ceiling and they both were hit and knocked to the floor. The roof fell in then and the heavy thatch helped to smother the fire." Ellen explained, her voice catching with emotion as she spoke. "It all happened so fast, Mr. Hawke, and I don't think they suffered a great deal."

Ellen wiped her eyes with her handkerchief. Peter did not speak.

Mary entered the room just then with the baby, his tiny hands flailing the air. She handed him to Ellen who held him gently in her arms. Peter put his cup down and moved closer to Ellen to look at the child.

"So you are Henry Lowell Hawke," said Peter, looking down at the baby.

"He has your blue eyes," Ellen remarked. "Like yours and your mother's," she added quickly.

Ellen never blamed Peter for loving Margaret. She was jealous and unhappy at first, but she felt no man could be blamed for succumbing to a woman with Margaret's beauty. In fact, now it seemed to have been inevitable, living together in the same house.

Peter had taken no notice of her words. She could have no knowledge of his and Margaret's love for each other, he thought.

"What am I going to do about him, Ellen?" he asked, solemnly, taking the child's tiny hand in his own.

249

Ellen's eyes were full of love as she looked at Peter and he stared at her, almost as if seeing her for the first time. Ellen's heart was beating so fast she dared not speak. She did not trust her own voice. Peter must know, she thought, he must.

"Will you go with me to Woodbridge, Ellen?" he asked. I want to see the house and find out what can be done."

"If you want me to, Sir," Ellen replied.

"There's so much to do all at once, Ellen, I feel somewhat overwhelmed. We shall have to talk with Mr. Barnes too about the property and the shipping company."

Ellen noticed his use of the word "we" as he spoke, including her in his plans. No doubt he was quite unaware of having spoken in just that way.

"I think we'd better see Mr. Barnes tomorrow, if possible, and plan to take the coach to Woodbridge on Thursday," Peter continued. "Could Mary keep the child, do you think?" he added.

"I'm quite sure of that," Ellen replied. "She adores him."

Peter knew that returning to Woodbridge was going to be a difficult experience. With Margaret and William both gone and the house and land he loved in a disastrous state, there could be little joy in going back to the village. Nevertheless, he had to see for himself. Either he could rebuild the house or sell the land to someone who might raze the remains of Hawkes Nest and start over.

As the coach neared Woodbridge, Peter looked anxiously out the window. Ellen sensed his apprehension.

"It's not a total loss, Sir," she said. "Many things are still there. The trees, the roses, most of the front part of the house."

He nodded his head but did not speak.

The coach swayed to a stop and Peter helped Ellen descend to the road. Together they started up the cobbled path towards the house. Neither spoke. Now the blackened timbers of the kitchen and the workroom could be seen protruding from under the heavy thatch roof which had fallen to smother the flames.

Ellen trembled suddenly and looked at Peter. His jaw was stiffened and he had clasped his hands behind his back. He stood motionless, just staring at the blackened house.

"How sad for them," he said, finally.

Then he turned to Ellen.

"Well, shall we see what can be done?"

"Reverend Thomas has the keys to the front bedrooms. That's where everything is stored," said Ellen.

"Very well, I'll walk down and get them. You can wait here if you like. Or perhaps you want to come and see some of the folks in the shops."

Ellen shook her head.

"No, I'll just wait here. There's still a bench in the garden. I can sit there."

"I'll be back as soon as possible and I'll see about getting rooms at The Bell for night," Peter remarked.

"But I still have my cottage, Sir," Ellen said quickly. "I did not give it up to go to Bristol."

"Of course. I think of you so much a part of Hawkes Nest that I had forgotten you had the cottage."

Ellen smiled at him but made no further comment. Watching Peter disappear down the path, Ellen realized in that moment that she actually was enjoying herself and she had no right to under the circumstances. Two people were dead, a lovely house was badly damaged, Peter had lost his brother, and a child was left without parents. How could she sit there and feel almost happy. Ellen knew it was only because she had Peter to herself.

For the first time since their picnic in the garden almost two years ago, she had Peter alone.

Believing that he would remain in America, she had given up hope of ever seeing him again. Now that he was here to talk to, listen to, be close to, she hardly could believe it was really happening. If only she could make Peter love her as she did him. If only she knew the way.

As Ellen sat looking at the half-burned house she thought of the many things she could do to help Peter if he would only let her. She wondered what he would say if she suggested helping him with the house and caring for baby Henry. He surely needed someone and she was already there. Maybe she should just gather up her courage and come right out and ask him. Still, she did have pride and such an arrangement could only bring her more frustration, she decided.

Peter was a long time in returning, but Ellen guessed that everyone he saw in the village would stop to speak to him and of course she was right. Most of all, they were curious about America, and they wanted to know if he had come back to Woodbridge to stay.

When Peter finally returned to Hawkes Nest he was very apologetic to Ellen.

"I'm really sorry to have been so long. You must have become chilled sitting out here," he said.

"A little, but I'm quite all right," Ellen responded, getting to her feet.

"I've made arrangements for us to have supper at The Bell," Peter stated as they went into the house.

Even the recent rains had not covered up the strong smell of smoke and ashes in the rooms. Ellen's eyes filled with tears as she recalled the awful scene of the fire all over again.

The sight appeared even worse to Peter than he had imagined. His eyes wandered about the rooms as he and Ellen walked through the house. The rain and dampness since the fire had given everything a gloomy, depressing appearance and the smell of smoke and mildew and charred wood was most unpleasant.

"It's hard to recognize the place, isn't it?" Peter said, finally.

"Yes, Sir," Ellen replied, her voice soft. "But it's a bit better upstairs," she added.

Unlocking the door to his own bedroom, Peter recalled vividly the night Margaret had come to him, passionately beautiful, warm and loving. Now the room was piled with goods salvaged from the rest of the house.

"Reverend Thomas and I put as much in here as we could and the rest in Mr. William's room," Ellen explained. "There was more space in here since you had taken most of your things," she continued.

The light of day was beginning to fade as they moved on into William and Margaret's room, adding to the despair Peter was feeling. He went down on one knee by the large blanket chest at the foot of the bed and raised the lid. The chest was empty, but still had a faint smell of lavender.

"What happened to the things that were in here?" he asked.

"I put all of Mrs. Hawkes clothes in with Mr. William's in the trunks in the spare room, Sir," Ellen replied. "This had no lock."

"I see." said Peter, closing the chest.

"Everything smelled of smoke, Sir, so I had to hang the clothes out in the air for a while. I don't think it's so noticeable anymore."

"I think we'd better leave now, Ellen. It's getting dark and we can come back in the morning," Peter said, his voice sounding tired.

As they started down the stairs, Peter remarked that Ellen might as well have Margaret's clothes.

"You can make good use of them, I'm sure, Ellen."

"Oh, Sir, they're much too fine. Where would I wear them?" Ellen responded.

"Just wear them for whatever you do."

Ellen laughed heartily, and her voice seemed to echo in the house.

"My, I'd be the fanciest, most elegant housekeeper in all of England."

Peter saw the humor in that and joined in the laughter.

"Oh, it's good to hear you laugh, Sir," said Ellen.

They looked at each other then for a brief moment, Peter's blue eyes intense. Ellen's heart was pounding as she held his gaze and she felt the color rush to her cheeks.

"Do you know you've become very pretty?" Peter remarked.

Starting down the path, he stopped and looked back. He stared at the house a long time before he spoke.

"You know, Ellen, I don't think it can ever be what it was. Nothing can make it the same. Everything has changed too much. It might be best to sell the land and forget about the house."

"Oh, Sir, do you really think so?"

Ellen's question was almost a wail.

"Yes, what was once here is long gone. I have no more family. I could never carry on William's business now that I'm involved in trade. There's really nothing here, Ellen. I've got to forget what was. Nothing can ever bring back the Hawkes Nest I knew. Nothing."

Peter sounded so certain of what he was saying that Ellen could make no response. Yet she knew that if he did leave Hawkes Nest behind, his need for help from her would be considerably lessened. Still, there was baby Henry. He might be her last chance.

The next morning when Peter and Ellen again went to

254

Hawkes Nest it was clear that Peter meant what he had said about disposing of the house and land.

"I just came from a visit with John Perkins, Ellen, and he is going to handle the matter for me. The land has considerable value, but obviously the house will need a lot done to it. The furniture that is usable will be sent to Bristol in care of Mr. Barnes. Now I want you to pack up all of Margaret's clothes in that big chest in my old room while I gather up what I want of William's and we'll take those things back to Bristol with us on the coach, providing there isn't too big a load already. If so, we'll send in with the furniture.

Peter seemed so definite in his plans that Ellen needed only to follow instructions.

"By the way," Peter went on "thank you for turning the horses over to the people at the Crowley place. They want to buy them."

"It was all I could think of at the time," Ellen responded. "The poor things were panicked at the sight of the fire."

There was such a stillness in the house as Peter and Ellen went through Margaret's and William's personal belongings. Ellen was overwhelmed at the vastness of Margaret's wardrobe and decided there were far too many dresses she could not wear. Margaret had been a smaller person and Ellen felt many of the clothes should be given away. The cloaks and bonnets she could use, and the dressing gowns. If Peter did not object, she would suggest giving the bulk of the clothes to the ladies at the church for them to dispose of among the parishioners. Besides, she could readily imagine how they would cherish something which had been worn by the beautiful Margaret Hawke.

As she walked into the bedroom where Peter was working, Ellen saw that he was sitting motionless on the side of the bed, his head in his hands. She went to him, not speaking, but she put her hands on his shoulders very gently. He leaned forward, clasping her about the waist, drawing her close to him.

His voice was heavy with emotion as he spoke.

"So much was left unsaid, Ellen."

"You must not say that. It's too late to worry about things unsaid. You know you had a fine relationship with your brother and you know how pleased he was that you were doing so well in America. Anything not said is no longer important."

Peter still held onto Ellen and she wished he never would let go. Abruptly, he raised his head and dropped his arms from around her waist.

"Forgive me, Ellen. I should not have lost control of myself like that, but suddenly the enormity of the loss just settled in on me. My family is all gone."

Ellen straightened up and looked directly at him. Peter's eyes fixed on hers and he seemed to be studying her face.

"I'm so glad you're here, Ellen. You are such a help, I can't begin to tell you."

Then he smiled at her and added, "Also, I think it's about time you started calling me Peter. You're my family now."

"You poor stupid man," thought Ellen, "how can you sit there and not see that I love you, that I want to help you?" but she merely replied, "I want to help in any way I can."

Peter stood up, his body close to hers, and he cupped her face in his hands.

"You're very sweet, Ellen."

His voice was gentle as he smiled down at her. Then he dropped his arms and moved away.

"Very well, shall we get on with it?" he said, matter-of-factly.

"He's treating me just like a child," Ellen said to herself.

She explained her idea about most of Margaret's clothes and Peter thought it might be just as well to do the same with William's.

When at last they had finished the sorting and packing, Peter made a statement which was totally unexpected and which caused Ellen to gasp aloud.

He said, "Ellen, how would you like to go to New York?"

Her face had such a startled look that Peter laughed and repeated his question.

"I said, how would you like to go to New York?"

"To America?" Ellen was breathless.

"Yes, I must go back. It's where I want to be now, where my future is. Mr. Barnes can handle the affairs in Bristol. He's been doing it for years anyway, even before Lowell Howard's death. Will you come?"

Ellen's face had turned pale. She felt as if she were about to faint. Her legs seemed weak, as if they could not support her. Peter was staring at her, an amused expression on his face.

"I'm afraid of the ocean," she said, finally. "I'm really afraid to go."

'Is that what concerns you? Is that all?" Peter laughed as he spoke. "Ellen, there's no need to be afraid. We can wait for the *Bristol Cloud*. She's a fine ship which has made many crossings.

Ellen looked at him as if for the first time, observing his handsome features, the curve of his mouth and the brightness of his blue eyes. His long slender arms and legs belied the strength of his body. To be with him was all that mattered to her.

"Will you come?" he asked again, earnestly.

Ellen nodded her head as she spoke.

"Yes, I'll come."

● 9 ●

The next few weeks were like a dream to Ellen. She had gathered up her few belongings from the cottage in Woodbridge and had notified the owner that she was leaving.

Gossipy tongues remarked how strange it was that Peter Hawke was taking her off to America and they not husband and wife.

Ellen really didn't care what anyone thought. She would be near Peter and that was the only thing that mattered. Let them think whatever they liked.

During their stay in Bristol, Ellen saw Peter only at supper. He was away early in the morning and returned at dusk, so involved were the many details regarding the property belonging to Margaret and to his little nephew.

Ellen tried not to think about the long trip on the sea, but she was very frightened at the thought of being out of sight of land for weeks on end. Also, she was afraid of being seasick. Then she would be of no help at all to Peter or to the baby. However, she guessed she could suffer even that to be with Peter.

That evening at supper Peter seemed quite happy and talkative, much like he was at Hawkes Nest when Ellen first became a part of the household.

"Have you ever been to a ball, Ellen?" he asked, suddenly.

"My goodness no," she replied, with a laugh.

"Well, get out your best frock. You're going to one just two nights off."

Peter's eyes were mischievous as he smiled at Ellen, knowing she was truly surprised.

"To a ball? But I don't have a best frock!"

"Of course you do. Wear something of Margaret's. Mary can fix it for you. Just ask her."

"Oh my!"

Ellen was so excited she could not eat another bite of her supper. Her stomach was fluttering inside and she felt a weakness in her knees. Then she looked across the table at Peter, her eyes wide and bright.

"But I don't know how to dance!" she said in dismay.

Peter laughed at her distress.

"You'll learn in no time. It's not all that hard," he said. "Besides, if you're like most women, you'll find it a very pleasant diversion."

The next day Ellen prevailed upon Mary to go through Margaret's dresses from Hawkes Nest and help her find something suitable for a ball. Some of the seams probably would have to be let out a little, Ellen thought, as she and Mary took the carefully folded gowns out of the trunks into which they had been packed.

They agreed on a pale pink silk with dainty embroidered flowers on the bodice and a deep flounce of ivory lace bordering the low neckline.

Ellen suddenly remembered the pink dress she had worn at the party in the garden at Hawkes Nest when William Hawke had introduced Margaret to his friends and neighbors in Woodbridge. Ellen had made that dress herself and several people commented that the color was most becoming. Even Peter had like it. So of course the pink silk was the correct choice.

Mary fitted and pinned and then let the hem down

259

two inches. She released the seams of the bodice since Ellen was fuller in the bust than Margaret had been. Finally the dress was ready.

The night of the ball Ellen was so nervous her hands were shaking and she had to ask Mary to help her dress. She was unable to fasten the small hooks at the back of the gown and perspiration was running down her face as she struggled. Mary wiped Ellen's cheek with a towel and patted her on the arm.

"Don't be so frightened, Miss Ellen. You're not goin' to a hangin', you know," she said, smiling.

"Oh, I'm so afraid I'll do something to embarrass Mr. Hawke," Ellen replied.

"Nonsense!" You'd better settle down now. No gentleman wants to take a lady out who's shining with sweat! Just sit down here and quiet yourself while I fix up your hair."

"Oh, thank you, Mary. I don't think I could manage without you tonight."

Ellen finally relaxed while Mary brushed and curled and fastened her hair up with some pink silk ribbons and flowers.

"Now just look at yourself," said Mary, obviously pleased with her handiwork.

Ellen stood up and walked over to the mirror. She scarcely could believe the image reflected back to her. She looked so pretty, really pretty. Not beautiful like Margaret, she said to herself, but prettier than she had ever thought she could be. Now Ellen felt cool and calm and was ready to go downstairs and face Peter.

He was in the library, standing with his back to the fire. He heard Ellen's footsteps and then she appeared in the doorway. Peter stared at her. When he did not speak, Ellen became anxious.

"Is something wrong?" she asked nervously.

"On the contrary. You look lovely, Ellen."

He walked towards her.

"Do you have a cloak?" he asked.

"Yes, it's in the corridor," she replied, turning from the door.

Mary was watching them as they prepared to leave.

"Doesn't Miss Ellen look beautiful?" she asked, her face beaming with satisfaction.

"Indeed she does, Mary," Peter replied.

Settled down inside Lowell Howard's carriage, Ellen asked Peter if they could just watch the dancing right at first before she tried it herself.

"If you like," he replied, "but I'm sure you'll do very well. I'll not scold you anyway if you step on my foot."

Peter was teasing her and Ellen turned to him with a smile. His face became solemn then and Ellen wondered why he looked at her with such a serious expression. She didn't know that Peter was disturbed at the unexplained emotion he was feeling towards her. She seemed so warm and thoughtful and he also was aware of her softness and femininity. She looked so lovely in the pink dress and the brown velvet cloak with its soft fur collar nestling against her chin.

When they reached the Imperial Hotel where the ball was being held, Ellen found that Peter had many acquaintances there and she was thankful that none of them knew who she really was.

It was some time before Ellen was willing to try a dance. She had watched the other dancers, noticing every step. It looked rather complicated she thought, but Peter had seemed so sure she would have no trouble. Now they joined the other couples out on the floor. Sometimes they faced each other, sometimes they were side by side, and sometimes they circled about. Ellen was enjoying herself tremendously and she had made no serious mistakes. Peter was very helpful in directing her. It wasn't long before some of the other gentlemen asked her to dance and Ellen knew she never had had such a glorious evening.

When she and Peter finally left in the carriage to return to Seagull's Point, Ellen was truly exhausted. She heaved a sigh and wriggled her feet out of her slippers.

Peter laughed as he spoke to her.

"The dancing did you in, did it?"

"Oh, it was wonderful, just wonderful, but I feel as if I could go to sleep right here!" Ellen exclaimed.

"Well, I'm glad you had such a good time. For your first ball, I'd say you did very well."

"It was lovely and I do thank you so much for taking me. It was most kind of you."

Ellen knew that Peter could have asked any number of girls in Bristol. In fact, she wondered why he had not.

When they reached the house Peter helped Ellen out of the carriage and they went up on the walk. Mary had not yet gone to bed and she was quick to open the door.

"A lovely ball was it?" she smiled as she spoke to Ellen.

"Oh yes, wonderful!" Ellen responded enthusiastically.

Mary turned towards Peter.

"There's a fire in the library, Sir. I thought you might like some hot chocolate."

"I think some sherry might be more to my liking, Mary, but I can manage. Thank you. You may go along to bed."

"Very well, Sir. Good night then."

Ellen was getting out of her cloak and was about to start up the stairway when Peter turned towards her.

"Won't you join me?" he asked.

He took the cloak from her arm and laid it on the settee. Ellen followed him to the library. She went over to the fire to warm her hands while he poured the sherry into two small crystal glasses.

262

"Are you still frightened about leaving England?" Peter asked as he handed her the wine.

"Not of leaving England, Peter. Just of being on the sea."

Peter noticed that her cheeks were flushed with color and he didn't know if it was from the firelight or the sherry. Whichever it was, she looked very desirable and suddenly he felt he would like to take her in his arms and kiss her. It had been several months since he had made love to a woman and his eyes could not help but linger on the full curves of Ellen's breasts and the smooth softness of her arms. Still, he wondered if she would be offended. She was, after all, in his employ, his housekeeper. That could cause some future problems. So he refrained from touching her. He finished the wine and set the empty glass on the table.

"Perhaps we should call it a night," he said, bending down to spread the coals in the grate.

"Yes, I'm feeling quite tired," Ellen responded. "Thank you again for the ball. I shall never forget it. Goodnight, Peter."

She walked quickly out of the room so that Peter could not see the tears of frustration welling up in her eyes.

The remaining hours of the night seemed unduly long to Ellen. She was unable to sleep even though she felt very tired. She tossed and turned restlessly in the bed, knowing it was because she wanted Peter's love so desperately.

Lately he seemed to look at her with a different expression in his eyes. Ellen felt that perhaps he did find her attractive after all. At least he had made no mention of anyone in America. So far as Ellen knew, Peter was not yet betrothed. Until that happened, she guessed there was still reason to hope. Yet, sometimes she wondered if any man could be worth the frustration and

263

anxiety and emptiness she felt in her relationship with Peter. Why should loving someone be so miserable?

The big clock on the stair landing struck five and Ellen knew it soon would be daylight. She punched the pillows hard with her fist and closed her eyes tightly, trying to shut out Peter and everything connected with him.

● 10 ●

The *Bristol Cloud* had arrived in port and Peter left the house early the next morning to go to the docks and meet with the Captain of the ship and with Mr. Barnes.

When Ellen came downstairs she found Mary in the kitchen feeding the baby, who seemed to be thriving on the woman's care.

"I must know everything you're giving him, Mary, and any advice will be most helpful. I'll be so frightened if he should become sick on the voyage," said Ellen.

"He'll take to the sea like it was a rockin' cradle. Don't you be worryin', Miss Ellen."

"I hope you're right."

The old woman thought Ellen looked rather sad and worried and she wondered if maybe the girl was having second thoughts about leaving.

"Is somethin' botherin' you, Miss?" she asked, quietly.

Ellen had poured herself a cup of tea and was seated at the kitchen table, staring out the window.

"Sometimes I'm not sure I should be going to New York at all," she remarked.

Mary studied the girl's face for a considerable time before she spoke.

"You know he ought to be marryin' you, don't you?" she said, matter-of-factly.

Ellen's eyes opened wide in surprise.

"You know it's true all the same. It just don't look

right takin' a young girl into a man's home and them not married. Besides, anyone can see how much you love him.

Ellen was greatly embarrassed by that remark and hid her face in her hands.

"Now, Miss Ellen," Mary went on "I'm not blind. He's fond o' you all right. You know that too. But sometimes men don't see what's right in front o' them. Always lookin' 'round for somethin' else."

"I don't know what to do, Mary," said Ellen.

She was trying hard to control the tears which glistened in her eyes.

"I'll tell you one thing. Even though I've remained a maiden lady, I've noticed a lot of peculiar things about men. Seems like the more a woman does or knows, the less they like her. Maybe you're just too ready and willin' to help Mr. Hawke. You don't give him a chance to do somethin' for you."

"But he's taking me to America, Mary!"

"Nonsense. That's not for you. That's for him. He needs you for the baby. How could he manage, I ask you? That's why I say he ought to marry you."

"But he doesn't love me."

"Rubbish! You're a very pretty girl and you're capable too. What more could he want?"

Suddenly Ellen laughed, long and heartily.

"Just listen to us!" she exclaimed. "Anyway, Mary, you do make me feel better."

"Mind what I said now," Mary went on. "Give him a chance to do somethin' for you."

Sailing day for the *Bristol Cloud* came up brisk and clear. They sky was cloudless and the wind blew fresh and not too strong. People milled about the docks, as was always the case on the day a ship sailed or docked.

Peter and Ellen and the baby Henry were at dockside

early to be certain all their belongings were put aboard ship.

Mary had said her goodbyes at Seagull's Point, fearing she would become too upset watching them actually leave the harbor and knowing it was unlikely she would ever set eyes on them again. She would be staying on in the house until Peter and Mr. Barnes decided what to do with it. In any event, Mary was to be taken care of.

Ellen looked unusually pretty in Margaret Hawke's brown cloak and velvet bonnet. Her blonde hair curled out from under the bonnet and lay soft against her cheeks which were pink and glowing, both from the cool air and the excitement she felt at starting the long voyage to America.

Peter suddenly saw Ellen in a new light. Holding the baby in her arms, she appeared very young and vulnerable. He realized in that instant that here were two people he was responsible for, two people who were depending on him for their safety and care. He looked down at Ellen as he stood beside her, waiting to board the ship.

"Still frightened?" he asked.

"Yes," Ellen replied. "Somehow I thought the ship would be bigger."

Standing a few feet away from Ellen and Peter was Ross MacNeil, a stocky, sandy-haired Scotsman, carpenter by trade. He had been watching Ellen intently. With the baby in her arms, it was natural to assume she and the tall man next to her were husband and wife. Still, there seemed to be an aloofness about the man and a somewhat reticent attitude on the girl's part which made him wonder what the arrangement might really be. He thought Peter almost too handsome, too self-confident, too self-assured. With almost five weeks at sea, Ross MacNeil was certain to find out all he wanted to know about the two of them. He still was staring at

Ellen when suddenly she turned towards him, becoming aware that someone was watching her.

Ellen's brown eyes were steady as she looked at him. She neither smiled nor frowned. Ross MacNeil bowed slightly and smiled at her.

"Do you know that man?" Peter asked, noticing MacNeil's obvious interest in Ellen.

"No, but he seems to think he knows me," Ellen replied, and she gave a faint smile to the stranger.

Peter glanced at Ross, curiously.

"I've never seem him before," he remarked, dismissing the incident.

He then put his hand at Ellen's elbow.

"Come, we can get aboard now."

Ross MacNeil stepped aside to let them pass, and again his eyes followed Ellen's every move.

"Why does he stare at me like that?" she asked herself.

Since Peter was familiar with the ship, he led directly to their quarters below deck. Ellen was dismayed to find how small and airless the cabin was where she and the baby were to stay, but she said nothing. There was one tiny porthole to let in light. Peter was quick to see her distress.

"I think you'd better move into my cabin, Ellen. It's a bit larger and I can come in here," he suggested.

"Oh no, Peter, I couldn't take yours. This will be quite all right," Ellen remarked.

"No, it won't do at all. You need more space with the baby. We'll just switch things around."

Peter seemed determined to make the change, so Ellen kept silent. She suddenly remembered what Mary had said to her.

"Let him do somethin' for *you*."

Well, Ellen thought, this was a beginning.

● 11 ●

The first few days at sea were fairly calm and the ship maintained a steady speed in the brisk wind. So far, the motion of the ship had not bothered Ellen as she had expected it would. However, she liked to be on deck as much as possible, for the fresh air.

There were only seven other passengers besides Ellen and Peter, but the ship was heavily loaded with cargo, indicating a handsome profit for the shipping company.

The detail of the goods on board kept Peter in his cabin with the necessary paper work, and Ellen saw him only briefly and at mealtimes. However, she knew he couldn't be working on papers for the entire voyage. In a few more days he should be caught up and would have more time to talk with her about America, and New York in particular.

"I shall have to find a house," he had said. "Perhaps I should build another Hawkes Nest."

"Oh, wouldn't that be wonderful!" Ellen had exclaimed, excitedly.

Peter chuckled then.

"I spoke in jest, Ellen. I could never do that. Besides it wouldn't be the same in a place like New York. Not the same at all."

So the subject was dropped and now Ellen didn't know what he had in mind.

They had made Ross MacNeil's acquaintance the first day out of Bristol. He was travelling alone, having left his home in Glasgow, and hoped to set up shop in New York or Philadelphia as a carpenter. Probably ten years older than Peter, he was a widower. Ellen thought him very pleasant and she enjoyed listening to his Scottish brogue.

Ross was pleased with himself for having guessed correctly that Peter and Ellen were not husband and wife. It was Ellen who had explained the situation to him and about the orphaned baby who was Peter's nephew and sole relative. They had been talking one morning when Peter was at work in his cabin.

"You seem a very young lass to be leavin' your home for so distant a land," Ross remarked.

"Not really. I'm twenty-two. Besides, I have no family either," Ellen replied.

Her smooth rosy skin and wide-eyed expression gave Ellen a youthful innocence that Ross found most appealing. He was enjoying her company immensely and already looked forward to seeing her each day.

After two weeks at sea Ellen had settled into a routine. With breakfast for herself and Henry out of the way, she would take the baby on deck for a while. There she would find Ross MacNeil and they would discuss the weather and the prospects for the day, and Ross would play with the baby and tell Ellen more about Scotland. She enjoyed these interludes very much.

"You seem to love Scotland so much, I'm surprised you are leaving," said Ellen one day.

"Well, with me lass gone, I find no joy there. So I decide to go. New land, new work," he explained, simply.

It was on deck under a grey, overcast sky that Peter found them talking. The wind was quite cold now and the air full of mist.

"Don't you think it's a bit damp out here for Henry?" Peter asked Ellen, taking no notice of Ross.

"But it seems so stuffy below," Ellen replied.

She saw at once that Peter was irritated about something and she quickly got to her feet, pulling the blanket closer about the child.

"Perhaps you're right. I'd best go inside," she said.

"We can talk later, Miss Davis," said Ross, ignoring Peter.

Peter followed Ellen and the baby to their cabin.

"If I've done something to displease you, Peter, I'm sorry," said Ellen, noticing the stern expression on Peter's face, something quite unusual for him.

"You haven't," said Peter "but I wonder if it's wise to spend so much time with Mr. MacNeil. We know nothing at all about him."

"He seems very nice to me, and I think he's lonely. Besides, those Germans never speak and I couldn't understand them anyway."

"Those Germans" were the other passengers on board, a family headed for Philadelphia.

A smile crossed Peter's face, much to Ellen's relief.

"You're right, Ellen. I don't know what came over me. Too much mucking about the figures I guess. Let's forget I ever mentioned Mr. MacNeil," said Peter.

The days passed with a dull sameness, except that each day the ship was becoming more odorous and unpleasant. Ellen found it increasingly difficult to keep the baby clean and she wished there was more water. Her hair felt sticky from the salt spray and the bedclothes seemed damp and musty. There were barrels of water, augmented by rain, which were shared by everyone on board, but it was never as much as Ellen would have liked.

Then in the fourth week there was a drastic change in the weather. The sky became so dark and ominous it was as if day and night were the same. The ocean swells were deeper and closer together, causing the ship to heel perilously from side to side. Going out on deck now was impossible. Everything was lashed down and lifelines were stretched fore and aft to protect any crewman from being washed overboard by the heavy seas.

Giant waves began to collide, sending spume in the air like clouds of smoke. Wind howled through the rigging and the ship creaked and groaned as it struggled through the storm. The cold was piercing as the rain turned to sleet and then snow.

Ellen was plainly terrified. Her body was shaking, both from fear and from the cold. She sat on the bunk wrapped in one of Margaret Hawke's wool cloaks, the baby next to her, bundled in blankets. Sleep was impossible, as well as eating. Her stomach felt so contracted from fear that she could not have swallowed a mouthful anyway.

"Ellen?" Peter called as he knocked at her door.

She sprang to her feet to let him in. As she did so, the ship gave a great lurch, throwing her into Peter's arms. She clung to him like a frightened child and began to cry.

"We're all going to die," she wailed.

Peter held her close, pushing against the door with his back to shut it behind him.

"No, we're not, Ellen. We'll be all right. I've been in storms before and so has the *Bristol Cloud*. She's a taut ship." Peter spoke reassuringly.

He released her and she again sat down on the bunk, still trembling. The baby was blissfully asleep, unmindful of all that was going on around him.

Peter never had seen Ellen's face so pale, nor her eyes so large. The golden hair had become unpinned and was hanging in curls and tangles about her neck and shoulders. He thought she looked lovely, even with her frightened, tear-stained face.

"Will you stay with me?" she asked, her voice tremulous.

272

"Of course, Ellen, if it will make you feel better."

Peter smiled down at her troubled face and felt a very real tenderness and sympathy towards her as she spoke.

The ship heeled sharply again and Ellen reached for Peter with both arms as she cried out in terror.

They sat close together on the narrow bed, Peter holding her tightly, trying to quiet her shaking body. As frightened as she was, Ellen didn't know if her trembling was due to the fierceness of the storm or to the fact that Peter was holding her in his arms. She could feel the hardness of his muscles through his coat and for the first time in hours she relaxed and her body became less tense. Peter felt this and gave her a gentle squeeze.

"Feeling better?" he asked, looking down at her.

Ellen raised her head and her face was very close to his. Then suddenly his mouth was on hers and she felt a tingling race through her body. It was a sensation she never had experienced before and she gasped for breath when he finally raised his lips from her soft mouth.

"Forgive me," said Peter. "I should not have done that."

"I didn't mind. Really I didn't," Ellen responded, looking directly at Peter as she spoke.

His eyes never left hers and he still kept his arms about her.

"You're very sweet, you know. I can see why Mr. MacNeil is so taken by you," Peter remarked.

"Do you think he is?" Ellen asked.

"You know very well he is."

For a few brief moments the storm had been forgotten. Ellen had ceased to notice the rolling and creaking of the ship. She almost wished it would go on and on just so Peter would stay with her and hold her in his arms.

Peter was pleasantly surprised when he kissed Ellen. He didn't really know why he had done it in the first place except she seemed so soft and helpless as she leaned against him. She had needed him at the time and he found that comforting her gave him an unexpected pleasure too. He wanted to kiss her again.

"You should try to get some sleep," he said, getting to his feet. "I think the storm is beginning to slacken."

The ship did seem to be rolling less heavily and the wind was no longer shrieking as it had been for several hours.

"I'm sure we're through the worst of it, Ellen. You try to rest now and if you need me I'll be in my cabin," Peter continued, and then he was gone.

Ellen did lie down on the bunk but sleep was the farthest thing from her mind. She thought about Peter's kiss and the tingling sensation returned over her body. Instead of being tired as she had every reason to be, she felt strangely exhilarated. Peter had kissed her at last and now she could only wait with anticipation, hoping it would happen again. She wondered if he could have felt the same excitement as she.

● 12 ●

When Peter returned to his cabin he felt certain that he must be in love with Ellen. Holding her in his arms and kissing her had been the most pleasant thing that had happened to him in a very long time. He had felt passion towards her and a strong desire. He loved her and wanted her.

For a brief moment he thought of returning to her cabin to talk with her. Peter was surprised at what was happening to him.

Lying on the bunk, always too short for his long legs, he began to realize that he must have been in love with Ellen for a long while and never knew it until now. Certainly she had been in his thoughts much of the time since he left Hawkes Nest, but with Margaret in the back of his mind and his passionate feelings towards her, he could not see what was happening to him. How foolish he had been to have wasted all those months. Ellen could have been with him in America all along.

He suddenly remembered Yancey Hamilton's words to him before he left New York.

"You should have a wife, Hawke, and a family. Make your place in the town."

And Ellen had been there all the time. Sweet, gentle Ellen. How could he have been such a blind fool?

Peter got to his feet and walked back to Ellen's cabin. He knocked lightly on the door and called her name There was no answer. She must have fallen asleep, he decided, and after knocking again with no response he returned to his own bed.

The next morning the sun was shining. Whitcaps dotted the sea as remnants of the storm, but the remaining clouds were high and scattered.

Ross MacNeil and Ellen were standing close by the railing of the ship.

"That was a bit of a blow," he remarked. "Were you frightened?"

"Indeed I was!" Ellen exclaimed. "I'd just as soon not see the likes of that again."

"We should have fair weather now the rest of the way," Ross remarked.

"I certainly hope so," said Ellen, although she couldn't imagine how he could know anymore about the weather than she did. He never had crossed the Atlantic before either.

"Where would you be stayin' in New York?" asked Ross, changing the subject abruptly.

"I really don't know. Mr. Hawke hasn't said, except he did say he'd have to find a house."

"I'd be most pleased to see you in New York, Miss Davis," said Ross, quietly.

Ellen turned towards him, somewhat surprised.

"I thought you were going to Philadelphia," she said.

"I have no definite arrangements yet. I might even settle in New York," Ross replied. "Could I see you there?"

Ellen was flattered by his attention and interest, but didn't know quite know what to say to him.

"It's possible, Mr. MacNeil, but I don't know where I'll be or how you could find me," she replied.

"I could find you right enough. Mr. Hawke bein' an officer of the tradin' company, they'd know where he was."

Ellen laughed at his assumption.

"Very well, Mr. MacNeil."

Peter was not unaware of the attention Ross MacNeil was bestowing on Ellen, nor of the laughter and camaraderie between them. Now as he came on deck and saw them again in conversation he made up his mind in that instant that he must speak to Ellen.

"Ellen, could you come to my cabin, please?" he asked as he approached her and Ross MacNeil.

She looked somewhat startled and wondered what Peter could have on his mind concerning her that could not wait. Ellen followed Peter below deck and he held the door open to his cabin so she could enter. She turned to face him. She had managed to get enough water to wash her hair and it hung loose and shining about her neck and face. Her eyes were bright and clear as she looked at Peter. The bodice of her dress fitted snugly over her rounded breasts and now she clasped her hands together waiting for him to speak. Peter thought she was truly adorable.

"Ellen, I'm in love with you and I want you to marry me."

Ellen could hardly believe what she had heard. She had waited so long for those very words, hoping against hope that they would one day be said. Now she was speechless. She just stared at Peter in astonishment.

"Did you hear what I said? Do you think you could love me?" Peter asked when she did not speak.

Ellen's face broke into a broad smile and her eyes were twinkling as she moved towards him, putting her arms up around his neck.

"Oh yes, I think I could, Peter. I really think I could."

Peter held her tightly against his chest and kissed her long and hard, feeling the softness of her body close to his.

Ellen experienced a rapture she never had known and she surrendered fully to Peter, surprising him with the intensity of her response.

"I do love you, Ellen. Perhaps I have for a long time and didn't realize it," said Peter as he released her.

Ellen was incredulous at the thought. She had found the way to make Peter love her and she didn't even know when or where it had happened. Men, she thought to herself, were indeed strange and unpredictable creatures at best. And Peter most of all.

She tightened her arms about his neck, her lips barely touching his, so softly. Her happiness was something she doubted he ever could know or understand.

"I love you, Peter, love you, love you," she whispered.

Peter looked down at her upturned face and as he clasped her even more tightly against him he knew how very much he wanted this girl.

"Ellen, my darling. How could I not have known long ago? I do love you so and nothing can separate us now. Nothing."

Peter kissed her again, long and tenderly. When he released her, Ellen looked up at him and touched his face with her hand.

"Peter, couldn't we build another Hawkes Nest? Please, couldn't we?" she asked, plaintively.

He smiled at her as he realized she was serious in her request. Then he hugged her again, as if she were a little girl.

"Of course, Ellen, if that's what you really want. We'll build a Hawkes Nest on the finest piece of land we can find and it can be just what you want it to be."

And so Ellen Davis would someday soon be Peter's wife and the mistress of a Hawkes Nest just as she had always dreamed.

MISTRESS OF GLORY
Lorinda Hagen

BT51279 $1.95
Historical Romance

The glory that was Greece was on the wane, but for one last moment it shone again. Alcibiades and Timandra—their love for each other was the force that drove them in their epic struggle to regain the Golden Age of Athens. It was a passion that shaped the world!

SAVAGE PASSAGE
Gardner Fox

BT51270 $1.95
Historical Romance

In the middle of the nineteenth century, the New World was the magnet for the hopeful ones of Europe—there they could find a new life, a new freedom, new love. But first they must find—and survive—passage across the Atlantic on a sailing ship whose crew recognized no law but its own desires. From the moment they board the *Dreadnought,* the immigrants are committed to whatever the future may hold, and there is no way to turn back. Through the perils of storms and their own conflicting passions, they must still face a band of desperate mutineers. The chemistry when passengers and crew meet makes for explosive passions!

FAREWELL TO THEE
Marian Forrester

BT51309 $2.25
Historical Romance

Hawaii was a strange new world to Parrie Dobson, but the governess was soon caught up in the life of the island paradise, and its politics. Tyrone Hamilton, her employer's son, became her ally—and her lover. Together they would struggle to restore the glory of ancient Hawaii.

CHARLOTTE　　　　　　　　BT51271 $1.95
Amanda Hart Douglass　　　Historical Romance

Not even New York was immune from the turmoil of the Civil War, and Charlotte Bourne's life was no exception. She loved beneath her station, and she saw her lover march off to war in her brother's place. War and the rules of society said they could never be together—but somehow, somewhere, they would find a way. In the aftermath of the war, suddenly alone, she sought her beloved Liam through all the obstacles which the world could put between them—even her own marriage—until nothing could keep them apart!

UNTAMED HEART　　　　　　BT51321 $1.95
Julia Greene　　　　　　　Historical Romance

Kate Penhallow didn't want love or fame—she wanted to be respectable. Her father's background as a smuggler didn't help, but the money she made in his trade did. She never thought she'd give it up for a man—until she met Beau D'Auberge!

SWEET SINNER　　　　　　BT51330　$1.95
Lorinda Hagen　　　　　　Historical Romance

Julia Bernard was the Queen of the Comstock, the prostitute who became the leading madam—and first citizen—of Virginia City. She led a life that first scandalized, and then earned the respect of, all of the Old West, and she set a pattern for three generations of descendants.

ECSTASY'S CAPTIVE

Nelle McFather

BT51380 $2.50
Historical Romance

Dispossessed, Valentina Cortivanni fled to Venice, where she soon faced a difficult choice—the love of her guardian, D'Angelo, or that of the famous Nicolo Polo. Together they journeyed to Cathay, facing perils from bandits—and betrayal!
Setting: Venice, Asia, 1200's

UNDER CRIMSON SAILS

Lynna Lawton

BT51401 $2.25
Historical Romance

When Ryan Deverel first met Janielle Patterson, he raped her. Each of them tried to escape the destiny that threw them together, but the stormy passion of their first encounter pursued them across an ocean and beyond the law!
Setting: South Carolina, the Caribbean, 1790's

MELLONA

Kathalyn Krause

BT51360 $2.25
Historical Romance

Mellona Jolais had disappeared thirty years earlier, but everyone at the artists' colony agreed that Laurie Mathews could be her double. Even Laurie could not deny the resemblance—especially when she fell in love with the son of Mellona's lover. Laurie had to discover Mellona's secret in order to free herself!
Setting: Mariposa Beach, CA, 1901

THE FLAME OF CHANDRAPORE

Aaron Fletcher

BT51342 $2.25
Historical Romance

Half-English, Half-Indian, Aeysha Owens-Neville was accepted in both worlds but found love in neither. With her mother long dead, when her father and brother were killed in battle she decided to go to her last relatives in England. But before she got there, she would face terrible dangers at sea—and find a man she could love! Setting: India, 1760-90

THE MUSIC ROOM
W.E.D. Ross

BT51223 $1.50

Gothic

Lovely Enid Graham thought she was marrying for love. But when her husband—handsome, brilliant, wealthy Pierre St. John—took her to his lonely chateau, she discovered the real reason for this marriage. She was a bride of fear—wed to terror—and haunted by the terrible secret of the room!

THIRTEEN TOWERS
Celeste Caldwell

BT51286 $1.50

Gothic

Eve Prescott barely knew of the St. Amand Family, but she was a distant relative, and she had to go down to Thirteen Towers to help settle Old Pierre's will. But the family intrigue proved to be more complicated—and more dangerous—than she thought!

POINT VIRTUE
Anne Tedlock Brooks

BT51370 $2.25

Historical Novel

Dr. Sage Harland came to Point Virtue because he believed in healing the sick and protecting the weak. Winthrop Morley was in Point Virtue because he believed in power, wealth, and progress. When Morley tried to bring in the railroad, the battle lines were drawn—and Morley would use any weapon to drive Dr. Harland out of town!

Setting: Oregon Coast, 1880's

JOSEPHINE
Hubert Cole

BT51351 $1.95

Historical Romance

Who was the older woman who captivated General Bonaparte? She started as a girl of no prospects, married the son of a marquis, went to prison during the Revolution—and became Empress of the French. Even after their marriage was anulled, Napoleon depended on her advice. The mysterious Josephine is revealed at last!

LOVE'S DARK CONQUEST
Ralph Hayes

BT51260 $1.95

Novel

From the moment the captive Indian princess first set eyes on the golden-bearded Cortez, she knew her world would never again be the same.

In the name of love, Marina abandoned her people, betrayed her country and desecrated her gods. She gave up everything for her lover, but she began to fear that he was a dangerous and driven man who could never belong to any one woman.

Swept along on the bloody tide of Cortez' assault on the proud and warlike Aztecs, Marina fought an even greater battle with her own rebellious heart.

This book will be foiled.

THE GOLD OF KARINTHY
Diana LaPoint

BT51261 $1.95

Novel

When Maurella Duncan met Imre Karinthy, the darkly handsome Hungarian several years her senior, it was love at first sight. The carefree life they'd planned was drastically altered when Imre was called back to his family home to assume the management of the estate upon the sudden death of his older brother.

Maurella found herself completely lost in an alien world, as she tried to cope with a variety of challenges that were to tax her to the limit of her strength.

The course she chose would mean the difference between life and death for the man she loved.

SWEETER THAN CANDY
Cynthia Wilkerson

BT51290 $1.95

Novel

Roger Sinclair had a lot of nerve, to walk out on Vivian for one of his Columbia students. She promised to get her revenge, even if it meant the sexual destruction of every man in New York!

WORLD IN THE MORNING
Lewis Banci

BT51229 $1.95
Modern Novel

She loved her husband, but she wanted to be free of him—and there was no reasonable way she could explain it. The break-up of their marriage would be hell for both of them, yet she felt it had to be done. He was a good lover and a good father, but that didn't seem to matter. There would be problems for which she didn't have answers, yet she knew there was no turning back. Right or wrong, she had to be her own woman. A fascinating modern novel about a bright, beautiful woman determined to find her true identity.

THE WIDOW
Charity Blackstock

BT51219 $1.95
Novel

Sheila and Tom Armstrong knew each other just well enough to fall deeply in love—and busy, crowded lives left time for little else. Then one terrible day Tom was dead—and Sheila realized she'd married a stranger. Strange memories haunted her, and she knew her only hope for survival lay in the truth about her husband's past—in the place where he was born. But every moment of her journey back seemed to bring her closer to a reality she didn't want to face.

"Highly readable fiction filled with interesting people in an unusual setting."

—*New York Times*

JEANNE
Katharine Howard

BT51331 $1.95
Novel

Suddenly, she was an unmarried woman. The comfortable world Jeanne Oliver had worked so hard to build had been utterly destroyed by her husband's divorcing her. Now she had to start over, meeting new people and proving to herself that she could make her life meaningful!

EVERYTHING HAPPENED
TO SUSAN

BT51221 $1.50

Barry Malzburg

Novel

She came East to become a Broadway star—and became queen of the cheapo skin flicks—and roommate to a sadistic, unpublished writer instead. How to save Susan of the casting couch from obscurity? Well, there was this extravaganza in the planning—the "Ben Hur" of skin flicks—"The Sexual History of The World." A BT Original.

THE THOUSAND FIRES

BT51291 $2.25

Anne Powers

Novel

Napoleon's wars swept across Europe changing its face. The social world was turned upside down, and the unthinkable became real. A love blossomed between a countess of the *ancien regime* and an officer of the upstart Emperor. It was a passion to defy the world!

COME SLOWLY, EDEN

BT51322 $1.75

Charlene Keel

Novel

The roommates—Julie was given everything and wanted nothing but pleasure; Janine had nothing, and wanted an education. For both of them, sex was the way to get what they didn't have. After them, college would never be the same!

THE VELVET BUBBLE

BT51325 $1.75

Alice Winter

Novel

Dorrie's mother is dead, and Dorrie is delighted—now she has Daddy all to herself. But people don't leave them alone, and then Daddy falls in love with the new housekeeper. Dorrie can't let that happen—something has to happen to the housekeeper.

HEROES DIE YOUNG
BT51361 $1.75
Rick Sandford
War

When Jeff Parton got to France he knew nothing about combat, and he figured he was lucky to have battle-hardened Gil Ryder for a buddy. Ryder would teach Parton what he needed to know to stay alive—and sooner or later this education would pay off!

Setting: France, 1944

MISSION INCREDIBLE
BT51346 $1.50
Lawrence Cortesi
War

The five-man crew of the downed B-25 survived the crash, but they were separated. Each one had to fight his way out of the New Guinea jungle alone. And when they got home each one had a different story to tell. Somewhere in those stories was the truth about a Japanese ambush!

Setting: New Guinea, World War II

ESPIONAGE
BT51363 $1.95
William S. Doxey
Spy

The leaks were impossible. The only way the Russians could have gotten the information they had was if they could read minds. James Madderly, parapsychologist, was given an order: Find out if it was true, and, if it was, stop it from happening again!

Setting: London, Finland, Leningrad, contemporary

MAYHEM ON
THE CONEY BEAT
BT51353 $1.75
Michael Geller
Crime

Angel Perez took round one—he had Bud Dugan busted down from detective to patrolman. But Dugan wasn't throwing in the towel yet, and when his ex-partner was found dead—apparently of an overdose of heroin—Dugan was back on the case, with a big reason to nail the heroin kingpin Perez.

ONE OF OUR BOMBERS IS MISSING
Dan Brennan

BT51140 $1.50
Novel

A searing graphic account of an air mission over Europe in World War II.

"...one of the best, most moving war novels..."
—*Minneapolis Tribune*

"It is a moving salute to the heroes who nightly endure the tension and terrors that are here so graphically described...stark honesty and marked artistic skill."
—*Liverpool Evening Express*

THE CAMP
Jonathan Trask

BT51214 $1.50
Novel

A group of right wing military officers were running a top secret operation deep in the woods of New England. Its written purpose was to toughen soldiers against torture, but its real purpose was more nefarious...The Camp would threaten the very security of the United States. A BT Original.

DEADLY COMPANIONS
Bob Sang and Dusty Sang

BT51243 $1.50
Novel

Jacob Pendleton was a latter-day James Bond who would take on just about any dangerous job...provided the price was right. This latest assignment called for him to deposit a million dollars worth of gems in Vault Box 211 in a Geneva bank, and then to repeat the proceedings in banks all over the world. All within 72 hours, no questions asked. The Chicago-based adventurer knew he could get killed, but that was part of the job.